Kate Sedley was born in Bristol and educated at The Red Maid's School, Westbury-on-Trym. She is married and has a son and a daughter and three grandchildren. THE SAINT JOHN'S FERN is her ninth historical mystery, following DEATH AND THE CHAPMAN, THE PLYMOUTH CLOAK, THE HANGED MAN, THE HOLY INNOCENTS, THE EVE OF ST HYACINTH, THE WICKED WINTER, THE BROTHERS OF GLASTONBURY and, most recently, THE WEAVER'S INHERITANCE, all featuring Roger the Chapman and available from Headline.

D0813800

The
Saint John's
Fern

Kate Sedley

HEADLINE

First published in hardback in 1999 by
HEADLINE BOOK PUBLISHING

First published in paperback in 2000 by
HEADLINE BOOK PUBLISHING

10 9 8 7 6 5 4 3 2 1

ISBN 0 7472 6810 X

Printed and bound in Great Britain by
Clays Ltd, St Ives plc

HEADLINE BOOK PUBLISHING
A division of the Hodder Headline Group
338 Euston Road
London NW1 3BH

www.headline.co.uk
www.hodderheadline.com

The
Saint John's
Fern

Chapter One

Clouds were gathering on the horizon, the first indication of a squall rolling in from the still distant sea, and a sharp tang of salt was borne on the freshening breeze. All about me lay the low curves of the moor, rising steeply in places to rocky outcrops of granite, poised between heaven and earth like mysterious elfin castles. Patches of fern and bracken glowed faintly bronze-coloured in the fluctuating light, a reminder of autumn, in spite of the warmth of the October morning.

Looking back now from the safety of old age – and seventy-five is a good ripe age for a man to reach – I can see myself clearly as I was then: young, vigorous, healthy, having just achieved my twenty-fifth birthday. And I marvel how unafraid of life I was. It never worried me what that fickle jade might have in store for me, for I had the utmost confidence in my ability to extricate myself from any and every untoward situation. (This is a slight exaggeration, perhaps, for I put my faith in God as well; but then, it was usually He who landed me in all my difficulties in the first place.)

Those of you, my children, and, maybe, grandchildren, who have taken the trouble to read these chronicles of mine so far, will know that when I flouted my dead mother's wishes and forsook my novitiate with the monks at Glastonbury for the freedom of the open road, it seemed that God had determined to

1

make use of me in some other fashion. He wasn't going to let me escape my obligations quite so easily, and decided to employ my talent for unravelling those mysteries which had defeated the powers of other people, to bring various evil villains to book. That may sound somewhat conceited, but I believe we all have a special aptitude, an accomplishment not shared by everyone, and the ability to solve knotty problems was mine.

Mind you, I can't pretend that I was always, if ever, a willing tool in the Almighty's hands, and I had a good many one-sided arguments with Him, which, naturally enough, He totally ignored, simply giving me the choice to do His will or not – which, of course, as He knows full well, is no choice at all. And I had an uneasy feeling, as I made my way along the ancient ridge-road running across the great empty spaces of Dartmoor towards the town and port of Plymouth, that some agency other than my own free will was directing my footsteps.

To begin with, in this early October of 1477, I had been less than four months married – and very happily married – to my second wife, Adela. With her little son, Nicholas, now only two weeks short of his third birthday, and my daughter, Elizabeth, a mere four weeks younger again, I found myself, for the first time since early childhood, at the centre of a warm and happy life. The one-roomed cottage that I rented from Saint James's Priory in Lewin's Mead in the city of Bristol was undoubtedly cramped, partly because of my great height and girth, but we failed to notice it, unaware that we were treading on each other's toes or that we were falling over one another. The two children had been friends from their very first meeting, while my love for Adela grew deeper by the day, as I had every proof that hers did for me. In addition, my mother-in-law from my first marriage was a kinswoman of my present wife, and was more than content to play grandmother to us all, visiting us from her home in Redcliffe at least two or three times every week.

In these circumstances of domestic bliss, with no sense that they were about to pall or grow stale, why had I suddenly been seized with my old, familiar restlessness? Why had I felt a terrible urge to visit Plymouth once again? My mother-in-law – for, having no other, I should always think of Margaret Walker as that – made no effort to hide her disappointment and disapproval, understandably regarding my desire to be off on my travels as a typical attempt to shirk my husbandly and parental responsibilities.

'Put your foot down,' I had overheard her advising Adela. 'Start as you mean to go on or you'll find yourself bringing up Nick and Elizabeth all on your own.' I had imagined her lips folding themselves into an almost invisible line. 'I know. Haven't I raised Bess here practically single-handed since Lillis died? There's plenty of money to be made peddling his wares hereabouts if Roger would only put his mind to it. No need for him to be wandering off to foreign parts.'

But Adela had only laughed. 'Margaret, he's not my prisoner. Roger knows that he's free to come and go as he pleases. It was part of our bargain when we married, and, besides, I enjoy my own company now and then.'

No more had been said as the two women had, at that moment, become aware of my lurking presence, but I realized even more fully what I had known all along, that I had married a woman in a thousand; and I shuddered to remember how nearly I had let her slip through my fingers. Nevertheless, the desire to escape in no way abated, and at the beginning of August, a mere eight weeks after my wedding to Adela, I set out southwards, with Plymouth as my destination. But it wasn't until that warm October morning, the goal at last within reach, that I suddenly began to question this strange urge that possessed me. Why, in spite of my happiness with my wife and children, had I felt impelled to leave them?

And why had the town of Plymouth, which I had visited only once before, four years earlier, sprung so insistently and vividly to mind?

I stopped in my tracks, in the grip of a deep and most unwelcome suspicion. 'Lord,' I demanded aloud, 'is this Your doing? Tell me! Is it?' There was, unsurprisingly, no answer, but I had no need of one. I dropped my pack – now considerably lighter than when I had left home – to the ground and leant heavily on my cudgel in order to ease my aching shoulders. 'Very well!' I muttered angrily. 'That's that! I'm retracing my steps. You can't force me to continue.'

The unexpected sound of wheels made me jump and glance around, and there at my elbow, blowing gustily through its nostrils, was an old brown cob harnessed to a cartload of peat. The driver, perched on his box and looking down at me with a pair of smiling blue eyes, was almost the same colour as his horse, his deeply tanned face surmounting leggings and tunic of coarse brown homespun, a piece of sacking draped over his head to protect it from all weathers.

'I'm going as far as Plympton Priory,' he informed me. 'If you'd care for a ride, chapman, jump up.'

He must have thought me a great gaby for I had neither seen nor heard the cart approaching until it was alongside me, and consequently I stood goggling at its driver for several seconds in open-mouthed astonishment.

'Th-thank you,' I stammered at last, and before I had time to recollect my resolve to proceed no further, I had clambered up beside him, my pack and cudgel lodged uncomfortably at my feet.

'Where are you making for?' the carter enquired, as, in response to a flick of the reins, the old brown cob moved sluggishly forward.

'Plymouth. Er – that is,' I faltered, 'I haven't quite made up my mind.'

'Know the town, do you?' my companion asked, ignoring my indecision. 'Been there before, perhaps?'

'Once,' I acknowledged.

'Get around a lot in your trade, I dare say. Where have you come from?'

'Bristol. My wife and family are there. But I was born and brought up in Wells.'

My companion shook his head. 'Don't know the place. Nor Bristol, though I know *of* it, of course. What's the news in that part of the country, then? You must have plenty of truck with London. What's happening there?'

I eased my cramped legs. 'Word is that all's quiet in the capital at the moment. The Duke of Clarence is still a prisoner in the Tower. Do you know about that?'

'A rumour or two has reached us,' said the carter, nodding, 'even in Tavistock, where I live, but that was some time ago. What's the upshot?'

'At the moment, there is none. It seems the Duke has neither been released nor yet brought to trial, and what will be the outcome no one can say for certain. The King's forgiven his brother so often in the past that the general opinion is that he'll do so again. But for the time being, at least, while Clarence is imprisoned, we're spared the threat of further civil war.'

My new acquaintance grimaced. 'As bad as that, was it? We heard that the Duke had been making mischief again, but not how serious it was. Well, well! But I don't suppose it'll affect us much down here, whatever happens.' And the conversation drifted towards more trivial matters: the bad state of the roads the unseasonable warmth of the weather, the rapidity with which the nights were already drawing in.

As we approached Plympton Priory, my companion suddenly asked, 'Do you have anywhere to stay in Plymouth?' And at the first shake of my head he added, 'I'll give you my daughter's direction, in Bilbury Street.'

'That – that's very kind of you,' I stammered. 'But as I said just now, I haven't really decided—'

'Better still,' he interrupted, 'if you care to wait for me while I deliver this load of peat to the priory, I'll take you on to Plymouth myself. My wife was saying only last night that neither of us has seen Joanna for quite some time, nor our son-in-law and the grandchildren, and that one of us – meaning me, of course – ought to make the effort to find out how they're faring. So here's my chance. I've no more deliveries today and if you'll be so good as to give me your company, it'll make the journey that much less tedious, and you'll be fixed up with a comfortable billet into the bargain. What do you say?'

What could I say in the face of so much kindness and goodwill? God was forcing my hand and there was nothing I could do about it unless I wished to appear worse than churlish. Suppressing a sigh, I gave in with as much good grace as I could muster and thanked him with a spurious heartiness.

'If you're certain it's not too much trouble—' I added, but my companion cut me short.

'No trouble in the world. That's settled then.' He spoke with undisguised satisfaction.

Plympton Priory is an Augustinian foundation, and I was interested to note that the canons wore little black birettas on the crowns of their heads, which, upon enquiry, I was informed was because they were untonsured. Their cassocks were mainly woven from a very fine wool, and the whole place exuded wealth and luxury. I was reminded of something that I had either read or been told a long time ago, probably during my years at Glastonbury, to the effect that the Augustinian Black Canons were always well-shod, well-fed and well-clothed; that they went abroad in the world, mixed with whom they liked and talked at table. I recalled my youthful envy of an order whose rules were so far removed from those of the Benedictines, and my dissatisfaction with the life that my mother had chosen for me had increased.

'Well, let's be on our way,' said the carter, whose name I had by now learnt was Peter Threadgold, climbing up on the box seat of the empty cart and indicating to me that I should do the same.

We had been given a dinner of soup and bread and cheese in the priory kitchen, during which time, by the greatest good fortune, the squally shower that I had earlier noted on the horizon, had passed over Plympton and was now moving further inland, towards the heart of the moor. The spears of stinging rain had given place once more to a hazy, autumnal sunshine that made every leaf, every blade of grass sparkle with a myriad rainbow drops of moisture. The track was rutted and green with weeds, revived by their sudden drink, and the smell of the river running broad and deep on our left, was, for a furlong or two, all-pervasive. But then the salt tang of the sea assaulted my nostrils and other scents were lost as I experienced yet again the old, familiar prickle of excitement.

I'm not a good sailor and I'm far happier with my feet planted firmly on shore, so I don't know why I respond in the way that I do to the smell of the sea. But I've noticed throughout my life that I'm not the only confirmed landsman to do so. I can only suppose that it's because here, in this island, and in neighbouring Ireland, whichever way you travel, the sea is at the end of so many journeys, and has a meaning, a significance, even for those people who have never seen it. The mere thought of it quickens the blood, and the sight of it sends a thrill of anticipation coursing up and down the spine. I think all islanders must have a little salt in their veins, for I noticed that Peter Threadgold also raised his head and sniffed appreciatively as we passed through the Old Town Gate.

'Here we are then,' he said, as we traversed the main street of Old Town Ward before turning left into Bilbury Street, where his daughter lived.

This, as both the name of the gate and ward made obvious, was the oldest part of Plymouth, many of the houses and cottages in Bilbury Street having been built, so Master Threadgold somewhat apologetically informed me, well over a hundred years earlier. I had to admit, although not aloud, that most of them looked it, quite a few being almost derelict and others hovering on the brink of decay. One or two, however, were well maintained, the outside walls being washed with that mixture of potash and sulphur which turns them a delicate greenish-grey, and holes in the thatch having been patched with iris leaves, a plant which grew in abundance in some of the gardens.

To my relief, it was in front of one of these better-kept cottages that we finally drew up, having driven almost the entire length of the street.

'Whoa, boy!' my companion exclaimed, pulling on the reins, although the cob's pace was so steady that the order was superfluous, the lightest of touches being sufficient to stop him in his tracks.

Immediately ahead of us was another of the town gates – Martyn's Gate, Peter Threadgold said – which, as I was to learn later, gave access to the east-bound road that passed the Carmelite Friary just beyond the walls. The cottage before which we had halted was separated from the gatehouse by only one other dwelling, a two-storeyed edifice in excellent repair, its wooden frontage painted red and gold, and with a tiled roof from which no slates appeared to be missing. It was far superior to any other building in the street, money having obviously been lavished upon its upkeep, and no expense spared to ensure that it was at once recognizable as the residence of a gentleman. There was something not quite right about it, however, but it took a moment or two for me to realize just what it was. Then it dawned on me that every window in the house was shuttered in spite of the warmth and brightness of a sunny afternoon, and that the door was not only inhospitably shut, but the knocker had been removed, leaving merely the iron hook from which the clapper had been suspended.

Peter Threadgold, whose eyes had followed my gaze, remarked, 'That's strange! Master Capstick must have gone away, although at his age, I shouldn't have thought—'

He was interrupted by the emergence from the cottage of two very excited small boys, one about five, the other, I judged, a couple of years younger, and, hard on their heels, a woman whose plump, smooth face was wreathed in smiles.

'Grandda! Grandda!' The children reached up their little arms, trying ineffectually to drag their grandsire from his seat, while their mother laughingly admonished them.

'Robin! Thomas! That will do! Behave! Father, what a lovely surprise. Come down before the boys do you a mischief.' She caught sight of me. 'And . . . and your friend, also,' she added uncertainly.

Peter Threadgold leapt nimbly to the ground, catching up the two boys in turn and tossing them, squealing with delight, into the air. Then, as I was by this time standing alongside him, he turned to introduce me.

'Master Chapman, this is my daughter, Mistress Cobbold, and these two young imps of Satan are my grandsons. Joanna, my dear, our friend here is looking for a bed for the night, being more or less a stranger to these parts, and I thought you might be able to find him a corner.'

Joanna Cobbold dimpled. 'If he doesn't mind sharing a bed

with one of the children, he's more than welcome. Now, come along inside, the pair of you, and Father, I can't wait to hear all your news. How is Mother and when can we expect to see her again?'

The interior of the cottage was as clean and neat as the exterior had led me to believe it would be, and I was soon settled at the table with a cup of Mistress Cobbold's home-brewed ale in my hand. And in order to draw off the boys' overwhelming attentions from their grandfather, I opened my pack and allowed them to rummage through its contents, while Peter Threadgold and his daughter talked, uninterrupted, exchanging all the latest family gossip.

Later, as we were sitting down to a meal of savoury-smelling rabbit stew, followed by pippin tarts and goat's-milk cheese and chives, the master of the house returned, greeting his father-in-law with genuine affection and adding his voice to his wife's, urging Peter to stay with them overnight.

'No, no, lad, I daren't.' The carter shook his head regretfully. 'I told Martha I'd be straight home after I'd delivered my load at the priory. She'll have me overturned at the bottom of a ditch as it is. I must be going, I'm afraid, as soon as I've finished eating. But you'll oblige me by looking after my friend Roger Chapman here.'

John Cobbold made no further attempt to persuade his father-in-law to remain, and for the rest of the meal the conversation turned on the present parlous state of the wine trade in Plymouth, my host being employed, as I gathered, by a vintner who had a shop near the market cross. The expulsion of the English from Bordeaux twenty-odd years before, and the subsequent edict forbidding any Englishman to take up residence in that city, had, I learnt, started the rot; and now the trade was fast becoming the monopoly of the hated Flemings and the even more detested members of the Hanseatic League.

'In fact,' John Cobbold added gloomily, 'trade is generally bad altogether at present. Fishing isn't what it was. Even the hake business is losing money, and you know how plentiful hake's always been in the waters off this coast.' He sighed. 'There aren't any fortunes to be made from it nowadays, not like old Master Capstick's, next door.'

'May God rest his soul,' Joanna added, making the sign of the Cross.

Peter Threadgold clicked his tongue. 'He's dead then, is he, old Oliver Capstick? I noticed when we arrived that the house was boarded up and the knocker removed.' The carter rubbed his nose. 'I must say, I'm surprised. He was getting on in years, it's true, but he was always so healthy and active that I can't imagine him succumbing to illness. But there, it happens to us all sooner or later. When our time comes, it comes and there's no escaping it. Poor old fellow! A bit cantankerous and difficult, by all accounts, but he was very polite to me whenever I was here and we happened to meet in the street. And that isn't always the way of the rich towards the poor, as we very well know. What did he die of?'

I saw John and Joanna Cobbold exchange glances, then the former said, 'You two boys can go and play, if you've finished eating. I can hear some of your friends outside.' Robin and Thomas needed no further encouragement to leave the table and the tedious conversation of their elders to join the other boys and girls in the street, and were gone like a shot from a bow. But their father waited until the cottage door had closed behind them before answering Peter's question. 'Master Capstick didn't die of any illness. He was murdered – and very brutally murdered – last May.'

11

Chapter Two

Peter Threadgold flinched visibly, the shock of his son-in-law's words hitting him with the force of a blow. He was not old, having, I guessed, seen some fifty winters, but old enough to fear the horrors of a brutal death; to identify with the vulnerability that the waning of physical strength brings in its wake.

For my own part, I was unsurprised by John Cobbold's revelation. The suspicion that here, in Bilbury Street, was the reason for my presence in the town of Plymouth, had been growing steadily upon me ever since I had clapped eyes on the shuttered house next door. Consequently, I settled myself more comfortably on my stool, took another chive from the dish in the centre of the table and, chewing thoughtfully, prepared to listen while all was revealed.

'What happened?' Peter Threadgold asked, after a second or two's horrified silence. 'How – ' he cleared his throat – 'how did Master Capstick die?'

'He was bludgeoned to death in his bed,' Joanna answered, lowering her voice as though afraid that one of the children might have crept back into the cottage without her noticing. She added impressively, 'I saw his body,' and waited for a moment while her father and I looked suitably appalled. She then went on, 'I was in the yard, spreading out my washing to dry, when I heard Mistress Trenowth start screaming, so naturally, I ran next door to discover what was wrong. I found her upstairs in Master Capstick's bedchamber.' Joanna gave an involuntary shudder. 'It was horrible. Horrible! His head had been beaten to a pulp and the bedclothes were soaked in blood.' She began to cry, making little whimpering sounds like those of a wounded animal.

John Cobbold got up from his place to walk round the table and sit on the bench beside her, putting a broad, workmanlike arm around her shoulders and giving them a squeeze.

'We don't discuss it in front of the boys,' he said, 'and most of the time Joanna forces herself to forget all about it. But then, when she does remember, everything comes back afresh, and upsets her.'

'Who's Mistress Trenowth?' I asked, and was told that she had been the old man's housekeeper.

'She was with him a very long time,' Joanna said, pulling herself together and dabbing at her eyes with a corner of her apron. 'Ever since his wife died, which, I understand from neighbours, was some fifteen or sixteen years ago.' She gave another sniff and wiped her nose on the back of one hand. 'Mistress Trenowth was fond of him, I think, in spite of the fact that, when the mood took him, Master Capstick could be an old curmudgeon.' She smiled tremulously. 'In truth, we all found him a bit difficult now and then. He used to shout at the children if they made too much noise, playing in the street. But on other occasions, he'd thrown them sweetmeats out of his bedroom window.'

'And he wasn't proud,' her husband added. 'In spite of his wealth, he stayed here, in the house he'd been born in, instead of moving to Notte Street, where all the new buildings are going up, and where most of the people with money in this town are buying new properties. It didn't seem to worry him that many of the houses in Bilbury Street are falling into a state of disrepair.'

'But do they know who did this terrible deed, and why?' Peter

Threadgold demanded. 'You say the murder happened last May, and here it is October and you don't mention an arrest. Haven't the Sheriff's officers caught the murderer yet?'

'Yes to your first question, and no to your second,' John Cobbold answered. 'The murderer was Master Capstick's great-nephew, Beric Gifford of Modbury. We know that for certain because Mistress Trenowth met him at the foot of the stairs, as he was coming down, the front of his tunic all stained with blood – or at least, so she remembered later. She says she didn't really take much notice at the time. It seems she'd just come from the kitchen with the old man's breakfast, which she was carrying up to him on a tray, and wasn't expecting to see anyone else at that hour of the morning, not having heard Beric enter the house. He didn't return her greeting when she spoke to him, but let himself out of the front door without a word. Mistress Trenowth went on upstairs – and found Master Capstick lying there, in all his gore. That was when she started screaming.'

'She's sure that it was this – this what did you call him? – Beric Gifford?' I asked John Cobbold.

He nodded emphatically. 'Oh, yes! And she wasn't the only person to see and recognize him, both on his journey from Modbury to Plymouth, and on his ride home again. Any number of people saw him – including Joanna.'

I turned to my hostess, who had by now recovered her poise and was sitting bolt upright on the bench, her hands tightly clasped together on the table in front of her. '*You* saw him? And you'd swear that it was this great-nephew of Master Capstick?'

'Of course I'd swear! I know him well by sight. He and his sister have often visited their great-uncle in the past. Just before I went to spread out my washing, I'd been in the street, talking to Bessie Hannaford, my neighbour on the other side, and as I turned into the yard, Beric Gifford rode up on that big black horse of his.'

'A huge, showy, very spirited animal,' John Cobbold put in. 'Master Capstick told me once that his great-nephew was the only person who could manage the brute. He was quite proud of the fact, even though he strongly disapproved of the boy spending so much on a horse that no one else on the manor could ride. A shocking waste of money he called it—'

Peter Threadgold broke in impatiently, 'But if it's known he killed Master Capstick, why hasn't this Beric Gifford been arrested and hanged?'

His son-in-law shrugged. 'No one can find him,' he answered in a hushed voice. 'Since last being seen on the morning of the murder, he's seemingly disappeared off the face of the earth.'

There was silence for a moment, then I suggested, 'He's run away, do you mean?'

Joanna Cobbold stirred uneasily. 'He would have had to run very fast,' she said, 'to outstrip the Sheriff's men. On my and Mistress Trenowth's evidence, there was a posse after him within the half-hour, and it seems that when they arrived at Valletort Manor, Beric Gifford's horse was in the stables, still lathered after its ride. But there was no sign of Master Gifford himself, and he hasn't been seen since. The general opinion is that his sister's hiding him somewhere on the manor, for, by every account, the two of them have always been as thick as thieves.'

'But surely that's impossible,' her father protested. 'The Sheriff's men must have searched every nook and cranny of both house and demesne. If he's there, they're bound to have found him.'

John Cobbold grimaced. 'Well, they haven't,' he said, 'although they've been looking, on and off, these past five months. And there's also a reward offered for Beric's capture, but that's done no good, either. The countryside's been scoured for miles around, in all directions, but no one's ever found hair nor hide of him.'

He drew a deep breath. 'The truth is that quite a few of the Sheriff's officers, as well as a number of other people, are coming to the conclusion that Beric Gifford . . .' He hesitated before continuing, 'They're saying . . . well, they're saying that he must have eaten of Saint John's fern.'

The carter stared for a moment, his blue eyes wide with dismay, then he shivered and made the sign of the Cross. 'He's made himself invisible,' he whispered.

We all followed his example, crossing ourselves to ward off the evil spirits, for Saint John's fern is part of the world of magic, practised by those hobgoblins, elves and other sprites who inhabit the nether regions between earth and hell. Perhaps in this modern age, people no longer give as much credence to the powers of spells and witchcraft as they once did – leastways not in the towns and cities – but when I was young, there was an implicit belief in such things, in spite of the contrary teachings of the Church. It was well known that the hart's-tongue fern, which grows in damp, shady places such as woods and down wells and in fissures in the rocks, and is also called the fern of Saint John, can, taken in sufficient quantity, make people invisible. An infusion of its leaves is very good for hiccoughs, coughs and other winter chest complaints, but eat the leaves raw and the human body can melt into thin air for hours, or even days at a time, disappearing and reappearing at will.

I was not sure then, any more than I am now, that I really believed the tale; and even in those less enlightened days, there were many people, particularly in London and other big cities, who would have shared my doubts, while any self-respecting priest would have roundly denounced anything which smacked of magic as heresy. But at the same time, it is difficult to free ourselves of the beliefs of our ancestors; and those of us in whom the blood of the Saxon predominates over that of the Norman, accept from

17

birth the powers of the gods of the trees; of Hodekin, the wood sprite, of Robin Goodfellow and of the terrible Green Man. All Nature is a mystery, and the properties of Saint John's fern one of the greatest, for although the plant has leaves and spore, the flowers are never seen. They are invisible, and the belief is that they can pass on this attribute to humans.

There was a long silence after Peter Threadgold's last words while we contemplated the unwelcome idea of a brutal murderer escaping the law, and his just deserts, by unnatural powers.

Then, 'No,' I objected, all the common sense that I inherited from my mother reasserting itself, 'it can't be possible.'

'Why not?' demanded Peter Threadgold. 'And if Beric Gifford has made himself invisible, he could easily be many miles away by now.'

I shook my head. 'I don't believe it,' I said loudly and firmly, in order to convince myself as much as my listeners. 'I don't believe that Saint John's fern makes anyone invisible. It's just a story. As for what really happened, if this Beric Gifford returned home barely ahead of his pursuers, then what Mistress Cobbold said is right. He had very little time to escape, even if he took a fresh horse. And if he has not been traced elsewhere, then he must still be hiding on the manor.'

John Cobbold looked and sounded irritated. 'The house, outbuildings and lands have been searched from end to end, I tell you, and the Sheriff's men have found nothing. Although,' he added grudgingly, 'there have been claims by some local people that Beric has been seen. But the sightings have always been late at night, or sometimes very early in the morning, and never near enough for them to say positively that it was him.'

'Master Hannaford, next door,' Joanna Cobbold broke in, 'was one of the posse raised to go in pursuit of Beric Gifford. And he told Mistress Hannaford that the Giffords' groom told the sergeant that no horse was missing from the Valletort stables. None had been taken out that morning save the black and he was safely back in his stall.'

John Cobbold frowned. 'You haven't mentioned this before.' He sounded somewhat aggrieved that his wife had not kept him better informed.

'I'd forgotten it until now,' she answered simply, to which there was no satisfactory response.

'The groom might have been lying,' I suggested. 'But if he wasn't – and I suspect the number of the Giffords' horses is well known to their neighbours, and the information easily checked – then it's possible that, even if he is not within the manor pale, Beric is still somewhere close at hand. What of his parents? What do they say regarding the accusation against their son and his disappearance?'

'The mother and father have been dead these many years, I believe,' Joanna Cobbold said. 'But I really know very little about the family. If you want to know more, you will have to consult Mistress Trenowth.'

'Now why should the chapman wish to know more?' her husband chided her. 'If the Sheriff's men can't solve the mystery of Beric Gifford, I'm sure no one else can. Roger's only here to sell his wares and then move on.' He glanced anxiously at his father-in-law, who was still looking a little sick, and added hurriedly, 'The best thing we can do is to put the unsavoury business out of our minds. There's no need to trouble ourselves further. No random killer is on the loose. It was a family quarrel, obviously, and therefore nothing to do with anyone else. Whatever provoked Beric Gifford to murder his great-uncle is not our concern.'

Peter Threadgold nodded in agreement, a little of the colour creeping back into his cheeks beneath his tan. 'You're quite right, John,' he said. 'It's a terrible thing to have happened, but you mustn't dwell on it, either of you.' He pushed back his stool and rose to his feet. 'And now I must be going if I'm to reach Tavistock before midnight. Martha's probably on the lookout for me already and will be in a fine state by the time I do get home. Where are those two young rascals? Call them in to kiss their old granddad goodbye.'

The boys, hauled in from the street, were inclined to be sullen at first at being taken away from their friends, but upset and tearful when they understood that their grandfather was going home.

'Won't you stay, Grandda?' they begged, catching hold of his arms and attempting to detain him by sheer force.

By the time they had been detached, general farewells exchanged, fond messages for her mother relayed by Joanna Cobbold, and the cob, who had been put out to grass in the cottage yard, once more harnessed between the shafts of the cart, the day was on the wane. It would be another hour before it got dark, but Peter Threadgold was suddenly anxious to be off, and I noted how his eyes carefully avoided the shuttered house next door as he turned the cart about. He paused for one last kiss from his daughter and grandsons, punched his son-in-law playfully on the shoulder and raised a hand to me.

'Good luck attend you, chapman, and if you're ever near Tavistock don't go on your way without paying a visit to my goodwife and me. I'm well known in those parts and anyone will direct you to our cottage. Joanna will make you comfortable tonight. God be with you, my friend!'

We all stood and watched him trundle the length of Bilbury Street and turn the corner. One final wave and he had vanished from sight. I went back into the cottage with my hosts.

I was finding it impossible to sleep, and part of the reason was sheer physical discomfort.

I was sharing a truckle bed with Thomas, the elder of the two boys, and although, unlike his younger brother, he was a fairly quiet sleeper, and did not perpetually toss and turn from side to side, the bed was far too short for my great limbs. By day, it was kept, with its fellow, beneath the larger bed that stood behind a curtain in one corner of the cottage, and was, of necessity, of only middling length. It was also narrow, and, in addition, I felt obliged to lie rigidly still for fear of disturbing my companion.

The other reason for my restlessness was the story of Master Capstick's murder at the hands of his great-nephew, Beric Gifford. Once Peter Threadgold had departed, I should have liked to question my hosts further on the subject, but I suspected that my interest would be unwelcome. Moreover, the two boys had settled themselves by the fire for the evening, and I knew that neither John nor Joanna Cobbold wished to discuss the matter in front of them. And even when Thomas and Robin had gone to bed, they were still close enough at hand to hear every word that passed between their elders. So I had held my peace, and eventually retired, to fall into an uneasy slumber from which I had awakened an hour or so later, with no hope of going to sleep again for quite some time.

Bright moonlight filtered through the cracks in the window shutters, diffused by the inner screens of strong, oiled parchment. The fire had been banked with peat for the night and a few glowing embers were still visible between the turfs. I felt an urgent desire to get up and walk about, but for a long time I dared not, for fear of waking the others. But finally, in desperation, I pushed aside my share of the blanket and eased my feet to the floor, sitting quietly on the edge of the bed for a moment or two, my knees tucked almost beneath my chin. Then, stealthily, I reached for my tunic and boots, the only three items of clothing that I had shed, and put them on again, waiting with bated breath for someone to ask me what I thought I was doing, and where I was going, in the middle of the night.

But no one challenged me. Thomas rolled on to his stomach, reclaiming the half of the palliasse that I had abandoned; John Cobbold's rhythmic snoring never faltered; Robin murmured in his sleep, but did not wake; and from my hostess there was neither sound nor movement. Cautiously, I edged my way to the door and drew back the bolts, grateful for Joanna Cobbold's careful housewifery that kept them well oiled. With a swift, almost furtive glance over my shoulder, I stepped outside, gently shutting the door behind me.

The street was quiet: no one was abroad. A dog barked somewhere, once, twice, and then fell silent; an owl hooted in a distant barn. I could hear, not too far away, the hush and murmur of the sea. Oliver Capstick's house rose up, gaunt and black, against a moonlit sky; and just beyond it, Martyn's Gate was closed and locked until the porter's arrival to open it at daybreak.

I stared up at the eyeless windows, wondering who the house belonged to now, and why, five months after the old man's murder, it still remained shuttered and empty. Unlike the cottages in Bilbury Street, it had no fenced yard around it; outside it boasted only a well and an outside privy, but no stables, which was unusual in a gentleman's residence. At the back was open ground where judging by the churned-up mud, the children played, and where a tenter had set up his drying frames. In the distance, I could just make out the shadow of the Old Town Gate. I returned to the front of the house, feeling that familiar shiver of anticipation that heralded the start of any new adventure; for I was more convinced than ever that Oliver Capstick's murder was the reason God had brought me to Plymouth.

I walked up to the front door and, without the slightest expectation of it being unbolted, lifted the latch. To my utmost astonishment, it yielded to my touch and, trembling with excitement, I pushed it wide and stepped inside. Immediately, I was almost overpowered by the smell of dust and damp that permeates any house left unoccupied too long, and I stood unmoving for several minutes while my eyes grew accustomed to the gloom. When I could see again, I realized that I was standing in a small, square hall from which the stairs rose steeply to the upper storey. Two doors opened off this hallway, one to the right, one to the left of me, and, upon investigation the rooms they served proved to be the counting-house and parlour. A narrow passage, cautiously trodden in case some of the flags should prove uneven, led me to the back door and also gave access to kitchen, pantry and wash-house.

Softly I padded back to the foot of the stairs and closed the street door, but not before I had lit a candle that stood in its holder on a nearby shelf, using the tinder-box that lay alongside it. Then I mounted to the upper storey, which, I discovered, boasted three bedchambers. Two of them were of middling size and showed no sign of occupancy, all the cupboards and chests, when I peered within, being empty of any personal belongings. I guessed that one must have been used as a guest chamber and that Mistress Trenowth had probably occupied the other; but there was no doubt whatsoever that the third and largest room had been Master Capstick's.

A huge, canopied, four-poster bed stood in the middle of the floor, its curtains made of a heavy, richly woven damask silk. An elaborately carved chest, which I did not hesitate to open, still contained his clothes, now chill and damp to the touch and, in daylight, most likely showing traces of mildew. The rushes covering the boards, like the rushes in other parts of the house, stank to high heaven and had obviously not been removed or changed since the murder. But what eventually drew my eyes, and held them was the coverlet, roughly folded and placed in the middle of the mattress. It showed sinister dark marks which, at first, I tried to convince myself were merely a part of the pattern. However, the tips of my fingers assured me that the patches were stiff and brittle, the rusty stains of long-dried blood.

I drew back in disgust. Whoever was now the owner of Oliver Capstick's property seemed to have shut up the house without making any attempt to clean it properly or set it to rights since that terrible morning when Beric Gifford had murdered his great-uncle and then disappeared. The sour stench of decay emanated from almost every room, making the bile rise in my throat. I made a bolt for the bedchamber door, sweat breaking out on my forehead, and as I did so, my foot kicked against something solid. I stooped and groped about, very reluctantly, amongst the flea-infested rushes until one hand closed over something hard and metallic that was lying on the floor, partially concealed by the base of the bed.

I dropped whatever it was into my pocket and rushed headlong down the stairs, blowing out the candle as I ran and returning the holder to its shelf, before dashing out into the chill night air, where, to my astonishment and shame, I was violently sick.

Chapter Three

When I felt a little better, I went to the common well on the other side of the street and drew up a bucket of water. I washed my face and hands, and had a much-needed drink, after which, cleansed and refreshed, I sat down on the rim of the well to examine my discovery in the moonlight. As I drew it from my pocket it glittered, and I saw that it was an ornament, one of those brooches that the wealthy wear pinned to the upturned brims of their hats. It was made of gold, fashioned in the shape of two entwined letters, a B and a G, enclosed in a chaplet of laurel leaves. A large pearl drop, like a single tear, was suspended from the lowest leaf. B. G. They had to be the initials of Beric Gifford. The brooch must have come loose and fallen from the murderer's hat as he fled from the scene of his crime; and as I turned the jewel over in the palm of my hand, I saw that the clasp was indeed broken.

I restored it to my pocket and made my way back to the Cobbold's house, gingerly lifting the door-latch and tiptoeing inside. Everything was just as I had left it. The same snores and murmurs filled the room, Robin tossed from one side of his truckle bed to the other, and Thomas, with arms outflung, sprawled across the one I had previously been sharing with him. As quietly as I could, I bolted the cottage door and once more divested myself of boots and tunic, stretching out on the rushes nearest the hearth and using my pack, as I had done so often in the past, as a pillow.

Yet in spite of bodily ease, I still could not sleep. It was difficult for me to explain my recent physical weakness. Was I growing squeamish, I asked myself, that I was unable to stand the sight of a little dried blood, or the thought of corruption and decay? But there was something about the very recollection of that house next door that made my stomach begin to churn. Whoever owned it, now that Oliver Capstick was dead, seemed indifferent to the property, or perhaps just unwilling to set foot in it after what had happened there. But to whom *did* it belong?

I could make further enquiries of Joanna Cobbold at breakfast, but I had a feeling that my questions would be as unwelcome in the morning as they had been the evening before. Moreover, I had no wish to give any accidental hint of my midnight trespass. Then I remembered Mistress Trenowth, who had, according to my hostess, been housekeeper to Oliver Capstick for so many years that she probably knew most of his business. If she still lived in Plymouth, or within a reasonable walking distance of the town, a visit to her might satisfy my curiosity and, with luck, enlarge my knowledge of the circumstances surrounding her employer's death. If I could obtain her direction from Joanna Cobbold, I might be able to take my first tentative step on the road towards finding out what had really become of his murderer.

Having made this decision, I wriggled into a more comfortable position amongst the rushes, scratched myself in various places where the stalks and dried flower heads tickled, and was sound asleep within minutes.

Mistress Trenowth was a small, plump, motherly looking woman, with a pair of wide grey eyes, as clear and limpid as water. Her manner was calm and soothing, as though nothing in this life could ever ruffle her, as placid within, I conjectured, as she was without; and it was easy to see how she had managed to live in harmony with Oliver Capstick for all the years since the death of his wife.

After the murder, according to Joanna Cobbold, she had gone to stay with her sister, the Widow Cooper, in the latter's house in the Vintry Ward, close to the Franciscan Friary. 'And unless she's decided to move on in the last few days, that's where you'll find her still,' said my erstwhile hostess, eyeing me curiously. But she had asked no questions that might delay my departure, and had wished me God speed, relieved, I fancied, to be rid of me.

I had made my way to the Greyfriars, overlooking the harbour, and a very few enquiries had led me to the dwelling of the Widow Cooper, who, as good luck would have it, had gone shopping along the quay, a fresh catch having recently been landed by one of the fishing boats.

'But she'll be back soon, if you'd like to wait for her,' said my informant.

'No, no!' I protested. 'It's you I wish to see – if, that is, you're Mistress Trenowth.'

'I am Mathilda Trenowth, certainly,' she agreed. She looked me up and down. 'But I'm not the mistress here, and you should show your wares to my sister if you wish to make a sale. She'll know what, if anything, is needed. For myself, I'm in want of nothing just at present.'

'No, no!' I put in quickly. 'You're mistaken. I'm not selling. I've been staying with Mistress Cobbold and her husband overnight, and they've been telling me of the terrible murder of Master Capstick. There are . . . some questions about it that I should like to ask you – if, that is, you'll be so kind as to give me some answers.'

'You're a friend of the Cobbolds?'

'Yes,' I said, conveniently ignoring the fact that a few hours' chance acquaintanceship hardly entitled me to term myself their friend. 'It was Mistress Cobbold who told me where to find you.'

'But why do you want to question me about Master Capstick's murder?' Mistress Trenowth enquired, her smooth forehead creased in a puzzled frown. 'There's no doubt, I can assure you, as to his killer.'

'So I understand. But if you'll agree to let me in,' I said, 'I'll explain.'

She hesitated and, for a moment, I thought that she was going to refuse. But after studying me closely, she evidently decided that I was to be trusted and held the door wide enough to allow me over the threshold.

The house, although small, was two-storeyed and well furnished, arguing a modest degree of prosperity. The late Master Cooper had obviously left his widow comfortably off. I noted that the parlour into which I was shown by Mistress Trenowth faced out over the harbour, the warmth of the day having led to the opening of both the inner and outer shutters. There were two good carved armchairs, corner shelves on which were displayed some fine pieces of silver and pewter, a table, and a window-seat piled high with brightly embroidered cushions. Mistress Trenowth, not without some display of lingering doubt, invited me to be seated in one of the chairs and, taking the other, waited expectantly, her plump hands folded quietly in her lap. But her eyes were wary, and she was tense, on the alert for possible trouble.

Under that appraising stare, I found it a little difficult to begin, but decided in the end that it was easier to confess the truth than to prevaricate. I told her exactly how I had come to be in Bilbury Street, and of the circumstances under which I had met Peter Threadgold, his daughter and son-in-law. I also told her of my past successes in bringing to book villains who had, until then, gone undetected and unpunished. Whether or not she believed all my claims, I had no idea, but in any case it made no difference.

Once I had her trust, and she was convinced that she had not been hoodwinked into letting me into the house under false pretences, Mistress Trenowth was only too eager to talk about the murder and the inability of the Sheriff's men to trace Beric Gifford.

'It's scandalous, that's what it is!' she exclaimed in a soft, gentle voice that nevertheless managed to convey condemnation and outrage in equal measure. 'Beric *has* to be on Valletort Manor somewhere, and yet the Sheriff's officers declare they are unable to find him. What arrant nonsense! They're letting him and his sister make fools of them.'

'You don't believe, then,' I asked, 'this theory that the boy's eaten of Saint John's fern?'

Mistress Trenowth shivered. 'Perhaps he has done,' she admitted at last, hastily crossing herself to ward off evil. 'But it wouldn't make him invisible all the time. Nor would Beric want to be permanently invisible, now would he? Would you? Would anyone? Besides,' her natural common sense prodded into her adding, 'I know they say that St John's fern has the power to make people disappear, but in all my life, I've never met anyone who actually knew of a case of someone becoming invisible. I'm not saying, mind you, that it can't happen, or hasn't happened. There are strange and wonderful goings-on in this world that no one can explain, not even the Church.'

'But you feel,' I prompted, after a pause during which Mistress Trenowth seemed to have become lost in reverie, 'that the reports of invisibility due to eating the fern are always second-hand?'

She nodded. 'Or even third- or fourth-hand. Wouldn't you agree?'

'Yes, indeed.' I leant forward, my hands on my knees. 'But surely, having committed this terrible crime, Beric Gifford would have taken the earliest opportunity to escape. Once the initial search for him had proved fruitless, and he had managed to evade the Sheriff's officers for a day, maybe even a week or two, and once the scent had gone cold and enthusiasm for the hunt had begun to wane, then he must have slipped away under cover of darkness. He'd be a fool not to. Every day he spends in the vicinity of his home, he's in mortal danger of being seen, arrested and hanged. He must be miles and miles distant by now.'

Mistress Trenowth gave a decided shake of her head. 'Oh no! There's no way Beric would have left the manor while *she*'s still there. And she *is* still there. I know, because I've another sister who lives in Modbury, and she told me so.'

I frowned. 'Who are you talking about? Are you referring to Master Gifford's sister?'

'No, no! Although he and Berenice are close, and always have been. No, I was meaning Katherine Glover. She's the reason Beric and Master Capstick had that terrible falling-out the day before he killed his uncle.'

I drew a deep breath. 'I'm afraid, Mistress Trenowth, that if I'm to understand this story, you'll have to give me all the details of your master and his family, their past history and the events leading up to the murder. It would save me asking a lot of questions, which can only be a trial to both of us. Would you be agreeable?'

She thought for a moment, then graciously inclined her head. 'There isn't, in any case, a great deal to tell,' she said, 'but such as there is, you're welcome to know. Particularly,' she added, her eyes filling with tears, 'if it can help you bring Beric Gifford to justice.'

Oliver Capstick, Mistress Trenowth told me, had been the younger of two sons of a Plymouth vintner, owner of a flourishing business, importing wine from both Bordeaux and La Rochelle; wine that had subsequently been transshipped to Calais and the North Sea ports, as well as being supplied to London and the eastern counties. Those had been dangerous, but heady days, when dozens of vessels had sailed in convoy in order to beat off attacks from the Breton pirates, and when England had been the French vineyard owners' most valued customer. All that had changed now, of course, but then there had been great fortunes to be made in the wine trade, and Jonathan Capstick had become a very wealthy man.

The elder son, Henry, had followed in his father's footsteps, but the younger, Oliver, had elected to go into hake fishing, and had bought himself three boats with money left to him by his mother.

'As a foreigner to these parts,' Mistress Trenowth condescended to inform me, 'I must tell you that hake is in very plentiful supply in these waters.' And she nodded towards the open window through which could be seen the sparkle of sunlight on the golden-blue haze of the sea. 'Master Capstick once told me that the greater part of every catch is sent to Gascony, where it seems they have a partiality for hake when it's dried and salted. Mind you, it's very popular in this country, too. In fact, there's nothing I like better, myself, than a nice bit of hake on a Friday.'

'In short,' I said, 'hake fishing is a very profitable business.'

'It certainly made Master Capstick wealthy,' she conceded before resuming her story.

The Capstick brothers had, in due course, married, but between them, had managed to produce only one offspring, Henry's daughter, Veronica. Both couples had been fond of children, and so she had become the darling not only of her parents, but also of her uncle and aunt. And it had been the greatest desire of Oliver's heart, far greater than that of his brother's, that Veronica should marry well.

'Judging by what Master Capstick let drop,' Mistress Trenowth confided, settling down for a comfortable gossip, 'and from what

I've been able to gather from other people who knew them, Henry Capstick wished his daughter to marry for money and didn't much care about pedigree. But Oliver had different ideas and wanted his niece to be a lady; so when Cornelius Gifford came courting Veronica, he was all for the match and wouldn't hear a word against it.' The Giffords, it appeared, were related by blood to the Champernownes, who had been lords of Modbury and its environs since the beginning of the previous century. 'But the trouble was,' my companion continued, 'that this particular branch of the Gifford family were poor relations and as far as Henry Capstick was concerned, Cornelius's noble connections didn't make up for his lack of fortune.'

But Oliver had put pressure on his niece to agree to Cornelius's proposal of marriage by promising to double whatever her father gave her by way of a dowry if she did so. Otherwise, not a penny piece would she ever get from him, then or in the future. The combined bribe and threat had proved too difficult to withstand, and as her mother was also urging her to marry Cornelius, Veronica had duly accept his offer. 'But of course,' Mistress Trenowth added with a shrug, 'you don't need me to tell you the outcome.'

'Cornelius frittered away all his wife's dowry,' I hazarded, 'and was left just as penniless as before.'

She pursed her lips and nodded. 'The bulk of it he lost gambling and the rest went on impractical, grandiose schemes for enlarging Valletort Manor.'

In the end, there had been nothing left, but by that time Veronica had died giving birth to Beric, three years to the day after marrying Cornelius. The elder child, Berenice, had been borne within the first twelve months.

'What happened next?' I asked.

According to Mistress Trenowth, neither Henry nor Oliver Capstick had been prepared to throw good money after bad, and

Oliver had blamed himself bitterly for having insisted on the marriage in the first place. But there were other factors, also, why the brothers declined to assist Cornelius. First, when Berenice was three and Beric one, their Aunt Capstick had died, leaving her husband to mourn her passing by becoming almost a recluse. Secondly, the wine trade was not what it had been, and Henry Capstick's business had begun to fail. Consequently, when he died in the autumn of 1468, within three months of the death of his own wife, his fortune had been considerably eroded. The amount of money, therefore, left to Beric and Berenice had been substantially less than their father had been led to expect. Nevertheless, by the time that Cornelius himself had died, in the spring of 1475, of a surfeit of drink and hard living, he had managed to whittle away his children's inheritance still further, and Valletort Manor was once more slipping into a state of decay.

Berenice Gifford – eighteen years old at the time she lost her father – and her brother were now almost entirely dependent on their Great-Uncle Oliver for the luxuries, and even, on occasions, the necessities, of everyday life.

'And Master Capstick was only too willing to supply them with what he thought was right and proper,' Mistress Trenowth said, getting up to close the inner shutters, for the October morning had suddenly clouded over. She returned to her chair and went on, 'He felt it to be his duty, you understand, for having more or less forced his niece into marriage with Cornelius Gifford.'

'But was that the only reason?' I interrupted. 'Wasn't he fond of his great-niece and -nephew?'

Mistress Trenowth frowned. 'He didn't dislike them,' she answered cautiously, 'but he was old and they are young, and they didn't pay him the attention that he thought was his due. The elderly grow exacting, Master Chapman, as you probably know. They get lonelier than they'll admit to. It happened with the Master.

Oh, his neighbours would have visited him as often as he could have wished, but there again, old people never want what they can have, only what's not on offer.'

'You mean that Beric and Berenice Gifford were neglectful of him?'

'No, no! I wouldn't say that. One or the other of them visited Master Capstick at least once or twice a month, and sometimes they rode over together. But very often the reason for their visit was because they wanted more money.'

'And their uncle objected to giving it to them?'

'It depended what it was for. If they said it was to mend the roof of some leaking outbuilding, or to rebuild a wall, or simply to keep them in clothes, he'd part with the amount in full without a murmur. But it's what I said to you just now. They're young, and the young need to have their moments of fun and extravagance. The master kept them on too short a rein because he was so afraid that they were going to prove profligate like their father. If Beric spent more than he thought he should have done on a horse or a hawk, or if Berenice bought silk and satin when he considered that she only had need of wool or linen, or if she purchased some extravagant jewel for her personal adornment, then Master Capstick would absolutely refuse to reimburse them by so much as a groat. "If they get into debt for such fripperies, that's their look out," he used to say to me.'

'And did they? Get into debt, I mean.'

Mistress Trenowth sighed. 'Almost certainly, because in the final year of his life, Master Capstick stopped giving them any financial help whatsoever, after he found out that most of the money they'd had from him for repairs to the manor had not been used for that purpose at all.'

'And how did he happen to make the discovery?' I wanted to know.

'One day, he took it into his head to pay them a surprise visit. No one who knew him would ever have expected him to do such a thing, for he hadn't been out of the house for years except to visit his man of business, down by the Dominican Friary. I was amazed when he told me to go to the livery stable and hire a wagon and horses.'

'And did this refusal to lend them any more money lead to bad blood between Master Capstick and his great-niece and -nephew?'

'He was very angry when he returned home,' Mistress Trenowth admitted. 'I do remember that. What had passed between the three of them, I could only guess at from the fact that they didn't come to visit the Master for quite a long time afterwards. But then, towards the end of the April just past, Berenice arrived in Bilbury Street, all smiles, just as though nothing had happened, to tell her uncle that she was betrothed to Bartholomew Champernowne, a young relation – although how distant I'm not quite sure – of the Champernowne family.'

'And did this news please Master Capstick?'

'There was a sort of reconciliation between them,' nodded Mistress Trenowth, 'and the Master promised her a handsome dowry when the marriage should eventually take place. But he told me after she'd gone – and he admitted saying this to her face – that he wasn't parting with any money beforehand in case her story was a trick, or in case this Bartholomew Champernowne should prove to be as impoverished and feckless as Cornelius Gifford had been. "Once bitten, twice shy," I remember him saying.'

'And Berenice wasn't angry at such plain speaking?'

'She didn't seem to be. Indeed, I don't recall ever having seen her look so happy.' A little smile lifted the corners of my companion's mouth, and she heaved a romantic sigh. 'She was obviously very much in love, and I believe that Master Capstick himself was half-persuaded that there was no foundation for his suspicions. But experience had taught him caution.'

A day or so later, however, all thoughts of his great-niece's betrothal were temporarily driven from Oliver Capstick's mind by the return to Plymouth of an old friend of his youth, a certain Edwin Haygarth, who had made his fortune in London, in the glass-making trade. This Master Haygarth had a granddaughter of marriageable age, his only remaining family, and almost as soon as he had renewed acquaintance with Oliver, he had proposed a union between this granddaughter and Beric Gifford.

'The Master was delighted with the idea,' Mistress Trenowth continued. 'His early mistake with his niece had convinced him that, after all, money was of far more importance than breeding. And marriage to this Jenny Haygarth would have made Beric rich for life.'

Beric, now a handsome, self-willed youth of eighteen, was summoned to his great-uncle's house and the proposition put to him.

'Well, to be honest, it wasn't so much put to him,' my companion said, 'as that the lad was told what was expected of him. Jenny Haygarth was rich and pretty. I don't think it so much as crossed Master Capstick's mind that Beric would refuse to do as he wished.'

Chapter Four

'But he did refuse?' I asked, although it was more a statement than a query.

'He refused point-blank,' Mistress Trenowth confirmed. 'He told his uncle to his face that when he took a bride, it would be one of his own choosing.'

'And what did Master Capstick say to that?'

My companion shrugged. 'He didn't take Beric seriously at first. He thought he was just being awkward and asserting his independence, so he told him not to be a fool.'

'You heard all this?'

Mistress Trenowth coloured faintly. 'They were in the parlour and took no trouble to lower their voices. The door was standing wide and so was the door to the kitchen. I couldn't choose but hear. Indeed, it became impossible not to, when they began to shout.'

'Master Gifford proved adamant, then, in refusing to accept this Jenny Haygarth as his bride?'

Miss Trenowth sighed. 'More than adamant! He abused his great-uncle roundly for trying, as he put it, to dictate whom he should marry. He called him a tyrant and other worse names. For a little while, the master still tried to reason with him – I was in the counting-house by this time. Dusting,' she added defensively.

I inclined my head. 'These chores have to be done.'

She looked suspiciously at me, but I kept a straight face, which seemed to satisfy her. 'Indeed, they do. Well, as I say, Master Capstick attempted to reason with his nephew, extolling the young lady's virtues; her beauty and docility and wealth, and impressing upon him that once he met her, he would be only too happy to take her for his wife. And that's when Beric really lost his temper. He said he was already promised, and that nothing and no one on this earth would persuade him to change his mind or to give up his betrothed.'

'Did he say who this young woman is?' I asked, as Mistress Trenowth paused to draw breath. But, of course, I knew the answer. My companion had already named her.

'He did. It was his sister's maid, Katherine Glover.'

'A choice not approved by his great-uncle, I assume.'

'Of course the Master didn't approve!' The ex-housekeeper was scathing in her condemnation. 'A common serving girl with neither money nor breeding to recommend her! What future is there in such an alliance for a young man without any fortune of his own?'

'What happened next?'

'When he'd calmed down a little, Master Capstick told Beric to go away and think about it. He also told him that if he didn't return the following day to say that he'd changed his mind and was willing to do his great-uncle's bidding, then he, Master Capstick that is, would alter his will. "At present," he said, "my money, when I die, is to be shared equally between you and your sister. But if you persist in refusing to marry Jenny Haygarth, I shall rewrite my will and leave everything to Berenice. She, at least, has had the good sense to betroth herself to a Champernowne."'

'And then?' I prompted, as Mistress Trenowth once again drew breath.

'And then,' she said, pressing a hand to her heart as she recalled the fright she had experienced at the time, 'there was this terrible scream and a gurgling sound. I ran into the parlour, hardly daring to imagine what I should find, to see the Master pinned against the wall with Beric's hands locked around his throat and his face beginning to turn a bluish colour.'

'What did you do?'

'I seized Beric around the waist with both arms, trying to drag him away and yelling at him that he was killing his great-uncle. At first, I don't think he was even aware of me, he was so furious; but then, suddenly, he dropped his hands to his sides and stood back, just staring at the Master with such malevolence that my blood ran cold.'

' "Make a new will, and be damned to you," he said. "I love Katherine and she loves me. We can live without your money." Of course they can't, and Beric thought they wouldn't have to. I've no doubt, and nor, I'm sure, had he, that Berenice would have shared everything with him once the money was hers.'

'What was Master Capstick's response?'

'As soon as he'd recovered sufficiently to be able to speak, he told me to go for Master Horner – that's his lawyer who lives down near the Blackfriars – immediately. "I'll draw up a new will this very afternoon," he said to Beric. "And I'll make it a condition of Berenice's inheriting my money that she settles none of it on you, so that you'll have to ask her for every last penny that you need. And once your sister's married, and her husband holds the purse strings, I doubt if you'll find it easy to get your hands on any of it. The Champernownes are a high-stomached race. There's not one of them who'd relish having a serving maid as a sister-in-law." '

'And did this threat give Beric second thoughts?'

Mistress Trenowth shook her head. ' "Do as you please, Uncle," he answered. "You won't stop me marrying Katherine. We love one another." He'd got as far as the parlour door when he turned round and added, "I just hope you won't live to regret this high-handed attitude of yours." Next minute, he'd gone and we heard the sound of his horse's hoofs on the cobbles outside. "Good riddance," the Master said. But he looked very white and shaken, and his legs were trembling so much that he had to sit down for a while. Beric had spoken with such vindictiveness it had plainly unnerved him.

'And did Master Capstick alter his will as he had threatened to do?' I asked.

'Oh, yes. I was sent for the lawyer as soon as Beric had gone, and the new will was drawn up that very afternoon, with myself and Master Horner's clerk as witnesses. Everything, including the house, was left to Berenice on the condition that Master Capstick had stated, and it was signed and dated the 30th of April. The next day was May Day, and the young people were clattering through the streets and disturbing everyone's rest very early in the morning, bringing in the may to crown the May Queen. That's why I remember the date of the quarrel and the making of the new will so clearly.'

I hesitated for a moment before asking as casually as I could, 'Did Master Capstick leave you anything in his will, Mistress Trenowth?'

'Oh, no!' She appeared genuinely shocked at the idea. 'The Master paid me generously while he was alive. I expected nothing further. Master Capstick was a great believer in the blood tie, and while there was a member of his own family living to inherit his money and property, he wouldn't have dreamt of leaving anything to anyone who wasn't kin.'

There didn't seem to be any underlying resentment in her tone, but I couldn't help wondering if Mistress Trenowth was simply disguising her true feelings. After more than fifteen years' faithful service, she might have expected to be left something, however small. I stored away the thought at the back of my mind to be considered later.

'When did the murder take place?' I asked. 'I know it was sometime in May. Mistress Cobbold told me.'

'Why, the very next day! May Day! I should have thought Joanna would have remembered that.'

'Maybe she mentioned it, but if she did, then I've forgotten. So! Beric returned the following morning, did he? Can you tell me about the murder – if, that is, it doesn't distress you too much?'

'No, it doesn't distress me, not now. I was upset greatly at the time, but after all these months, I find it easier to talk about.' Mistress Trenowth settled herself more comfortably in her chair, and I got the impression that she was, if anything, rather enjoying herself. 'That morning, I'd gone downstairs to prepare the Master's breakfast a bit earlier than usual. As I said, the May Day revellers had woken me and I hadn't been able to get back to sleep again. I wasn't the only one who'd been disturbed by them either. It turned out that both Mistress Cobbold and her neighbour on the other side, Mistress Hannaford, were also up and about betimes. Joanna had done her washing and was spreading it out on the fence and the grass to dry when she heard me scream and came rushing in to find out what was the matter . . .

'But I'm getting ahead of myself. I went into the kitchen and cooked the Master's breakfast. He was very partial to a herring fried in oatmeal, and I'd bought some nice fresh, plump ones only the day before. When they were ready, I put them on a plate and the plate on a tray, along with a mazer of ale and the heel of a loaf, and carried it all along the passageway, ready to go upstairs. Imagine my astonishment when I met Beric coming down. I nearly jumped out of my shoes, for I hadn't heard anyone come in.'

'How did Beric enter the house?' I asked. 'Wasn't the street door still bolted at that hour of the morning? You said that it was early.'

'I'd unbolted it as soon as I got downstairs. I always did.' She shrugged. 'There was nothing worth stealing in that house. All Master Capstick's money and bonds and papers and things were kept in a padlocked chest in Lawyer Horner's cellar. The Master told me so himself.' She added indignantly, 'I don't think anyone in Bilbury Street keeps their door bolted much after sunrise.'

Her manner had grown hostile. Mistress Trenowth obviously thought that I was accusing her of dereliction of duty, and so I hastened to reassure her.

'Of course!' I said. 'Of course! I wasn't reproaching you; you mustn't think that. Beric, then, wouldn't have expected to find the street door locked?'

'Probably not.' She was still a trifle antagonistic, so I gave her my most ingratiating smile and she visibly thawed. 'I don't really know. Perhaps if he had found it bolted, he would have thought better of his intentions and gone away again, and this terrible murder would never have happened. But trying the latch and finding it open, he just went in and ran upstairs to his uncle's bedchamber, where . . . where . . .' Her voice began to quaver, then faltered and died.

'Where he killed him,' I finished gently. She nodded mutely, her eyes full of tears, and I went on, 'Do you think Master Capstick was awake when his nephew entered his room?'

'If he was, he didn't cry out. Of course, he may not have had time before Beric was on him.'

'What weapon did his great-nephew use?'

My companion shivered. 'A weighted cudgel. The head had been split open and molten lead poured in before the crack was resealed with wax and resin.'

I nodded. I had often seen this done to make a truly lethal weapon.

She continued, 'Beric had made no attempt to conceal it, or carry it away with him, but left it on the bed beside Master Capstick's body. One of the Sheriff's men took it.'

'Joanna Cobbold said that when you met Master Gifford at the bottom of the stairs, you noticed that his tunic was stained with blood.'

'Not at the time,' Mistress Trenowth amended, confirming Joanna's actual words. 'Well, that is to say I suppose I *must* have noticed it, mustn't I, or I shouldn't have remembered it later on? But at that particular moment, I didn't realize just what it was. I was so surprised to see Beric, that I couldn't really take in anything else.'

'But afterwards, after you'd found the body, it dawned on you that Beric must have been covered in blood?'

She blinked at me, suspicious, without quite knowing why, of my form of words. 'The front of Beric's tunic was badly stained,' she answered. 'When I thought about it, I knew what it must have been.'

At that moment, the parlour door opened and a woman who might have been Mistress Trenowth's twin came in.

'Ah, good!' exclaimed the Widow Cooper, for it could not possibly have been anybody else. 'A pedlar! Just the man I'm wanting. I need some laces, if you have any, to replace those in the back of this gown.'

There was small chance of questioning Mistress Trenowth further after the arrival of the Widow Cooper, who was a voluble woman with a constant flow of small talk that required little more than the occasional nod or murmur of assent. In her favour, it must be said that she not only bought my entire stock of laces, but also invited me to share their dinner; an offer that I accepted readily enough, for I was by then extremely hungry. But although on two or three occasions during the meal I made an attempt to reintroduce the topic of Master Capstick's murder, I was unsuccessful, the widow seeming to have far more interest in the gossip she had heard along the quayside that morning, and which she wished, in her turn, to impart to her sister.

When we had finished eating, however, Mistress Trenowth accompanied me to the street door and asked in a low voice if I thought there was any chance of catching Beric Gifford and bringing him to justice.

'I shall do my best,' I said, 'but I can't promise to succeed in finding him where so many others have failed. You're sure that he won't have gone far while this Katherine Glover is still living at Valletort Manor? He might, after all, be planning to send for her once he has settled in some other part of the country, where he's unknown.'

She shook her head decidedly. 'What would they live on? They have to rely on Berenice for money, and she won't leave her home, especially not now she's betrothed to Bartholomew Champernowne.'

We both heard Mistress Cooper's voice upraised, calling to her sister, and Mathilda Trenowth turned to go. I shot out a hand to detain her, at the same time fishing in my pocket with the other. 'I have something to confess,' I said, and told her about my trespass of the previous night. 'I found this,' I went on, 'buried under the rushes in Master Capstick's bedchamber.' And I held out the brooch with its entwined initials, B and G, and its pendant, teardrop pearl.

Mistress Trenowth stared at it for a moment or two in silence. Then, 'Yes, that's Beric's,' she confirmed at last, speaking with difficulty as though the sight of the jewel had brought back too many memories that she would prefer to forget. 'He . . . he used to wear it in his hat.' She seemed upset and drew back against the wall as if for support, her plump fingers knotted together.

Mistress Cooper appeared from the parlour, anxious to join in the conversation and curious to discover what we were talking about.

'I was telling the chapman,' Mistress Trenowth said quickly, motioning me almost furtively to put the brooch back in my pocket, 'that if he should find himself Modbury way, he must visit our sister. She'll give him a warm welcome and a bed for the night if he needs one.' She turned to smile tremulously at me. 'Just ask for Anne Fettiplace. Anyone will direct you to her cottage, won't they, Ursula?'

'She's well known in Modbury, certainly,' Mistress Cooper cheerfully agreed. 'Where are you off to now, chapman? I should try Notte Street if I were you. Plenty of money to be made there.' I thanked her for the advice and was about to take my leave when she added, 'Wait! I'll come with you and show you the way.'

'But you've not long come home,' said Mistress Trenowth, plaintively.

'Well, and now I want to go out again,' laughed her sister. 'We can't let the chapman get lost, now can we?' She winked at me. 'You can wash the dirty dishes if you want something to do while I'm gone.'

The widow, ignoring her sister's indignant protests, took her cloak from a peg near the door, flung it around her shoulder and preceded me into the street. When we were out of earshot, she asked accusingly, 'Have you been talking to Mathilda about Master Capstick's murder?'

I admitted that I had. 'But it was with her permission,' I urged. 'Mistress Cobbold of Bilbury Street gave me the history of the case, but there were certain details I wished to know that I felt only Mistress Trenowth could supply. It didn't seem,' I went on in extenuation of my actions, 'that speaking of the murder at all distressed your sister. Naturally, I shouldn't have continued if it had.'

'Yet it does upset her,' Mistress Cooper insisted. 'She still gets nightmares and wakes up crying. I tell you this because, having overheard part of your conversation when I came in earlier, I guessed what you had been talking about. And you strike me as the sort of persistent youth who might well return to plague my sister again.'

'I don't think Mistress Trenowth would mind if I did,' I retorted, my temper beginning to rise. 'It appeared to me that she wanted to discuss what had happened.'

'So she may, but it doesn't do her any good,' the widow replied, with the know-it-all air of someone supremely confident of her own perspicacity and judgement. 'The sooner she forgets all about the Giffords, brother and sister, and everything that happened in Bilbury Street, the better it will be.'

I didn't protest that I thought it highly unlikely Mistress Trenowth ever would forget, because I didn't have time.

Mistress Cooper continued, almost without drawing breath, 'Not, mind you, that Capstick, the old skinflint, deserves to be remembered by her. Over fifteen years Mathilda looked after that man – and no wife could have looked after a husband better – and then to be left nothing at all in his will! It's disgraceful, and so I told her, although she pretends she doesn't care. But, of course, she does. She's bound to! She has every right to feel resentful, that's what I say!'

'Are you acquainted with Beric and Berenice Gifford?' I asked.

'I've met them on occasions at Master Capstick's house, when I've been visiting Mathilda. And I've seen them often enough around the town when they've come to Plymouth for other reasons;

mostly to buy things here that they can't obtain in Modbury. They're both of them fond of fine clothes. Not two groats to rub together, mark you, but decked out like peacocks, the pair of them. But then, that's typical of such people.'

We had by this time reached the entrance to Notte Street, close by the Dominican Friary. Two rows of houses, rising gently over the headland, faced each other, not one of them then more than twenty years old, their brightly painted façades not yet seriously weathered by the salt-laden wind and rain from the sea. The widow was right. There was money here for the taking, and I could put up my prices without compunction if I had a mind to.

'Well here we are,' Ursula Cooper said. 'This is where I must leave you. I trust I can rely on you, chapman, not to pester Mathilda again, simply in order to satisfy your ghoulish curiosity.'

I did not answer her directly, but asked instead, 'Do you believe that Beric Gifford has eaten Saint John's fern?'

She snorted contemptuously. 'No, I don't! If he's any sense, he's escaped and is miles away by now. Ireland, perhaps, or Scotland! Although France is much nearer, and it wouldn't be all that difficult to find a boat whose master was willing to take him across the Channel – for a price.'

'But what about this Katherine Glover? Mistress Trenowth is certain that he wouldn't stir anywhere without her.'

'Nonsense!' The widow was dismissive. 'He's only to wait awhile and then send for her when the time is ripe.'

I sighed, thanked her, and stood looking after her as she walked away. A domineering woman, but one whose sole concern was for Mistress Trenowth's welfare, however mistaken she might be in that sister's needs. I wondered how long they would be able to tolerate one another before parting company. It was already over five months since the murder, a fair time for two women to share the same house.

As I climbed the gentle incline of Notte Street, I wondered if the Widow Cooper was not indeed correct in her assumption that Beric Gifford had fled to France. And yet, as Mistress Trenowth had pointed out, money would have proved a stumbling block, particularly before Berenice had come into possession of her uncle's fortune. Later, however, when the money was hers, had he gone then? Yet, according to Mathilda Trenowth, he would never have stirred without Katherine Glover, and she was still at Valletort Manor . . . Nothing seemed to make sense.

At least I knew now that the house in Bilbury Street belonged to Berenice Gifford. But why had she left it and its furnishings to rot? Before long, once people had overcome their horror of the killing, and when some curious person discovered, as I had done, that the street door was unlocked, the contents would gradually be stolen. If she wished to preserve her property, she would do well to look to it before it was too late.

I paused, my hand, upraised to knock on one of the Notte Street doors, arrested in midair. Perhaps I ought to return to Bilbury Street immediately and alert Mistress Cobbold to the fact that the neighbouring house was wide open to thieves and vagabonds. I should have to admit to how I knew this fact, but I felt that she had a right to be told. Consequently, I abandoned all thought of rich pickings in Notte Street and made my way back to Old Town Ward. But as I approached Martyn's Gate, I saw that there was a horse, a light-coloured palfrey, tied to the hitching-post outside Master Capstick's former dwelling.

I was still some few yards distant, when the door of the house opened and a young woman emerged.

Chapter Five

I saw at once that this could not be Berenice Gifford. The woman's garments were too plain and too sober for one who had recently acquired a fortune and who, by reputation, had a liking for finery. The clothes were more suited to those of a lady's maid, so I felt justified in my assumption that this was Katherine Glover. And who would be more trusted with the key of the house than a future sister-in-law?

And I could see that the girl *did* have the key, for, having closed the front door behind her, she inserted it in the lock; but her subsequent vain attempts to turn it gave me my opportunity.

I lengthened my stride. 'Can I be of help?' I asked, pausing beside her. 'You seem to be having trouble.'

She turned a delicate, flower-like face towards me, a strand of pale golden brown hair escaping from beneath her linen hood. Startled grey eyes, widely spaced on either side of a small straight nose, regarded me with a certain amount of apprehension while a softly bowed red mouth completed an enchanting picture. It was easy to see why Beric Gifford had been unwilling to give her up, even for a wife with a substantial dowry.

'Thank you. You're most kind,' she answered in tones that were deeper and stronger than I had expected from so fragile-looking a creature. 'The lock's rusty and the wards are stiff. Sometimes the key fails to do its job properly and the house remains open to any passing thief. If you would be good enough to make sure that the door is indeed secure, I should be very grateful.'

I checked, but this time, the key had behaved satisfactorily, so I smiled, withdrew it and handed it to the girl, noting as I did so that her fingers and nails were none too clean. I remarked as casually as I could, 'I was told that the person who lived here was murdered.'

Her whole body stiffened and the delicate features grew rigid with anger and disdain.

'This town is a hotbed of gossip. Every passing traveller is made free of all its scandals. No doubt you have been told the name of the murderer, too.' And she turned away abruptly, mounted the patiently waiting palfrey and rode off through Martyn's Gate.

A woman's voice said, 'That was Katherine Glover.'

I glanced round to see Joanna Cobbold, who had come out of her cottage and was now standing inside the paling that fenced its surrounding plot of ground. I retraced a few steps so that we could speak more comfortably.

'I guessed as much,' I nodded. 'I've seen Mistress Trenowth so I know who she is. Did you have any conversation with her?'

'A little. I saw her arrive half an hour since and pretended to be suspicious, particularly when she had a struggle to unlock the front door. It turned out, by the way, that it was already open. Whoever visited the house last hadn't managed to fasten it properly on leaving.'

I made no comment on this, merely asking, 'What did she have to say?'

'She told me her name when I asked her, and when I pressed for further information, I learnt that Mistress Gifford is at last thinking of selling the house. Before she does so, however, she needs to know what condition it's in after remaining empty these past five months. But that was all. When I would have put more questions, the girl ignored me and went inside and shut the door.'

'You say you asked her her name. Have you never previously seen Katherine Glover, then? Did she never accompany Berenice on any of her visits to Oliver Capstick?'

Joanna shook her head. 'Not that I recall. If she did, she made no impression on me. Berenice usually rode alone, and I remember Mistress Trenowth once telling me that she – Berenice that is – is a headstrong, fearless sort of girl, not much given to regarding the womanly conventions. So, making a journey of some twelve miles, from Modbury to Plymouth, unaccompanied, wouldn't worry her unduly, I imagine.'

I ventured another question on the subject of Oliver Capstick's murder, neither of the Cobbold boys being within earshot as far as I could tell.

'Were there many sightings of Beric on the morning that he killed his great-uncle? Or did the identity of the murderer rest simply on the testimony of yourself and of Mistress Trenowth?'

'It most certainly did not,' Joanna retorted, incensed. 'My neighbour, Bessie Hannaford, also caught a glimpse of Beric on his arrival. And as my husband told you yesterday at supper, quite a few people recognized him, both on his ride from Modbury to Plymouth, and again on his journey home. I know for a fact that a husband and wife, who live on the far side of the White Friars, beyond Martyn's Gate, saw him pass by on both occasions. And there was a smallholder who lives near Yealmpton. He was on his way to Plymouth market when he met Beric returning. Oh, and he was seen earlier by a woman near Brixton church, travelling westwards; so, on that occasion, he must have been on his way here. And a friend of his – whose name I've forgotten, if I ever knew it – recognized him in the distance, close to Sequers Bridge, but whether coming or going back I've no idea. So you see, the Sheriff's men had no need to rely only on the word of Mistress Trenowth or myself. But even if they had, can you doubt for a moment that either of us could have failed to recognize Beric when we were as near to him as I am now to that hitching-post?'

I assured her that I had never seriously entertained the notion that she and the housekeeper had been mistaken. I was just making certain in order to satisfy my own curiosity. 'But I have one further question,' I added. 'I should have asked it of Mistress Trenowth, but unfortunately her sister came in and I forgot. Although I have to admit that I wouldn't expect her to have known the answer any more than I expect you to know it now. Nevertheless, you might have some idea, some opinion of your own.'

Joanna Cobbold raised her eyebrows. 'And what is this question? I must say that you seem very interested in this murder, Master Chapman.'

I ignored her last remark and continued, 'I'm assuming that you know all the circumstances leading up to the killing. Mistress Trenowth, I feel sure, confided in you as she has since done in me.' When Joanna nodded, I went on, 'In that case, you must be aware that the day prior to the murder, Beric Gifford had made it clear to Master Capstick that nothing, neither blandishments nor threats, would persuade him to marry any girl but Katherine Glover. He was very angry with his great-uncle, and, according to Mistress Trenowth, physically attacked the old man. But, in the end, not much harm was done and he rode home to Modbury.'

Joanna shifted her position and leant against the outer wall of the cottage, as though her back was hurting. 'Well?' she demanded curtly.

'I was only thinking,' I said, 'that anger arising out of a quarrel usually cools with time and distance, especially if a person is conscious of having won the argument. But in this particular instance, even though he had had a night's sleep to calm him, Beric got up at first light the following morning and, without making the smallest attempt at secrecy, rode back to Plymouth with the fell intent of murdering his great-uncle in cold blood. Now, what could possibly have happened between his arrival home the previous day and his departure some ten or twelve hours later, to make him act in such a way?'

Mistress Cobbold was interested in spite of herself. A few moments ago, her growing impatience had been palpable, but now she pushed herself away from the cottage wall and came to stand by the paling again, so that we were once more directly facing one another.

'Perhaps,' she said at last, after careful consideration of the matter, 'Beric didn't really believe that Master Capstick would carry out his threat to change his will that very afternoon. He knew that if he continued to defy him, his great-uncle would indeed alter his will, but didn't think he would do so immediately. He thought it an idle boast and not one to be taken seriously. And as far as I can recall Mistress Trenowth's story, she had not left the house to fetch the lawyer before Beric quit it.'

'No,' I agreed. 'My recollection is the same. So, your theory is that Master Gifford determined to kill his great-uncle before, as he thought, Oliver Capstick actually carried out his threat to change his will. But if that is so, why did Beric commit the murder so openly? Surely, secrecy was vital to such a plan. All the money in the world was no good to him once he had put a noose around his neck.'

Joanna looked crestfallen as she was forced to confront this new problem, but after a little consideration, she perked up again.

'Very well,' she said. 'I take your point. In that case, he killed Master Capstick so that his sister could inherit the money straight away. Valletort Manor – so I understand – is falling down around their ears, and he wants to marry Katherine Glover. But she won't bring him any dowry. He decided that if he ate Saint John's fern, he could become invisible at will and so escape the consequences of his crime. Later, in a year or so, maybe, when the hue and cry has died down and people have more than half-forgotten about the murder, he and Katherine Glover can escape to France or Brittany or maybe even further – perhaps as far as Scotland – where no one knows them or their history, and they can live comfortably on the money that Berenice has shared with them.'

'That is, if she *is* willing to share her inheritance with her brother. And you're forgetting that by then she might well be married to this Bartholomew Champernowne, to whom she claims to be betrothed. He might not be willing for his wife to divide her fortune.'

Nevertheless, this particular argument would have had a certain merit had I for one moment truly believed in the magic properties of Saint John's fern. But, I thought suddenly, supposing there was a secret hiding place somewhere on Valletort Manor itself or in the surrounding countryside; a place known only to the Gifford family, the knowledge of its whereabouts passed on under oath of secrecy from father to son. Such a theory would by no means answer all the questions that needed to be asked about Oliver Capstick's murder, but it seemed to me to be as close an answer to the riddle as I was going to get at present.

I leant across the paling and lightly kissed Joanna Cobbold's cheek. 'Thank you,' I said.

She flushed with pleasure, but looked bewildered. 'What for?' she wanted to know.

'I think your second idea might contain some seeds of truth,' I told her. 'And without you, I shouldn't have seen the possibilities.'

Her face turned an even deeper shade of pink and she grew flustered. 'I must go and find out what my two young limbs of

Satan are up to,' she said hurriedly, holding out her hand.
'Goodbye, chapman. Don't forget to visit my father if ever you're
Tavistock way. He would be most disappointed if you didn't.'
And she disappeared into the cottage.

I smiled to myself, hitched up my pack, grasped my cudgel
firmly in my right hand and made my way out of Plymouth by
Martyn's Gate.

I crossed Bilbury Bridge and took the road eastwards. Noticing
the Carmelite Friary on my left, I remembered Joanna Cobbold's
words concerning a husband and wife who lived nearby, and who
claimed to have recognized Beric Gifford as he passed their door,
both going towards, and, later, returning from Martyn's Gate.

I glanced around me, but there was only one dwelling anywhere
near the friary, and that was a single-storey, stone-tiled cottage
some hundred yards further on, on the opposite side of the track,
close to the shoreline. It was surrounded by a small garden in
which grew a plentiful supply of samphire and sea beet, both
good for the cooking pot, and, I guessed, the occupants' means of
livelihood, sold by them either in Plymouth market or door to
door.

While I hesitated, wary of intruding, the goodwife emerged
from her cottage carrying a knife, and began to cut the now
flowerless plants, stripping them of their fleshy leaves which she
packed, layer upon layer, into a basket. She glanced up briefly as
I approached, then, finding me of no great interest, stooped once
more to her task.

I coughed in order to attract her attention, and when she again
looked up, I asked politely, 'Do you need anything today, Mistress?
Needles, thread? Silks, laces? Knives or spoons?' I slid my pack
from my back and shook it enticingly.

It was her turn to hesitate while she considered. Then, reaching a decision, she jerked her head towards the cottage door and said, 'Come inside.'

After the brightness of the afternoon sun, the interior of the little house was very gloomy, and all I could see for several moments was a galaxy of stars and whirling orange circles. When my sight cleared, however, the first thing I noticed was a table ranged against one wall, and a man sitting at it, having a meal and, at the same time, counting a pile of coins. The latter he quickly whisked out of sight, into his pocket, as soon as he saw me.

'A pedlar, Jacob,' the woman said, 'come to show us his wares. Clear the table, now, so he can spread them out.' And, with a single movement of her arm, she swept aside the tin plate and mug from which her husband was eating and drinking. The man seemed used to this sort of treatment and made no demur, except to grimace at me when he thought his wife wasn't looking. I smiled at him sympathetically.

'I haven't all day,' the woman admonished me sharply. 'I've more harvesting to do before sundown, so just let me see what you're selling.'

I unbuckled the straps of my pack and laid out its contents for her inspection. Whilst I did so, I cudgelled my brains for the most natural way in which to introduce the subject of Oliver Capstick's murder and their sighting of Beric Gifford. In the end, though, I need not have worried. It was the man, Jacob, who mentioned the subject without any prompting from me.

'You've been hawking your goods around Plymouth, have you? Not much joy to be had there, I'll be bound. Tight-fisted lot! Never want to pay a fair price for anything. Which way have you come? By Martyn's Gate and Bilbury Bridge?' I grunted assent and he went on, 'Did you happen to notice a house just inside the gate, painted red and gold? There was a very nasty murder there, five months back. At the very beginning of May it was. The owner,

Oliver Capstick by name, was bludgeoned to death by one of his own kinfolk; by his own great-nephew, Beric Gifford.'

'I did hear something of the story,' I said, keeping a close eye upon the goodwife who, I felt, was not above slipping one or two of the smaller items into her apron pocket while my attention was engaged elsewhere. 'There seems to be no doubt in anyone's mind that the killer was this young man you've mentioned. And yet surely it would be too foolhardy for anyone to commit such a crime so openly. Perhaps people are mistaken as to his identity.'

'There's no mistake,' the goodwife said tartly, picking up and putting down a length of cream silk ribbon on which she left earthy fingermarks. 'Jacob and I both saw him that very morning, the first time on his way to do the deed, and the second time on his way back.'

'And you're certain that it was Master Capstick's great-nephew? You know him well enough, do you, to recognize him? You weren't persuaded into thinking it was him, after others has named him as the culprit?'

The goodwife swelled up like a frog and almost burst with indignation.

'How dare you question my judgement?' she cried. 'Why, I've known Beric Gifford since he was in his cradle, even if my husband hasn't. Before I wed Jacob, I was laundress to Mistress Gifford, who died, poor thing, when Beric was born. And since my marriage, many and many's the time I've seen him and his sister pass by on their way to visit Master Capstick. They both knew us by sight as well as we knew them, and Beric would always wave to us if we were outside the cottage. Not recognize him, indeed! What would you know about it?'

'And did you ever think him capable of murder?'

The goodwife took a sudden, deep breath and looked unhappy. 'Of course I didn't! You can't imagine someone you know –' she did not add the words 'and like' although I could tell that they were on the tip of her tongue – 'doing something as . . . as horrible as that.'

'So why do think he did it?'

She shrugged. 'There's talk in the town of a family quarrel. Something to do with his great-uncle wanting him to marry money and Beric wanting to marry his sister's maid.'

'Money's really at the bottom of it, you can be certain of that,' the man, Jacob, said, patting his pocket and making the coins in it jingle. 'There are more murders committed for money than love.'

His wife snorted. 'And what would you know about love, pray? Answer me that!'

I decided it was time I left before a family dispute erupted and entangled me in its coils. 'Have you found anything you wish to buy?' I asked the goodwife.

She shrugged. 'No. Put your stuff away. There's nothing there that tempts me.'

In normal circumstances, I should have been irritated by this contemptuous dismissal of my wares, especially after so much careless handling of them. But I had not come to sell and had learnt what I wanted to know. The goodwife and her husband were both as sure that they had seen Beric Gifford on the day of Master Capstick's murder as were Mistress Trenowth and Joanna Cobbold.

As I gathered my goods together and restored them to my pack, I asked, 'You say that this young man always waved to you as he passed your cottage. Did he do so on the morning of the murder?'

The couple looked at me in some surprise, and then at one another.

'Yes, I fancy that he did, now that you remind me of it,' the woman said at last. She laughed. 'Odd, when you come to think of it, considering what he must have had on his mind.' She turned to her husband. 'Can you remember, Jacob? You were with me in the garden when he rode by. Did Master Gifford wave to us? Your memory's better than mine.'

Jacob thoughtfully scratched one side of his nose. 'I believe you're right,' he finally agreed. 'He did wave, the first time, same as he always does. Force of habit, I suppose. But not on the way back.' He slewed round on his stool, repeating Joanna Cobbold's observation almost word for word. 'You seem very interested in this murder, chapman.'

I fastened the straps on my pack. 'It's an intriguing case,' I said. 'From what I learnt in Bilbury Street, the young man has never been brought to justice, although everyone believes him to be responsible for the crime. He has, it seems, disappeared without trace, in spite of the posse being after him before his great-uncle's body was cold. Some people reckon that he's eaten Saint John's fern.'

The goodwife gave another of her raucous laughs. 'Gone abroad more like. France, perhaps. Or Brittany, to join that troublemaker, Henry Tudor.'

Her husband said nothing, but crossed himself.

'I'm sorry there was nothing here to your liking, Mistress,' I said as I shouldered my pack. 'Another day you could be luckier. If I'm ever this way again, I'll knock on your door.' But privately, I vowed never to go near them if I could help it. They had not even offered me a cup of water, let alone a stoup of ale. They might be down on their luck, but most poor people observed the laws of hospitality.

'We shall be pleased to have your company,' the goodwife said with a small, secretive smile of satisfaction. And I guessed then that she had managed to pocket some item from amongst my stock while I wasn't looking. I should discover later what was missing.

At the cottage door, I paused and looked back at the husband, who had taken the coins from his pocket and was once more counting them.

'You say Beric waved to you when you first saw him, riding into Plymouth, but not on the return journey. On that occasion, did either of you call to him, or try to attract his attention?'

Jacob looked up and frowned. 'Are you still here?' He laid a protective hand over his pile of money. 'There wouldn't have been any point calling out to him. He was riding as though all the devils in Hell were at his heels.'

The goodwife nodded in corroboration. 'He was riding so fast that he was having difficulty in controlling that great brute of a horse of his. Just for a minute, I thought he was going to be thrown.'

'But other than that, there was nothing suspicious in his appearance? You didn't notice any blood on his clothes, for instance?'

'We've told you,' the man said crossly, reaching for his tin cup and draining the dregs, 'he was riding so fast there wasn't time to notice anything.' And with that, he hunched the shoulder nearest to me, indicating that I should get no more from him. I had outstayed my welcome.

I said my farewells and, a few minutes later, was back on the road and once again walking eastwards.

Chapter Six

It was, by now, late afternoon, and the golden-blue haze of the middle distance had lost its radiance. A fine mist was moving in from the sea, and it would soon be time to find shelter for the night.

On the advice of a passing cowherd, whose instruction I sought, I struck out in a south-easterly direction across the Cattedown peninsula that divides Sutton Pool from the mouth of the River Plym.

'Ferry'll take you over the Cattewater,' the man told me, 'to Oreston, on the other side. There's a decent inn there, if you're able to pay your board.' He looked me up and down, while his cows, anxious to be milked, pushed and jostled one another along the homeward track, leaving him behind. 'On the other hand, a strapping, good-looking young fellow like you could well get free lodgings if he's civil to the landlord's wife. She's an eye for a handsome youth.' And with a nod and a wink, he set off in pursuit of his cattle.

I called my thanks after his rapidly retreating back and continued along the path he had indicated. There had been a time, and what an age ago it seemed now – although, in truth, it was far more recent than I imagined – when I might have been excited by the prospect of an older woman's admiration, but no longer. Nowadays, I was a happily married man, in love with my wife;

61

and at the memory of Adela, I found myself striding out, grinning like an idiot. Then, as there was no one to hear me, I pursed my lips and began to whistle happily, if tunelessly. (For as I have said somewhere before in these chronicles, I've absolutely no ear for music, and my pitiful attempts at it can drive listeners into a frenzy.)

After a while, however, I fell silent and my pace slowed as my thoughts again reverted to the murder of Oliver Capstick. I was by now thoroughly convinced that Beric Gifford had not rendered himself invisible by eating the leaves of Saint John's fern. Only the previous year, I had proved to my own satisfaction, as well as to that of others, that there could be a logical explanation for the disappearance of a young man, as if by magic. No, for me the most probable answer to the mystery was still that Beric had escaped to France or joined Henry Tudor in Brittany, and that he would presently send for Katherine Glover to join him. As for money, Berenice would see to it that her young brother and his future wife did not starve.

Yet the problem remained, why had Beric put himself in such an untenable position? He had gained nothing but a lifetime of exile and financial dependence upon his sister; a sister who was shortly to marry a high-stomached Champernowne. Of course, if it should prove necessary, there were plenty of ways in which a young man, in possession of his health and strength, could earn his living abroad, but why had Beric chosen to give up a pleasurable, leisured existence for one of constant hard work and insecurity? The simple answer, I supposed, was anger; that instant, uncontrollable rage which has caused many a man and – though far less frequently – woman to put a noose around his or her neck for the satisfaction of a single, brief moment of revenge.

But although Beric Gifford's instant rage had resulted in his almost choking the life out of Oliver Capstick, he had been prevented from killing his great-uncle partly by Mistress Trenowth's intervention, and partly, surely, by his own good sense and better judgement. 'Suddenly, he dropped his hands to his sides and stood back,' the housekeeper had told me. So why had he gone away, only to return the next morning in order to resume his murderous business? Something must have happened that last day of April, after he reached Valletort Manor, to rekindle his anger and make him determined to complete the deed; something that had so inflamed him that he had grown careless of all normal precautions to conceal his identity, causing him to ride out there and then to finish what he had failed to do the previous afternoon.

Following this line of reasoning, it was possible to assume that Beric, filled with an all-consuming hatred, had not paused to consider the consequences of his action until he was on his way home again. The realization that he had been seen and recognized beyond the slightest shadow of a doubt, and the knowledge that, in the circumstances, it would not be long before a Sheriff's posse was hard on his heels, must have hit him like a thunderbolt, making him urge his mount forward at breakneck speed. Small wonder, then, if the resentful animal had tried to throw him, for the horse was probably unused to such harsh treatment from his master.

But however much panic Beric was in, he must have decided on his course of action by the time he reached Valletort Manor, where Berenice and Katherine Glover would presumably have been awaiting his return in great anxiety. (It seemed to me unthinkable that they could have been ignorant of his intention towards Master Capstick, or of the reasons for it.) And whatever instructions had been issued by Beric had been carried out quickly and efficiently – perhaps even anticipated? – by his sister and her maid. Certainly, there was no sign of him by the time his pursuers arrived not long afterwards.

But this was as far, at present, as I was prepared to speculate.

I must rein in my imagination for a while, until I had accumulated some facts to support my theory. And there were more important things to think about just at the moment, for while I had been descending Cattedown towards the stretch of shore where the ferry boat was beached, the sea mist had thickened and was now turning to a persistent drizzle. The breeze had freshened, too, and the daylight grown murky, presaging an evening of wind and rain. It never ceases to astonish me how swiftly the weather of that south-western coast can change, as happened on that October afternoon. It was less than an hour since it had been warm and sunny, but now, although the day was not greatly advanced, I was eager to seek out food and shelter and be under cover as soon as possible.

The ferryman, fetched from his cottage, was none too pleased to be called out in such inclement conditions, particularly as I was the only person in need of his services. But I promised to pay him double his usual fare if he would row me to the Oreston side, whereupon, although still muttering grumpily under his breath, he returned to his cottage, reappearing a few moments later in a thick, hooded frieze cloak. I had in the meantime wrapped my own cloak about me, and together we dragged the boat into the choppy water.

It was not a pleasant crossing, the wind and rain getting stronger and heavier with every minute, the waves lapping over the sides of the little vessel and drenching our feet. But, thanks to the ferryman's skill, we arrived safely on the opposite shore, where I paid him his promised fee before waving him off on his journey homewards, silently thanking Heaven that I had not to endure it a second time. Then I turned and walked towards the inn, whose outline I could just make out, looming through the mist.

The Bird of Passage Inn stood in the lee of some arthritic, wind-blasted trees, whose remaining leaves were floating sadly to the ground to add to the piles already there. In sunlight, no doubt the place had a welcoming enough appearance, but in the murky dankness of a late, wet and misty autumn afternoon, its granite exterior looked somewhat cheerless. I approached it with no great enthusiasm, but a night's lodging was all I required and it would probably prove sufficiently comfortable for that.

The inn was of modest proportions, but there was a stable to the left of the building; a row of three stalls that, I suspected, were rarely occupied, the Bird of Passage being primarily frequented by travellers on foot, using the ferry. But even as the thought entered my head, and just to prove how fallible my deductions could be, I heard the whinny of a horse coming from the stall closest to the inn. So, unless the animal belonged to the innkeeper, I was confident of having company at supper.

Sure enough, as I ducked my head beneath the lintel, I could see a woman sitting at a bench near the fire holding her slender hands to the blaze, the skirts of her coarse, woollen gown steaming gently in the heat. She looked around as I entered, and I was surprised to see again the person I had encountered an hour or so earlier, outside Oliver Capstick's house. My fellow guest was none other than Katherine Glover.

For a moment or two, I was nonplussed as to why she was not much further ahead of me on the road to Modbury, until I realized that, travelling on horseback, she must have ridden some way northwards after passing through Martyn's Gate, in order to cross the Plym. But, having done so, why she had returned to Oreston instead of striking out across country, I had no idea.

I took off my cloak and shook it, the raindrops iridescent in the firelight, before advancing to warm my own hands at the leaping flames.

'We meet once more,' I said, smiling.

Katherine Glover frowned. 'I'm not aware that we have met before, sir,' she answered.

This was a severe blow to my self-esteem, for most people remember me, if only because of my height. I should have to remember, when I got home, to tell Adela, who would laugh and say that I needed to be shorn of some of my conceit.

'Outside Master Capstick's house, in Bilbury Street,' I reminded my companion. 'You were having trouble turning the key in the lock of the front door, and I was able to do it for you.' She inclined her head slightly, but made no response, so I continued with an assumed ignorance, 'I imagined you to be well ahead of me by this time.'

'You no doubt came by the ferry,' she said. 'I had to ride northwards a way, in order to cross the river by the Ebb Ford, at Crabtree.'

Curiosity made me impolite. 'And you returned to Oreston?' I frowned. 'Surely there are easier ways of reaching Valletort Manor?' I was half-hoping that she might reveal in which direction the manor lay.

Her face flushed a deep crimson, that had nothing to do with the heat of the fire.

'You seem to have learnt a great deal about me, chapman. How do you know where I live?'

'I spent last night with Mistress Cobbold, Master Capstick's neighbour.'

Katherine Glover curled her lip. 'That explains everything,' she sneered.

'I also have a passing acquaintance with Mistress Trenowth,' I added.

The sneer became more pronounced. 'Then you probably know as much about my affairs as I know myself.' Katherine Glover, whose wide, grey eyes had been raised to mine, now looked away, staring into the heart of the fire. 'As to why I didn't ride straight home after crossing the ford, the answer is simple. It's obvious that a storm is brewing. It was growing dusk early and those cross-country tracks are rough and lonely. It would be easy enough for the horse to stumble in the dark, and there are footpads and outlaws about to add to the danger. A woman on her own is never really safe. So I decided to ride here, to Oreston.'

I recalled my own crossing of the Ebb Ford the previous day, travelling in the opposite direction in the company of Peter Threadgold. 'There's an inn at Crabtree,' I said, 'to the best of my recollection.'

'Well, I prefer this one,' she snapped. 'The owners are my uncle – my father's brother – and his wife.' She was angry now, as she had every right to be at my unwarranted questioning of her arrangements. 'I'll thank you to mind your own business and leave me to manage mine.'

At that moment, the landlord entered the taproom and, hearing Katherine's raised voice, looked at me with hostility.

'This pedlar annoying you, Kate?' he demanded.

She hesitated , then shook her head. 'It's all right, Uncle. He's come from Plymouth, and has been listening to gossip about Master Capstick's death, with the result that he regards me as being under suspicion for harbouring a murderer. And he thinks this gives him the right to quiz me on all my movements. He's not the first, however, nor will he be the last to make such an impertinent assumption.'

'No, no!' I protested feebly, knowing that she was right, and guessing that she had probably suffered from public calumny and intrusion into her affairs ever since the killing and Beric's subsequent disappearance.

'Well, if that's the case, you can be on your way, chapman,' the landlord informed me belligerently. 'My niece has had enough to put up with from neighbours and folks in these parts generally, without perfect strangers giving her offence.'

'Now, now, Maurice, let's not be too hasty,' said a voice behind him, and the goodwife of the establishment glided into view. A pair of very bright, almost black eyes looked me up and down, and the full, sensuous mouth curved into an approving smile. 'Let's not be turning good money away from the door. The lad didn't mean to be inquisitive or rude, I'm certain. People's interest is always aroused by a murder, and there's no denying that Katherine's name will be bandied about in connection with it, whether she likes it or not.' She moved forward and laid a bony hand on my arm. 'But whatever you've been told by the Plymouth gossips, our niece knows nothing of Beric Gifford's present whereabouts, nor does she wish to. Her betrothal to him is at an end. Is that not correct, my dear?' she added, glancing towards Katherine with raised eyebrows.

'If you say so, Aunt Theresa,' the girl answered, but did not turn her head.

'I tender my apologies, Mistress,' I said. 'There is no possible justification for my prying into your affairs, or for questioning you as I did. I hope you'll forgive me.'

'Of course she will,' the goodwife, whose name I now knew to be Theresa Glover, assured me before Katherine had a chance to reply. 'That's settled, then.' She smiled at me. 'Are you looking for a bed for the night, chapman? You'd be wise to stop here if you can afford it. The weather's getting worse by the sound of it.'

At her words, we all paused to listen. Great gusts of wind, smelling of the sea, were hurling themselves against the shutters, which rattled dismally, like the loose teeth in an old man's head. The rain drummed on the roof of the inn in a steady, relentless rhythm, and the quiet firelit taproom seemed a haven of warmth and security in the surrounding stormy darkness.

'I'm hoping for supper as well as a bed, Mistress,' I answered. 'I can pay for both.' And I patted the pouch at my belt.

Mistress Glover nodded briskly, not doubting my word. 'In that case, I'll go and prepare your room. As for food, there's fish broth, half a cold capon, a pigeon pie, and some apple pasties that I baked myself only this morning.'

She hurried away, leaving me facing the still antagonistic landlord.

'What do you say, Kate?' Maurice Glover asked his niece after a moment or two. 'Do you want him to stay? Because if you don't out he goes, storm or no storm.'

'Oh, let him stay,' Katherine Glover answered indifferently. 'He's harmless enough. I can stand up for myself. Here, chapman, sit down and get dry.'

Her uncle grunted. 'Oh well, if you're happy . . . Do as she says, my lad. Sit down and I'll fetch you a cup of ale.' He took a wooden beaker from a shelf and went across to a row of barrels ranged against a wall of the room. Turning the tap of one of them, he filled the beaker with a flow of dark golden brown liquid, which he handed to me with the encouragement, 'Drink up!' and went away, presumably to help his wife.

'I'm sorry I was so rude just now,' I said, feeling the need to apologise yet again. 'And, of course, had I realized from the outset that this inn belonged to your aunt and uncle, I should never have thought it strange that you chose to make your way here rather than remain at Crabtree.'

Katherine Glover shrugged, but made no answer, continuing to stare into the fire where the logs, shifting every now and again, revealed caverns of ruddy gold and sea-green-blue. She made it perfectly clear that she had no wish to indulge in further conversation, so I respected her silence, sitting down at the opposite end of the bench and stretching my long legs towards the flames. It was a silence that she maintained throughout supper, a meal shared with the landlord and his wife, there being no guests other than our two selves staying that night at the inn.

When we had finished eating, Katherine announced that she was ready for her bed, and, with a kiss for her uncle and aunt and a brief 'Good night' to me, went upstairs.

'Your usual chamber,' her aunt called after her, but there was no response.

Theresa Glover sighed. 'This has been a bad business,' she said. 'Five months on, it's still the talk of Plymouth, and the gossip shows no sign of dying down yet. Well!' She rose to her feet and began collecting the dirty dishes together. 'I told my brother-in-law and his wife at the time that no good would come of allowing Katherine's betrothal to Beric Gifford. There was bound to be trouble over the inequality of the match. It stood to reason that old Oliver Capstick wouldn't tolerate it, and he held the purse strings. Oh, it's no good you frowning at me, Maurice, and shaking your head. The chapman'll hear worse than that from other people, if he's interested enough to listen. You go and make certain that all the shutters are secured against this wind. There's one with a loose catch in the corner chamber, where I've put Roger.' For she had prised my name out of me while we were having supper, and now used it, relishing the familiarity.

The landlord reluctantly departed to obey his wife's instructions, grumbling to himself, but plainly used to doing as he was bidden.

When he had followed his niece upstairs and disappeared from view, I asked Theresa Glover, 'What do *you* think has happened to Beric Gifford? The talk in Plymouth is that he's eaten the leaves of Saint John's fern and made himself invisible.'

I had expected her to deride this idea with all the contempt of which a strong-minded woman was capable. But, instead, she crossed herself and her eyes assumed a wary expression. 'I suppose it is possible,' she answered. She was silent for a moment, then said slowly, 'The truth is, that there are some people in these parts – sensible people, not given to extravagant fancies – who are ready to swear that they've seen Beric. Not close to, perhaps, but recognizable, even though he was in the distance.'

'I'd heard as much myself,' I answered, 'but was inclined to dismiss the possibility. But if these people are speaking the truth, then he must be in hiding somewhere, succoured by his sister and your niece.'

Theresa Glover shook her head emphatically. 'Katherine has assured both her uncle and myself, as well as her parents, that she has done with Beric and never wants to see him again.'

'Isn't that what she would tell you?' I asked sceptically. 'Especially if she's protecting herself and him.'

Mistress Glover looked uneasy, but said, 'Katherine has always been very truthful, even as a child. Far too truthful on occasions, to my way of thinking.'

'Everyone's capable of lying,' I argued, 'particularly if he or she is guarding something or someone precious.'

My companion was loath to agree, but eventually admitted, 'You could be right, I suppose.'

Her husband came back into the room, a disapproving look souring his face. 'Still gossiping?' he snapped. 'I thought you'd have had these dishes cleared away and washed by now.'

If he had hoped to discomfit his wife, he was mistaken. 'Are you certain that everything is secured upstairs?' she countered waspishly. 'Have you repaired that catch in the corner bedchamber?'

'I've done my best,' he answered sulkily. 'It shouldn't give you any trouble, chapman.'

I thanked him and said that, with his and Mistress Glover's

permission, I would retire. 'It's been a long day,' I added: and indeed it seemed an age since my talk with Mistress Trenowth that morning. Moreover, my previous night's sleep had been disturbed.

I was given a candle to light my way upstairs, and Theresa Glover insisted on accompanying me in order to show me my room. But when she would have entered with me to assure herself, as she said, that all was well, I bade her a firm good night and shut the door behind me.

As far as I could see, the Bird of Passage boasted only three bedchambers, and I guessed that the one at the front of the inn was used by the Glovers themselves. Its door stood wide open, showing an empty bed, whilst that of the chamber next to mine was tightly closed. Doubtless, the room was occupied by Katherine Glover, already sound asleep. There was little furniture in my own room, but the bed looked clean and comfortable and there was an iron chamber pot in one corner. Having relieved myself, I divested myself of most of my clothes and climbed thankfully between the sheets, tucking the coarse woollen blanket well up under my chin.

I lay for a little while, listening to the wind buffeting the house, soughing through the branches of the trees and rattling the shutters of my window. But I was too tired to stay awake for long, and with thoughts of Adela uppermost in my mind, I, too, was soon lost to the world.

Chapter Seven

During my years as a novice at Glastonbury Abbey, the discipline I most hated was having to leave my bed in the early hours of the morning for the service of matins, and again at sunrise for lauds. However uncomfortable my pallet, it was infinitely preferable to the chill of the night stairs and the empty, shadowed reaches of the great church, cold even in the heat of summer. Consequently, my worship was never more than half-hearted, and it was not unknown for me to fall asleep and have to be nudged into wakefulness by my neighbour.

But God has had His revenge. Although I long ago left the monastic life behind me, I frequently find myself, even now, in old age, waking up in the small hours of the morning, condemned to a period of restlessness before I can fall asleep again. And that night at the Bird of Passage Inn was no exception. But as I struggled back to consciousness through the clinging threads of dreams, I realized that there was another reason for my arousal. The faulty latch, mentioned by Theresa Glover, had obviously sprung again, with the result that both shutters were swinging loose in the wind, banging every now and then against the outside wall.

Cursing, I got out of bed, crossed to the window, opened the inner casement, then leant out to take hold of the shutters, one in each hand. The rain had ceased and a thin wisp of moon appeared from time to time, scudding across the sky between the blown wrack of clouds. Apart from the noise of the wind, which had considerably abated, and the distant hushing of the sea, all was quiet, so that the high-pitched whinny of a horse came clearly to my ears. Katherine Glover's palfrey was also restless, I thought, until a sudden flash of movement away to the left, drew my attention to the stand of trees.

I froze into stillness. I had almost closed the shutters, but not quite. A gap of some three or four inches remained between them, a wide enough aperture for me to see through without being seen in return. And provided that I held them still, I doubted if the fact that they were open would be noticed from the ground. I had no notion what I expected to happen next, but something was afoot, and I felt the hairs on the nape of my neck bristle in anticipation.

After a few moments, the figure of a man, muffled in a dark cloak and wearing a flat-crowned hat, emerged from the trees and approached the inn, stooping on his way to scoop up a handful of loose stones and small clods of earth, which he flung without hesitation against the closed shutters of the window next to mine. ('Your usual chamber,' Theresa Glover had told her niece.) He was forced to repeat this manoeuvre several times before he was rewarded with the cautious opening of the casement and the emergence of Katherine Glover's head. To be truthful, this was beyond my range of vision, but I guessed that she must have appeared when I heard her sudden, startled cry and the hiss of her indrawn breath.

'You fool!' she whispered. 'Whatever are you doing here? Get back and hide before anyone wakes up and sees you. Wait! I'm coming down.'

There was a low chuckle of amusement from below before the cloaked figure turned and did as he was bidden. Presently, there came the faint sound of the bedchamber door next to mine being opened, and the creak of a floorboard on the landing. I remained where I was, not knowing what to do. My impulse was to go after Katherine Glover, but if I finished closing my shutters or let them swing free, the movement would be noticed and the nocturnal visitor frightened into immediate flight. Furthermore, he and the girl would know that I had seen and heard them; and if the man was, as I suspected, Beric Gifford, I wondered how safe my life would be in the future. Someone who had already done one violent murder was unlikely to balk at committing a second.

In the end, I decided I had no choice but to stay perfectly still and simply be an observer of what happened. Nor did I have long to wait. Within minutes, Katherine's slender form, a cloak thrown over her night-shift, was running across the short stretch of ground between the inn and the trees. The man, who, meantime, had vanished, stepped once more into view, catching her in a smothering embrace. She responded by throwing her arms around his neck and covering his face with passionate kisses, before they both withdrew into the shelter of the copse.

Now was my chance to finish the job in hand and rouse the household. The thought had barely crossed my mind, however, when the man once again emerged from the trees, but this time on horseback, evidently persuaded that he was taking too great a risk by remaining longer. Katherine also reappeared, stretching up to embrace him as he bent towards her from the saddle. Another laugh reached my ears as the youth laid his whip across the big black horse's flank, then galloped off along the east-bound track, glancing round only once to wave and blow a kiss before being swallowed up by the darkness. The girl, gathering her skirt into one hand, ran swiftly back to the inn and passed from my sight.

At last I was able to finish closing the shutters before sitting down on the edge of my bed, my ears alert for the tell-tale sounds of her return. I heard again the creak of the landing floorboard and the gentle shutting of her door, but after that, all was silent. I found that I was trembling, but whether from fear or excitement, I was not quite certain. *I had seen Beric Gifford*: that was the thought uppermost in my mind. He had not gone to France or Brittany; neither had he taken refuge in some remote part of the country. He was still here, close to home, meeting with his betrothed and no doubt laughing up his sleeve at all attempts to find him.

I shivered as I recalled the way in which he had vanished into the trees without my noticing. Had my attention wandered for those few precious, vital seconds? Or had I become blinded by my racing thoughts, as happens when a person stares at something, but sees nothing? Or was he truly able to make himself invisible? Had Saint John's fern really bestowed that supernatural power upon him?

I sighed wearily. It seemed to me that I was almost back where I had started. But not quite. I knew now that Beric was somewhere in the vicinity and there for the taking, if only I could discover his hiding place. I returned to bed, settling down once more in the musty darkness, the wool of the blanket again irritating my chin. For a long while, I lay awake, the events of the past hour going round and round in my head; and when I did, finally, fall asleep, my dreams were haunted by hobgoblins and evil sprites, who chased me through never-ending woodland, jumping out from behind shrubs and thickets, or grinning down at me, disembodied faces, from between the leafless branches of the trees.

The sun was climbing in the sky when I eventually awoke the following morning. The latch of my bedchamber shutters had once again sprung open, and a soft golden glow was suffusing the oiled parchment of the windowpanes. From below, both in and out of doors, I could hear the sound of voices, Theresa Glover's louder than the rest; and from the subdued chorus of male tones, I gathered that the inn was open for trade and already doing business.

I fell out of bed and dressed as quickly as I could, descending to the kitchen, unwashed and unshaven.

'I'm afraid I've overslept,' I said to my hostess by way of apology.

She was busy preparing breakfast for a party of travellers just arrived by ferry, and only paused to direct me to the pump in the yard before bustling away to the taproom with laden dishes. 'There's a pan of hot water on the fire,' she called over her shoulder as an afterthought, 'if you want to scrape off your beard.'

While I made myself presentable, I wondered how I was going to face Katherine Glover without some chance word or expression of mine giving her a hint that I had been a witness to her meeting with Beric Gifford. But as I passed the stables, I noticed that the stall nearest the inn was empty. The palfrey had gone, and so, presumably, had its mistress.

Theresa Glover confirmed this to be so when I re-entered the kitchen and enquired after her niece.

'Oh, Kate's well on her way home by now. She got up early, afraid that Mistress Gifford may have been worried about her when she didn't return to Valletort Manor last night. Sit down, chapman, and have some porridge.' She eyed me shrewdly as she ladled the gruel from the iron pot hanging over the fire into a bowl. 'You don't look very refreshed to me. Didn't you sleep well?'

I had been considering whether or not to say anything to either of the Glovers about what I had seen, but had decided against it. Even if they believed me – which was highly improbable, regarding Katherine, as they did, as the fountain of all truth – they were members of the girl's family, and would be loath to accuse her of harbouring and succouring a wanted criminal. They were more likely to brand me a liar, and to tell lies themselves if necessary in order to prove me wrong. So I merely made some lame excuse for my tiredness and tucked into the bowl of porridge with apparent zest, although it was in fact neither very hot nor had much flavour.

Once I had eaten, I paid my shot, fetched my belongings from my room and said farewell.

'Which road are you planning to take?' Maurice Glover enquired suspiciously.

'Oh, I go as the fancy pleases me,' I answered cheerily. 'Maybe I'll go as far as Brixton and then turn inland, to Totnes.'

He seemed satisfied with this and went back indoors, calling to his wife that they needed to broach a new cask of ale. Meantime, I set out along the eastward path, but only to double back on my tracks once I was out of sight of the inn, approaching the stand of trees from the opposite side. I knew I was being stupid, yet I had to convince myself that the events I had witnessed early that morning had not been a dream. But it required only a moment or two to find the hoof- and shoe-marks of the horse and his rider imprinted in the rain-softened earth, and I upbraided myself for being a self-doubting fool. Then I picked up my pack and stepped out again along the path that leads eventually to the little town of Modbury.

After quarter of an hour's steady walking, however, fresh doubt's began to creep into my mind. How could I be so sure that Katherine Glover's nocturnal visitor had indeed been Beric Gifford? On the face of it, and in view of all the facts, it seemed the natural assumption to make. But supposing that, since Beric's disappearance, she had taken another lover and was frightened that word of her defection might reach Beric wherever he was hiding. Would there not then be a need for the kind of secrecy I had witnessed last night?

But I dismissed the idea almost as soon as it entered my head. Katherine was still living at Valletort Manor with Berenice Gifford, and it was extremely unlikely that she would be able to conduct a second romance without her mistress becoming aware of the fact. Nor was it plausible to suppose that the youth I had seen would be a party to such a clandestine affair. I remembered the careless laughter and the easy way he sat astride the big, black horse. This young man, whatever else he was, was afraid of very little.

His mount, too, was another reason why I had to believe that he was indeed Beric Gifford. What was it Joanna and John Cobbold had said the evening before last, at supper? 'Beric Gifford rode up on that big black horse of his.' 'A huge, showy, very spirited animal. Master Capstick told me once that his great-nephew was the only person who could manage the brute.' Well, the horse had certainly been big and black, although there had been no way to tell if it were spirited; but everything added up to make my doubts look as ridiculous as they really were. Nevertheless, I still had every intention of calling at the villages of Brixton and Yealmpton in order to discover, if I could, the two people who had seen Beric on the day of the murder, and find out what they had to say.

I reached Brixton around eleven o'clock in the morning, and my stomach was already protesting at the passing of the dinner hour without any sustenance. It was true that I had breakfasted late, but Mistress Glover had offered me no more than the bowl of gruel, being busy with her other guests and anxious, I suspected, to be rid of me.

I should have stopped at Plymstock, but I was eager to reach my destination and so, for once, ignored one of my most basic needs, the constant plying of my great frame with food. I would eat, I decided, when I got to Brixton; but Brixton was, disappointingly, little more than a huddle of cottages grouped around the church. At least, I thought, I should have no trouble in locating the goodwife who, according to Joanna Cobbold, had seen Beric Gifford pass by on his way to Plymouth, but I was wrong. Going from door to door, plying my trade as an excuse to set foot inside each dwelling – with the added bonus of making a little money as well – I could find no woman who admitted to seeing Beric on the day of the murder. Everyone knew about the killing and was more than willing to talk about it; and everybody had a theory as to what had become of Beric since. But no goodwife claimed, 'I saw him by the church.'

Finally, at the last cottage I visited, where the woman of the household was no more forthcoming in this respect than all the rest, I said, 'I was told that there was a witness, here in Brixton. Someone who saw Master Gifford pass by on May Day morning.'

'A stranger, then,' her husband hazarded, 'for to my knowledge, none of our neighbours has claimed such a thing.' And he glanced at his wife with raised eyebrows.

'I've heard nothing, either,' she agreed in answer to his unspoken question. 'When was it, do you know? About what time of day?'

'It was very early,' I replied. 'Beric Gifford was reportedly riding in a westerly direction, so he must have been on his way *to* Bilbury Street. Would there have been a stranger hereabouts at such an hour who might have seen him?'

The goodman stroked his beard. 'There'd be drovers and suchlike, taking their animals to market.'

'Perhaps I didn't make myself clear,' I said. 'The person who saw Beric was, according to my information, a woman. But whether old or young, I wasn't told.'

The goodwife rubbed her nose. 'A woman! Ah! That's different.

In that case, I can probably hazard a guess as to her name.' She turned triumphantly to her husband. 'Gueda Beeman.'

He nodded. 'Ay. You're right. That'll be who it was, not a doubt of it.'

'Who's Gueda Beeman?' I asked a trifle impatiently, when they showed no sign of offering further information, but sat smiling at one another, satisfied that they had solved the riddle I had set them.

'Eh?' They both looked at me, blinking in surprise. They had momentarily forgotten my presence.

'Oh, Gueda Beeman,' the goodwife continued. 'Of course, you wouldn't know. Some people call her a wise woman, some say she's a witch. But she's never done any harm to anyone that *I* know of.'

'Nor anyone else,' put in her husband.

'That's as maybe. There was a woman once, Kitley way, who reckoned as how Gueda'd put a curse on her. Mind you, she could never prove it, and live and let live's what I say, as do most of the folks around here.'

'And you think it might have been this Gueda Beeman who saw Beric Gifford on May Day morning?' I was growing even more impatient.

'Most likely,' the goodwife replied, once more nodding her head. 'She lives in an old, broken-down cottage, over to Wollaton, and walks into Brixton most mornings, early, to see what she can forage. She knocks on doors, and people'll give her a bit of stale bread or a few vegetables that are in season, or a cup of milk or an egg. It sees her through the day. Otherwise, she lives on roots and berries and anything else she can grub for in the woods.'

'A strange name, Gueda,' I remarked.

'It's Saxon,' the goodman told me. 'There are descendants of the Saxons everywhere in these parts. Modbury, as they call it nowadays, was once the moot burgh; the meeting place of the district. Before *they* came.' And he gave a vague jerk of his head. 'The Valletorts and the Champernownes, with their fancy foreign names.'

I nodded understandingly. I had come across this phenomenon several times before during my travels, happening upon little enclaves where the traditions and memories of our Saxon forebears continued to be cherished, and where they were talked of as though they had only ceased yesterday, instead of four hundred years ago.

I asked, 'Can you point me along the path to Wollaton? I'd like to speak to this Gueda, if she'll let me.'

'Why?' the man demanded abruptly. 'What's your interest?'

'Now, Wilfred!' his wife admonished him. 'That's none of our business. If the chapman wants to consult with the wise woman, that's for him to decide. Come outside, lad, and I'll show you the way. It's a bit northwards from here, but not that far, and won't take you any time at all with those long legs. You'll find her cottage easily enough.'

'He might not,' the man Wilfred objected, knitting his brow. 'I'd better go with him, just to make certain.'

'I shall be quite all right,' I assured him hurriedly. I laughed. 'I'm used to finding my way about on my own.'

'Of course you are,' the goodwife agreed, and turned to glance suspiciously at her husband. 'What do you want to go prancing about the countryside for? You're up to something. You're trying to get out of chopping that wood. I know you, you lazy good-for-nothing!'

'I'll have the scold's bridle on you, woman,' he retorted, 'if you don't watch your tongue.' But it was said without any great venom, and the snort of wifely scorn that greeted the remark made it plain that Wilfred's bark was far worse than his bite.

Nevertheless, he carried the day, and when I finally left the cottage, he went with me. But first, I had managed to persuade the goodwife to provide me with bread and cheese and ale, having given her a heart-rending tale of how I had come to miss my dinner, and of the poor breakfast I had received at the Bird of Passage Inn.

'Aye,' she had sniffed, 'they're a grasping lot, those Glovers. That Katherine, now, the one who's mixed up in the murder of this Master Capstick, she set her sights on marrying Beric Gifford as soon as his sister took her into the household as her maid. And how she wangled herself into Mistress Berenice's employ in the beginning, nobody knows, for her parents are common fisherfolk, down in the bay, close to Burrow Island.'

'You don't want to take too much notice of my goody,' Wilfred said as, thanks given and farewells taken, he and I set out along the track to Wollaton. 'It's nigh on seven miles to Modbury, and another mile or so south to Valletort Manor, and news loses its freshness over such a distance.'

'Don't worry,' I said. 'I always swallow everything I'm told with a grain of salt.' I turned my head and looked curiously at him. 'Why did you insist on accompanying me? I don't somehow think that it had anything to do with a reluctance on your part to chop wood.'

He laughed and admitted that I was right. 'I was afraid that once you'd found Gueda's cottage, you might go blundering straight in, for the door to the place has been off its hinges for months. I've noticed it the last twice I've had occasion to pass that way.'

'So?' I queried, puzzled.

Wilfred took my arm, dropping his voice to a conspiratorial whisper, although there was no one to overhear him.

'Gueda Beeman isn't just the local witch or wise woman,' he

said. 'She's the local whore, as well. Mind you, she never charges for her services. She likes men, so what she does, she does out of the goodness of her heart. In short, men might be said to take advantage of her, although I don't think she looks at it that way. But it's a fact not generally known by the womenfolk of these parts. If they did discover the truth, they'd run her out of the neighbourhood, if nothing worse. So the men keep quiet about it. That's why I thought I'd better come with you and explain, otherwise there could have been an embarrassing misunderstanding between you and her.'

I was grateful for the warning, and said so.

Gueda Beeman's dwelling was barely a mile north of Brixton, in a woodland clearing a few yards from the main track. It was, as I had been told, a ramshackle place with a hole torn in its roof of twigs and moss, and a rotten door fallen in on its hinges. Drifts of dead leaves lay scattered over the grass, and the swaying, sighing trees crowded all around us. Every now and then, a stray shaft of sunlight penetrated the latticed branches overhead, but for the most part, the surroundings were as dismal as the cottage.

'Here we are then,' my guide informed me unnecessarily. 'Do you want me to stay while you ask her these questions of yours? Everything's quiet, so it doesn't look like she's got anyone with her.'

But even as he spoke, we noticed two horses tethered close at hand: a dark bay gelding and a sturdy cob. Attending them was a sullen-faced youth wearing dark green livery, a hawk, with silver bells on its jesses, perched on one gloved wrist. A moment later, a young man, richly dressed, strode out of Gueda Beeman's cottage, pulling up short at the sight of Wilfred and myself.

He ignored my companion, but gave me a long, hard stare, almost as though he recognized me, before turning away and mounting his horse. He made no reply to my courteous 'Good day!' and rode off, his man following astride the cob.

'That was Bartholomew Champernowne,' Wilfred said.

Chapter Eight

Before I had properly assimilated the information, a tall, fair-haired woman came out of the cottage, and, much as Bartholomew Champernowne himself had done, paused to look me up and down. Again, Wilfred was accorded the most cursory of glances.

If this was Gueda Beeman, as I supposed it must be, she was not at all what I had expected. When the wise woman had originally been mentioned, along with the fact that many people thought her a witch, I had imagined an old crone, wizened and repulsive. Later, when Wilfred had told me that she was also the local whore, I had amended this picture, although I don't know why, to that of a somewhat younger woman, but one still well past the first flush of youth.

Instead, Gueda was not only young but also beautiful, in spite of the layers of dirt that grained her skin, and the filthy, tattered gown that she was wearing. She had huge, grey-green eyes, thickly fringed with lashes the colour of ripe corn, the same shade as her hair – or the shade her hair would have been had it been washed. Her figure, too, was one to make the angels jealous, and her bare feet were as small and delicate as her hands. But when she spoke, the illusion of some fairy princess fallen upon hard times was rudely shattered. Her voice was harsh, her speech coarse, thickly larded with its Devonshire burr.

'What do you want, then, chapman?'

I noticed that she was jingling some coins in her right hand, and I muttered in Wilfred's ear, 'I thought you said she gave her favours free.'

'So she does usually,' he muttered back. 'But perhaps Master Champernowne insisted on paying.'

'What are you two whispering to one another about?' Gueda demanded sulkily. 'If you have anything to say to me, pedlar, say it out loud.'

It was true that I was carrying my pack on my back, but I had the feeling that this was not the only reason that she had so readily divined my calling. I smiled placatingly before replying, 'I'd be grateful for a few words with you, Mistress, if I may.'

'Very well.' She stared at me belligerently, but made no attempt to invite me inside the cottage, for which I was truly thankful.

So I put my question regarding her sighting of Beric Gifford on the morning of the murder, without anticipating any reply but a confident affirmation. I was therefore astonished when she shook her head and answered with an emphatic, 'I saw nothing.'

'You mean it wasn't you who told the Sheriff's officer that you'd seen Master Gifford riding towards Plymouth on May Day morning?' I demanded, disappointed.

'I've told you so, haven't I?' she spat at me. 'I never said any such thing. And besides, I don't know this . . . this Beric Gifford.'

'Are you certain of that?' I queried angrily.

She tossed her head. 'Yes. I'm certain.'

But I could see by the way her eyes refused to meet mine that she was lying, and I was suddenly struck by the significance of the coins she was still jingling in her hand. Bartholomew Champernowne had not been enjoying the lady's favours; he had been bribing her to deny her evidence concerning his future brother-in-law in the event of a tall, far too nosy pedlar finding his way to her door and asking questions. But how had he known of me? The answer, of course, was simple: Katherine Glover. He must have been at Valletort Manor when she returned home that morning, and had heard enough of my curiosity concerning Oliver Capstick's murder to make him determined to try to silence the local witnesses. He no doubt felt that interest in the killing was on the wane after all those months, and the last thing he wanted was for a stranger to revive it with his unwelcome meddling.

Master Champernowne's interference, however, only stiffened my resolve to seek out the other two who claimed to have seen Beric on the fateful morning: the smallholder who lived near Yealmpton and the friend who had sighted him close to Sequers Bridge. And even if Bartholomew got to them before I did, and was able to command, or pay for, their silence, I hoped I could judge for myself whether or not they were telling the truth, just as I had done with Gueda Beeman.

I thanked the wise woman, (witch, whore, however she preferred to be known) with elaborate courtesy.

'Please forgive me, Mistress, for wasting your time.' I added with heavy sarcasm, 'I can see now that the information I was given concerning you was false. I shall therefore not inflict myself upon you any further.'

She regarded me with deep distrust, for she was not used to such talk and, guessing that she was being mocked, rightly resented it.

'I didn't see Beric Gifford!' she bawled after me as, grasping Wilfred's arm, I turned to go.

'She was lying,' my companion said positively as we made our way along the path leading from the clearing to the Wollaton track.

'Undoubtedly,' I agreed. 'Master Champernowne has paid her to deny her story. That's why she has money.'

'Of course!' Wilfred's honest face shone with sudden

enlightenment. 'I hadn't thought of that. What will you do next?'

'Carry on about my business,' I answered truthfully, even if I was being less than candid. 'I have a wife and children to support, and although I love a mystery, this one is already over five months old and I fear the trail has gone cold. It's time for me to be moving on.' But I was careful not to say where to. There seemed no point in involving Wilfred and his goodwife in my plans.

I walked with him the short distance back to Brixton and the main east-bound track, where, with some regret, we took our leave of one another.

'God be with you, then.' My new acquaintance reached up and patted me on the shoulder in a gesture that was affectionate as well as valedictory. 'You're wise not to try to cross a Champernowne. They're a family who make good friends but implacable enemies.'

'Give my regards to your goody and thank her for the dinner,' I said. 'If ever I'm this way again, I'll look you up.'

'Do, lad! Do! We'll be pleased to see you.' And with that, he smote me again on the shoulder before turning and walking in the direction of his cottage where his wife was waiting for him, wood-chopper in hand. I saw her gesture towards the pile of logs, and, smiling to myself, I set out once more on the next stage of my journey to Yealmpton.

It was little more than an hour's walk from Brixton to the neighbouring village, and I could have done it in less time had the track not led through some dense woodland, where the afternoon sun could barely penetrate the cathedral-like vaulting of the trees. The going was slow there, and twice I stumbled and almost fell over roots that snaked across the path. It was not easy trotting for horses, either, although the several riders I encountered, travelling in both directions, guided their mounts over the obstacles with all the confidence that familiarity with the ground inspires.

Eventually, however, the trees began to thin and give way to more open pasture. A spiral of smoke in the distance told me that I was nearing a homestead or outlying farm, and that Yealmpton could not be far away. I judged from the position of the sun that it was now about mid-afternoon, and my stomach was telling me that it would soon be suppertime. It was a few hours now since my belated dinner at the home of the goodman and his wife, so I decided to stop at the first dwelling place I came to, where I would try to buy or beg something to eat. I might also, if I were lucky, learn the name of that smallholder who had been on his way to market when he had encountered Beric Gifford returning from Plymouth and his murderous mission. Then I recollected Bartholomew Champernowne, and wondered if he would have been before me, suborning yet another witness into denying his former evidence.

Ten minutes more brought me to the cottage with smoke spiralling through the hole in its roof. It was surrounded by an expanse of comfrey, that useful plant whose root, pulped, strained and packed inside a splint, is invaluable for setting broken bones, and whose juice cleanses wounds, helping them to heal. There was also a bed of coltsfoot, which makes a soothing decoction for all ailments of the chest, and another of coriander, whose seeds disguise the unpleasant taste of physic. Undoubtedly, the owner of this holding sold his produce to the physicians and druggists of Plymouth and other nearby towns; everything was grown in too great a profusion to be merely for his own use or for that of his immediate neighbours.

At the back of the cottage was a small enclosure containing several geese and chickens, and a nanny goat tethered in one corner. A tall, very thin man, with sparse straw-coloured hair and pale blue eyes, was scattering corn from a bucket hooked over one arm. Assuming him to be the cottager, I did not bother to knock at the door, but approached him directly. Before I even had time to hail him, however, he glanced up, saw me and said, 'Ah! You must be the pedlar I was warned about. I've been expecting you.'

I smiled grimly. 'In that case, you must be the man who encountered Beric Gifford on the morning of his great-uncle's murder.' He looked disappointed at my lack of surprise, and I went on, 'Bartholomew Champernowne has already bribed Gueda Beeman to deny the evidence she gave to the Sheriff's officer five months ago, as I discovered this afternoon when I went to see her.'

The man upended the bucket to get rid of the last of the corn, then walked across to join me at the fence. He frowned, sucking his yellow teeth consideringly. 'So, what's your interest in stirring the matter up again, just when the Law is beginning to lose interest in the killing?'

'I don't like villains who get away with murder,' I answered promptly. 'Do you?'

He regarded me speculatively for a moment or two before jerking his head in the direction of the cottage.

'My name's Jack Golightly. You'd better come in. You can share my supper, if you're hungry,' he offered.

I needed no second invitation, and when he had shut the enclosure gate behind him, I followed him indoors as fast as I could, before he changed his mind.

'I'm a childless widower and I live alone,' he said by way of explanation, and with a sweeping gesture that embraced the unmade bed, the still unwashed dishes, the plain, beaten earth floor that needed brushing, and the dust lying thick on every surface. But to offset all that, there was the most delicious, savoury smell emanating from the iron cauldron hanging from a hook over the fire in the middle of the room. I could have tolerated a great deal more disorder than I saw about me to sample a plateful of Jack Golightly's stew.

'You seem very snug, all the same,' I answered, slipping my pack from my shoulders and heaving it into a space between the water butt and a wooden rack where some apples were set out, coated with melted beeswax to preserve them for the winter. I looked thoughtfully at my host as he wiped two bowls clean with a handful of grass, then filled them with stew. 'If you can cook like this, you have no need of a wife.'

He raised his eyebrows but made no comment on this rather crass remark, merely motioning me to draw up a stool to the table and pushing aside the remains of his previous meal, which had not yet been cleared away. He gave me a spoon and a slice of black bread, bidding me 'Fall to!' and pulling up a second stool for himself. For several minutes, there was no sound except the two of us eating.

Eventually, however, when I had blunted my appetite with two helpings of stew, I wiped my mouth on the back of my hand, propped my elbows on the table and said thickly, 'I guess that Master Champernowne must have been here. And did he try to bribe you to deny the truth of your story concerning Beric Gifford, should I pay you a visit? I think he must have done, or you wouldn't have been expecting me, would you? Did he give any reason for his request?'

Jack Golightly laid down his spoon and picked a sliver of meat from between two of his front teeth with a grubby fingernail before replying to my questions with one of his own.

'You say "try to bribe". What makes you think that he didn't succeed?' he asked with a grin. And fishing in the pouch at his belt, he produced three or four coins, piling them up on the table in front of him.

I looked from his face to the little pile of money and back again. 'You neither act nor speak like a man who is about to tell me a pack of lies,' I said. 'And yet . . . Are those your own coins or his?'

'Oh, his!' my host exclaimed cheerfully, picking them up and returning them to his pouch with every indication of pleasure. 'But you're quite right. I don't aim to mislead you, or tell you anything but the truth. I did meet Beric Gifford on my way to Plymouth market. So, what else is there that you want to know?'

'But . . .' I protested feebly, and Jack Golightly laughed.

'You wonder why I took young Master Bartholomew's money,' he said, 'when I had no intention of doing what he asked of me. Well, for one thing, I'm a poor man and must take my chance where I can to eke out an uncertain livelihood. For another, I made him no promises. It's not my fault if, in his arrogance, he assumed that I would bow to his demands. But if you want the real reason why I deceived him, it's because he's a Champernowne.' And he uttered the last word with such a weight of loathing that it was almost like a curse.

There was a moment's silence. Then I said, 'You obviously dislike the family. Can I ask why?'

My companion got up and poured two cups of ale for us from a pitcher standing on a smaller table where a few more dirty dishes were stacked. When he returned and had seated himself once again, he answered, 'I don't mind telling you. There's no secret about it.' He took a swig of his ale, which, to my mind, was rather tasteless and flat, and wiped his mouth on the sleeve of his smock. 'My family have always been loyal to the Courtenays, and therefore to the Lancastrian cause. The Champernownes are for the House of York.'

I grimaced. 'In that case, perhaps I should point out that you see before you a man devoted to King Edward IV and all his family.'

Jack Golightly shrugged. 'That doesn't worry me, chapman, although I think you're misguided. But many years ago now, when I was young – that same year, in fact, that Edward of Rouen was crowned in London as our present king – the French sent a force into Plymouth to help our cause. As soon as the Champernownes got wind of it, old William Champernowne sent his men to repel the French, but they were intercepted here, at Yealmpton, by the Courtenays and their followers.' The strangely pale blue eyes glittered with unshed tears. 'The Courtenays won the skirmish and the Champernownes were forced to retreat, but not before they'd fired this cottage out of revenge. My father and I managed to douse the blaze, but the shock was too much for my mother. She died not long afterwards. The Champernownes killed her as surely as if they'd put a knife through her heart.'

I don't know whether or not he expected me to sympathize with him, but I could not bring myself to do so. A great many common people had suffered grievously during the civil war that had torn this country apart for so many years; but, as I had just told him, I was sufficiently devoted to King Edward and, above all, to his younger brother, the Duke of Gloucester, to be unmoved by the plight of their enemies. So I took refuge in silence and buried my face, as far as I could, in my cup as I finished my ale.

'You see, therefore,' he continued at last, 'why I make no bones about serving any Champernowne a backhanded turn if the opportunity arises.'

'I do, indeed,' I said, setting down my empty cup. 'You don't deny, then, that you met Beric Gifford on the morning of May Day as you were going towards Plymouth and he was returning. Were you on foot?'

My host smiled sourly. 'Of course I was on foot. I'm not rich enough to own a horse, or even a mule. I have a shoulder yoke from which I suspend my baskets. He was riding, though; that great, black horse of his that he was so proud of. And still is, as far as I know.'

'Where did you encounter him? Were you close to him or at a distance?'

Jack Golightly repeated the habit he had of sucking his teeth before replying.

'It was in the forest near here. I expect you came through it. I had to jump aside, into the trees, to get out of his way. He was riding at a great pace, in spite of the roughness of the ground, bent low over the animal's neck, the reins all bunched up in one hand and the fingers of the other knotted's in the black's mane, as though he were scared to death he was going to fall off. I remember thinking to myself: One day, my boy, you'll break your neck, and serve you right, going at such a speed. But when I arrived at Martyn's Gate and found Bilbury Street swarming with Sheriff's officers and people who had just arrived to gawp, and when I learnt of the murder and was told the murderer's name, I understood his hurry. And I was able to tell one of the sergeants that I'd seen Beric Gifford heading, as far as I could tell, in the direction of Modbury and Valletort Manor. But a posse had already been sent that way after him.' My companion sounded cheated.

'You hadn't met the posse on your journey?'

'No, for I took the road to the ferry. They'd have gone north to the ford, or further on, to the bridge, if it were floodtide, just as Master Gifford must have done, before riding southwards again to join this track at Brixton.'

I asked, 'When Beric passed you in the forest, did you notice if he was wearing a jewel in his hat? Gold with a teardrop pearl.

My companion laughed. 'He was riding too fast for me to take notice of anything he was wearing.' Nevertheless, Jack wrinkled his brow as he obligingly tried to remember, but after a while he shook his head. 'If my life depended on giving an answer, I'd say that he wasn't. But if his life depended on it, I'd have to say that I can't be certain.'

Beric wasn't wearing the ornament that was now in my pouch, of course, for it had fallen from his cap in the bedchamber, where it had been lost among the rushes, and my host's testimony in some part confirmed this. I saw the curiosity in Jack Golightly's eyes, guessed the question hovering on his lips and made haste to divert his attention.

'Are you acquainted with Beric Gifford and his sister?' I asked.

He shrugged. 'I know them by sight well enough to recognize them when I meet them. And I listen to all the gossip. I know that they're famed for their prodigality; that they both spent far more money than they could afford until one of them murdered their uncle and the other inherited his fortune. I know that Berenice Gifford is betrothed to that young coxcomb who was here this afternoon, and that her brother is – or was – determined to marry her maid, Katherine Glover, which was the cause of his falling out with old Oliver Capstick. In short, I know as much as most other people do concerning their neighbours.'

'And what do you think has become of Beric Gifford since he killed his uncle?'

My host shrugged. 'If he's any sense, he'll be miles away from here. France, Brittany, Scotland.'

I thought for a moment, before deciding to take him into my confidence. 'If I told you that I'm certain I saw him last night, talking to Katherine Glover outside the Bird of Passage Inn at Oreston, what would you say to that?'

Once more, Jack Golightly pursed his mouth and sucked on his teeth. 'I'd think him the biggest fool in Christendom,' he answered slowly.

'You wouldn't think that he'd eaten Saint John's fern and could render himself invisible or visible at will?'

My companion laughed. 'No, I shouldn't! I'll tell you something, chapman. I ate the leaves of the hart's-tongue fern once, when I was a boy – and nothing happened! I waited all day to become invisible, but not so much as a fingernail vanished. If you believe that story, you're more gullible than I take you for.'

'I didn't say I believe it,' I answered. 'But I was speaking the truth when I said that I saw Beric Gifford last night. Unfortunately, it was impossible to apprehend him. Where do you think he's hiding?'

Jack Golightly had stopped laughing and was regarding me earnestly. 'If what you say really is true—' he began, but broke off to protest, 'No! Impossible! I find it hard to accept that he'd be so foolish. Do you have proof positive that it was him?'

'I have to admit that I don't know Beric Gifford except by report,' I confessed. 'But this man and Katherine Glover – who was spending the night at the inn, as I was – were behaving in a very lover-like fashion. And he was riding a black horse. I could tell that, even in the darkness.'

My host scratched his head. 'It sounds as though it could have been Beric you saw, I'm bound to agree. But if that's the case . . .' He chewed his nether lip and pondered. At last, he went on, 'If that's the case, there's only one place where he could be lying low with any measure of safety, and that's in Valletort Manor itself.'

Chapter Nine

'Why do you say that?' I asked, frowning. 'Surely the Sheriff's men have searched Valletort Manor more than once and failed to discover Beric Gifford?'

'And for that very reason, they are unlikely to search it again,' Jack Golightly argued. 'So what safer place for him to lie concealed?'

'I don't think you can rely on that. Furthermore, there must be servants,' I persisted. 'And however loyal the majority of them might be, there has to be one whose attachment is questionable, or whose devotion could be bought if the inducement were sufficient.'

My companion shook his head. 'After their father's death, the Gifford children fell on hard times. Servants were turned off one by one until, I believe, only three remained: three, that is, until Mistress Berenice decided to employ Katherine Glover as her personal maid.'

'And who are these three?' I asked. 'Do you know their names or offices?'

Jack Golightly wrinkled his brow. 'I understand there's an old nurse, who has been with the Giffords since Noah was a lad, and who, no doubt, is completely trustworthy, as such women generally are. They regard each succeeding generation of the family children as their own, and lavish a parent's love and care upon them. Of the remaining two, one, I think, is a groom, who has also been in the Giffords' employ for many years, and the other is an ancient who was once the household steward, but who is now semi-blind, and probably deaf as well.'

'But who does the sweeping and cooking and dusts the place?' I asked, with all the newly married man's awareness of such day-to-day practicalities. 'Surely Berenice Gifford doesn't clean the house herself?'

Jack Golightly shrugged. 'These are questions I can't answer, I'm afraid. My knowledge of Valletort Manor is limited to such gossip as comes my way.'

I forbore to comment that a great deal of gossip concerning the Gifford domain did apparently come his way. Instead, I gave voice to a sudden thought.

'Where exactly is Valletort Manor situated?'

I half expected him to reveal that the Giffords were his nearest neighbours, but it appeared that this was not the case. By my host's reckoning, the manor was a mile or two south of Modbury, on the peninsula of land that is bounded on two sides by the rivers Erme and Avon, and on the third side by the sea. I knew, from having been in the locality, some years previously, that that particular stretch of coast was populated by several closely related families, all of them fishermen, whose isolation encouraged in them a disdain for the laws and customs of the outside world, and who ran their community according to their own self-imposed rules. And had not the cottager's wife told me that Katherine Glover's parents were fisherfolk? Was it not possible, then, that Beric Gifford had found sanctuary among these people, and was being protected by them?

But yet again, that one word 'Why?' returned to tease me. *Why* had Beric Gifford not escaped to France or Brittany by now, taking Katherine Glover with him? *Why* had he placed himself in such jeopardy that he was forced to put his safety in the hands of others? *Why* had his anger against his great-uncle not cooled overnight, after his first abortive attempt to murder Master Capstick?

The answer to that last question remained, as always, the same. Something had happened, some revelation had been vouchsafed to him, between his return home on the last day of April and the morning of May Day that had turned him into an avenging fury, whose anger against his kinsman could only be assuaged by the most extreme violence. But what it could be, I was unable to imagine, and I asked Jack Golightly if he had any idea.

'I can't tell you that,' he answered, his face brooding and dark. 'But I will say this: I can understand Beric Gifford's feelings. Maybe the hatred for old Capstick had been building up inside him for many a long year, and to be informed that he must give up Katherine Glover for a woman of his uncle's choosing was the final insult.' My companion leant forward across the table to tap the back of my hand, and the pale blue eyes were suddenly as hard as flint. 'I tell you, chapman, that I could barely keep my hands from grabbing young Champernowne by his scrawny neck this morning and throttling the life out of him. Instead, I had to content myself with taking his money, knowing that I'd no intention of doing his bidding should you show up, as he prophesied you would, asking questions. But it was touch and go. And I have no especial dislike of Bartholomew Champernowne, except that he is a member of that family I abhor above all others. The passage of the years hasn't cured my detestation of them. My mother's death is as fresh in my mind as if it had happened yesterday, and I loathe every member of their race. One day, maybe, I shall do one of them a mischief and end up like Beric Gifford, a hunted criminal.'

I was a little taken aback by the vehemence of this speech, but I had to admit that Jack Golightly's interpretation of the events leading to the death of Oliver Capstick might have something to be said for it. Slow-burning rage can, on occasions, suddenly burst into flames. Nevertheless, I was unable to rid myself of the notion that there was more to Beric Gifford's actions than a simple explosion of anger could account for. I had no rational explanation for this conviction – it was purely intuition – but I had learnt over the years to trust my instincts.

'I must be getting on my way,' I said, rising to my feet. I paused, resting my hands on the tabletop. 'I was told that there was yet another witness in these parts, who saw Beric Gifford on May Day morning, either going towards, or returning from, Bilbury Street. My informant didn't know his name, but said the man concerned was a friend of Beric's, who recognized him in the distance, close to Sequers Bridge. You don't happen to know who that could be, or where he might be found?'

Jack Golightly shook his head. 'I've probably misled you into believing that I know a great deal more about Valletort Manor and its inhabitants than I really do. My knowledge is confined to such gossip as I pick up when I go to Modbury to sell my goods. You may have noticed that I grow comfrey and coltsfoot and coriander, all plants necessary to people's health, and I do a fair trade both there and in Plymouth. But as to being able to name any of Beric Gifford's particular friends, I'm afraid I can't help you. You'll have to enquire of those who know him better than I do.'

'Maybe not,' I argued. 'Try to think of any young men in this vicinity of whom you've heard mention, who could possibly be friends of Beric. Young men of birth, of about the same age, who follow the same pursuits. There can't be that many of them, I'll warrant. Above all, is there such a one living in the neighbourhood of Sequers Bridge? Wherever that may be. Is it far from here?'

'Some two to two and a half miles,' Jack Golightly answered

slowly. 'It crosses the Erme about a mile or so this side of Modbury.' Once again he puckered his brow. 'Now you jog my memory, there is a young man of about Beric's age, Stephen Sherford, who lives near Edmeston, not far from the bridge. He's the son of Sir Anthony Sherford and probably the only youth hereabouts who would answer your requirements.'

'Can you direct me to Sir Anthony's house?' I asked eagerly. 'I should like a word, if I'm allowed it, with young Master Sherford.'

'Yes, I can put you on the right path,' my host replied. 'But what do you hope to gain from asking all these questions? Why do you suppose that you can run Beric Gifford to earth when the Sheriff and his officers have failed?'

'Because,' I said, answering his last query first, 'in the past, I have had some success in bringing to justice felons who would otherwise have escaped the rigours of the law. As to what I hope to gain from all my questioning, I don't always know that until I hear it. It's like searching through a pile of dross for a diamond that I'm not even sure is there in the first place.'

Jack Golightly didn't look as though he really understood, but he smiled politely and nodded his head. 'I'll set you on your way to the Sherfords' house,' he added, moving towards the door.

But when he opened it and we stepped outside, we found that a steady rain had begun to fall, and that black clouds were piling up in the western sky, threatening a further downpour. My host glanced dubiously at them.

'You'd do well to stay with me tonight, chapman,' he advised, 'and continue with your journey in the morning. Otherwise, you're going to get uncomfortably wet.'

I was bound to agree with him, for the rain was increasing in volume with every succeeding minute. If I insisted on going further that evening and could find no shelter for the night – and who could guarantee that Sir Anthony Sherford or his steward would offer me a place to sleep? – I should be forced to take refuge in a barn, or even beneath a hedge, a foolish thing to do when I had the chance of warmth and a roof over my head.

'Thank you,' I said. 'You're very kind. I gratefully accept your offer.'

So we went back inside the cottage, and in return for Jack Golightly's hospitality I entertained him for the remaining hours of daylight with accounts of my past adventures, although I felt obliged to omit some of the details. But he was happy enough with what I told him and, apart from deploring my unswerving loyalty to the reigning House of York, enjoyed the stories and thanked me for enlivening what would otherwise have been his usual dull and dreary evening. Then, after we had consumed another cup of ale and braved the rain in order to relieve ourselves, he offered me a share of the palliasse and blankets, which he unrolled and laid before the dying embers of the fire. Once more, I accepted with gratitude, and minutes after shedding my boots and tunic, I was curled up beside my host and fast asleep.

I was suddenly wide awake, staring into the still-warm ashes of the fire, a few inches distant from my nose. At my side, Jack Golightly lay on his back, snoring loudly.

I wasn't sure what had disturbed me – apart from the fact that, as I said before, I so often wake in the early hours of the morning – until I heard a faint scratching sound coming from the direction of the cottage door. I raised myself on one elbow, peering through the darkness and trying to free myself from the coils of sleep that still wreathed about me. All was quiet. I strained my ears, waiting for the sound to come again, which, eventually, it did. I rose quietly to my feet and padded across the room, trying to make sense of what it was that I was hearing.

I realized after a second or two, during which the last vestiges of sleep deserted me, that it was the scrape of metal against metal; and it came to me suddenly that someone on the other side of the door was trying to pick its lock. Earlier, before we went to bed, I had watched Jack Golightly withdraw a key and hang it on a nail protruding from the cottage wall; a key I now lifted down, replacing it in its wards. (I understand enough about locks to know that it is almost impossible to open them from one side while the key remains in the other, for I had been taught the art of lock-picking by a fellow novice at Glastonbury, one, Nicholas Fletcher, who had spent his youth among rogues and vagabonds before hearing God's call.)

Continuing to tread softly, I returned to the mattress to wake my host, who was still oblivious to the world, shaking him gently by the shoulder. At the same time, I placed a hand across his mouth to prevent him from crying out.

'Hush,' I hissed in his ear, as he showed signs of struggling. 'There's someone trying to break into the cottage.'

Immediately Jack lay quiet, his eyes growing at first wide and questioning, then narrowing to angry slits as he, too, became conscious of the metallic scraping noises. I removed my hand, feeling it now safe to do so, and sat back on my haunches.

'I've put the key in the lock,' I whispered, and explained my reason for doing so. 'But whoever it is trying to force an entry may realize what I've done at any moment if he looks through the keyhole and finds it blocked. Unless he's a complete fool, he must have checked it first, so he will be alerted to the fact that he's discovered and that will probably be sufficient to frighten him off. If we want to find out who our would-be intruder is, we'll have to move at once, and quietly.'

Jack Golightly nodded, and I could tell from the direction of his glance that our minds were working in unison. The cottage was unusual in that, although it had only a single door, it boasted a brace of windows, one set alongside the entrance, the other in the wall opposite, overlooking the beds of comfrey and coriander and the pen where the animals were kept. Before Jack was even on his feet, I was lifting the bar from the shutters of this second window, laying it on the floor and pushing the wooden slats outwards. The chill night air rushed in to greet me, for there were no horned panes here to keep out the cold when the windows were open. I had one leg across the sill when I was joined by my host, who, considering his years, showed unexpected agility in following close on my heels and actually overtaking me on our dash around the outside of the cottage to apprehend the burglar.

In spite of the fact that we must have made some noise, the man crouched in front of the door was so intent upon his task that we were on him before he knew that we were there. He gave one strangled cry of fear as Jack wrestled him to the ground, but was unable to utter more because my companion was sitting athwart his chest, and his splayed arms were pinioned by the wrists.

'Who is it?' I asked, bending down to take a closer look at our captive. 'Do you recognize him, or is he a stranger?'

'Go and light a lamp and bring it here,' Jack ordered. 'And while you're about it, unlock the door.'

I was a little annoyed by his peremptory tone, but did as I was bidden, climbing back through the window and re-emerging through the door a minute or so later, a lighted rush-lantern in one hand. I held it up, and by its feeble glow managed to make out the features of the man on the ground. I had seen them once before, early yesterday afternoon.

'It's Bartholomew Champernowne's groom,' I said. 'He was with his master at Gueda Beeman's cottage.'

'Is it indeed?' asked Jack grimly, increasing his weight on his victim's chest. 'I knew Bartholomew had a man with him when he came here, but he left him outside with the horses and I didn't get to see his face.' He leant forward, releasing the man's wrists and placing both his hands about the other's throat. 'Tell me why you were trying to break into my cottage. If you don't, I'll squeeze the life out of you and leave your corpse for the carrion crows to mangle.'

Jack and I must have looked wild enough for anything, partially dressed as we were, our hair unkempt and standing on end, eyes still dark-rimmed and hollow from interrupted sleep. At any rate, our captive seemed to think us capable of carrying out Jack's threats, for he made another gurgling sound and, instead of trying to beat off his attacker, flapped his arms to indicate surrender. Jack eased his pressure on the man's windpipe just enough to let him speak.

'My master sent me,' the groom croaked, drawing a long and painful breath. 'My horse is tethered over there, amongst the trees.'

'Never mind your horse,' Jack answered roughly. 'Just tell us why Master Champernowne sent you here. If you'd managed to enter the cottage without waking either one of us, what were your instructions?'

There was a pause of perhaps a minute while our prisoner plainly debated in his mind whether to admit the truth or not. But now that we knew his identity, there was small hope of his pretending to be a common or garden thief, and what other purpose could he claim that would be believed, except the true one? He turned his head and looked at me.

'Young master wanted him silenced.'

'Bartholomew Champernowne sent you to kill me?' I asked incredulously. 'In God's name, why? What wrong have I ever done him?'

There was another pause, then an agonized gasp as Jack, first raising himself slightly, let his whole weight drop again on to the groom's chest and tightened his grasp about his captive's throat. This time the man did make some attempt to defend himself, lifting his arms and clenching his fists; but before he could use them on Jack, I knelt down behind his head and once more pinioned him to the ground.

'Why?' I repeated.

The groom made one last, desperate effort to squirm free of our restraining hands, but he knew it to be hopeless before he tried.

'Why?' I asked for a third time, and, emulating Jack's example, applied extra pressure to the groom's wrists.

The man yelped. 'All right! All right!' he panted. 'Young Master wants you dead because you're asking too many questions about Beric Gifford's disappearance and raking over the matter of the old man's killing, just when everyone's beginning to forget about it. He's betrothed to Beric's sister, Mistress Berenice, and he doesn't want her made unhappy.'

'And how did your master know I was here, in Master Golightly's cottage?'

There was another silence, then Jack said softly, but in a voice charged with menace, 'I, too, would wish to hear the answer to that question.'

'My master didn't trust you,' the groom told him savagely. 'He set me to watch you and see what happened when the chapman did turn up. Well, it was plain, when you let him inside the cottage, that you hadn't sent him away with a dusty answer, so I went home and told Master Bartholomew what you'd done. He rode back here with me, and just as we arrived, you both came to the door. It was raining steadily by then, and you went back inside. When you –' he nodded at Jack – 'began closing the shutters, Master guessed that the chapman had been invited to stay for the night. That's when he had the idea that I should force my way in while you were both asleep and – and—'

'And murder me,' I finished scornfully. 'Did he really believe that you could do it? Do *you* really believe you could have done it? Killing a man in cold blood is more difficult than you and your master might think.'

The man tried to spit at me, but when you are flat on the ground, spitting isn't easy and the saliva merely dribbled down his chin. I laughed and released his arms, but Jack Golightly was not amused. He advanced his face to within an inch of the groom's face, his lips drawn back from his teeth in a snarl of rage.

'You can go back to your master and tell him this. If he comes so much as within half a mile of this cottage, he'll be a dead man. No one violates the sanctity of my hospitality and gets away with it! Especially not a Champernowne!' Once again, he succeeded in making the name sound like the vilest of imprecations. He stood up, releasing his prisoner, but also delivering a swift, hard kick to the man's groin. The groom doubled up in agony.

Taking the lantern, we left him to hobble back to where his horse was tethered as best he could, and returned to the cottage once again, locking the door behind us. We also shuttered and barred the open window.

'Did we ought to make certain that he's gone?' asked Jack.

I shook my head. 'He won't hang around. He's too frightened. You've put the fear of God into him if it wasn't there already. I can almost feel pity for the poor oaf, for it was plain he didn't relish what he'd been ordered to do. I don't suppose he's ever killed a man in his life. I'd guess that petty thieving is the most his talents have ever run to.'

We were both shivering with cold now that the excitement was past, and with the bellows Jack tried to blow a spark of life back into the fire. After a while, a flame caught some of the unburnt wood, and he put a pan of ale to mull over the heat. Meanwhile, I found our two dirty beakers from yesterday's supper and within half an hour, we were able to sit on the mattress, the blanket pulled over our knees, and feel the warmth creep back into our bones.

'Well, all's well that ends well,' I said lightly. 'At least I'm still here.'

But my host refused to be mollified. When he spoke, his voice was harsh with unsuppressed hatred.

'I swear to you, chapman, that if ever Bartholomew Champernowne comes near this place again, I'll have his life and count my own well lost in ridding the world of such a worm!'

'That's foolish talk,' I said, draining my cup. 'It's wrong to take life, be it your own or another's. You're tired and upset. Lie down and get some sleep. You'll feel differently in the morning.'

I reached across and put out the lantern that I had left near us on the floor. Darkness muffled us once again. I stretched my length on the palliasse and, a moment or so later Jack did the same. He hadn't answered me, but I was too sleepy to press the matter. Besides, within minutes, he was snoring.

Chapter Ten

I awoke the following morning with aching limbs that felt as heavy as lead and an incipient headache that nagged behind my eyes.

It was as much as I could do to sit upright on the mattress, and my first thought was that I was suffering from an ague, contracted since coming into Devon. Then the truth dawned on me: I had had three disturbed nights, one after the other. Last night, Bartholomew Champernowne's groom had tried to break into Jack Golightly's cottage in order to kill me; the previous night, I had witnessed the nocturnal meeting between Katherine Glover and Berle Gifford at the Bird of Passage Inn, and the night before that again, I had paid a visit to Oliver Capstick's house in Bilbury Street. Lack of rest was no good for either my wits or my strength, and I decided that when I said my morning prayers I should have to have a word with God about it. It was all very well for Him to give me these signs and show me the path that I must follow, but if I were to be of any use in doing His will, He really would have to allow me to get some sleep.

Jack was already up, frying thick, fatty slabs of bacon in a pan over the now brightly burning fire and, at the same time, stirring porridge which was bubbling away merrily in an iron pot.

'You've slept a fair while,' he remarked, as I yawned and stretched my arms until the bones cracked. 'But you were so dead to the world that I didn't like to wake you. Not that you look much better now, with those dark circles under your eyes. Go and stick your head in a bucket of water; it might revive you. There's a stream that runs close to the animals' pen. Breakfast'll be ready when you get back.'

He was as good as his word, and by the time that I had washed and cleaned ny teeth with my willow bark, a bowl of gruel and a plate of bacon collops awaited me on the table. My host, seated opposite, had already started on his meal and greeted my return with a grunt, too busy eating to talk yet awhile. At last, however, he had cleared both plate and bowl, and patted his stomach with a sigh of repletion.

'Are you still of the same mind today as you were yesterday?' he asked. 'Do you intend calling upon Master Sherford?'

I nodded. 'And you? I can only hope you're *not* of the same mind as you were yesterday as regards Bartholomew Champernowne. You've been kind to me and I like you. I'd hate to see you dangling at the end of a rope.'

'That's up to him,' Jack replied grimly. 'Don't worry! I shan't go searching him out, but if either he or that groom of his comes bothering me again, I might not be answerable for my actions.'

'I doubt if he will come bothering you again,' I said. 'He'll guess that I've gone on my way this morning, and I'm the one he's after, not you.'

'Take care, then,' Jack warned. 'Watch your back. Live by this maxim: never trust a Champernowne.'

'Will he warn this Stephen Sherford, do you think, of my probable arrival? For he seems to know the name of everyone hereabouts who gave evidence to the Sheriff's officers after Oliver Capstick's murder. But even if he does, I fancy he'll hardly try to buy Sherford's silence, as he did yours and Gueda Beeman's.'

Jack grimaced and picked his teeth with a rusty nail that he kept handy for the purpose. 'He might go to see Master Sherford,' he conceded, 'but as you say, it's unlikely he'd attempt to bribe him. That might be regarded as too insulting. But it's likely he'd try to persuade young Sherford to have nothing to do with you for the sake of Mistress Gifford. Champernowne would appeal to his sense of chivalry in protecting a lady's name from further calumny.' Jack hesitated before adding, '*If* Master Sherford is the man you're looking for, of course. We don't know for certain that he's the one. It could possibly be some other.'

I finished my bacon and swallowed a mouthful or two of ale. 'But according to you there's no one else in these parts who could have been a friend of Beric's, so, in those circumstances, it's worth paying Stephen Sherford a visit. And even if he proves not to be my man, it's possible he can tell me who is.' I stood up, wiping my mouth on the back of my hand, and gathered up my pack and cudgel. 'I have to be on my way now. Many thanks for your hospitality. I shan't forget you.'

Jack Golightly warmly clasped my proffered hand.

'Take care,' he urged again. 'You're a good man, even if you do support that usurper Edward of Rouen, and all the tribe of the House of York.' He grinned. 'Tread carefully, and I hope you bring Beric Gifford to justice. You're right. There's no excuse for killing an old, defenceless man, whatever he may have done. God be with you, chapman, and I trust we'll meet again one day.'

He accompanied me to the door of the cottage, where he once more shook my hand before giving me instructions how to reach Edmeston and the home of Sir Anthony Sherford.

I crossed the River Erme by Sequers Bridge and then followed a track that wound its way between the trees in a slightly northerly direction. I had gone less than half a mile when, as Jack Golightly had predicted, I came upon Sir Anthony Sherford's dwelling.

Sir Anthony was obviously a man of some substance, for a

great many new buildings, a few of very recent construction judging by the rawness of the timber and the cleanliness of the stonework, had been added to the original house. This latter I guessed to be several centuries old and was built foursquare around a central courtyard and above an undercroft well stocked with provisions for the coming winter. There were also a number of servants in evidence, one of whom came forward briskly at my approach.

'Take yourself off to the kitchen, chapman. Either the cook or the housekeeper may have need of your goods. And if you have anything they think Lady Sherford might want, Dame Isabelle, the housekeeper, will let her know.'

'I was hoping,' I said, standing my ground, 'to have a word with young Master Sherford.'

The man was truculent. 'What do you want with him? He'll not be interested in your fripperies or your knives and spoons. Get away to the kitchen with you!'

'I'd like to speak to Master Sherford, none the less,' I repeated and, diving my hand into the pouch at my waist, I produced a coin, turning it over suggestively between my fingers.

The man, who had once more opened his mouth to refuse me, stood, suddenly irresolute, but with avarice winking in his dark brown eyes.

'What do you want with Master Stephen?' he demanded.

'That's my affair.' I handed over the coin, but then it struck me that I might be making a fool of myself and I added, 'If, that is, he's a friend of Beric Gifford.'

The servant's eyes widened abruptly, then one of them half closed in what might or might not have been a wink. At the same time, he slid the coin into his pocket. 'Got a message from Master Gifford, have you?' he asked in a carefully lowered voice. 'D'you know where he is?'

I made no reply, pressing my lips firmly together as an indication that I was not prepared to say more. The man still hesitated, and I realized that I had probably been foolish to hand over the money before I had achieved my object. But after a moment or two, he indicated an upturned barrel just inside the courtyard entrance and said, 'Sit there, and I'll see if I can find the young master for you. Mind you,' he added, swinging on his heel, 'even if I do, I can't guarantee he'll be willing to speak to you.'

He went away and, ignoring his offer of a seat, I withdrew into the shadows of the courtyard archway. No one else seemed to evince any interest in me, for which I was thankful. I had no desire to be hauled off to the kitchen to display my wares to the cook and housekeeper, or to have to explain my business over again.

The day, as days in early autumn often do, had turned suddenly warm, although it was not yet ten o'clock. I began to sweat, but whether as a result of the unexpected heat or because I was feeling the effects of my three nights of broken sleep, I was uncertain. Or was it simply that the events of the small hours of this morning had shaken me more than I cared to admit, even to myself? I suddenly had a great yearning for my home, for Adela, for my children, but I put the longing from me. There was work for me to do here, or God would never have given me that inexplicable urge to come to Devon.

There was a slight bustle in the main doorway of the house, which stood immediately opposite the archway where I was sheltering. A young man appeared, following the servant to whom I had already spoken, and, after what were obviously a few words of dismissal to his attendant, walked towards me across the courtyard. As he drew near, I could see that he was about eighteen or nineteen years of age, tall and slender, with hair so fair that it was almost silver in colour, and eyes that were of such an intense dark blue that in some lights they looked nearly purple. He was dressed for riding, and I surmised that he had been fetched from the stables, his expression suggesting that he was none too pleased at the interruption to his morning's plans.

I stepped out from the shadows and respectfully tugged at my forelock. Obsequiousness costs nothing and, in my experience often obtains me what I want with less effort than I should otherwise have to expend.

'Master Sherford, I'm sorry to intrude upon your time in this fashion. It's generous of you to take the trouble to speak to me.'

His annoyance was tempered with nervousness. 'Matthew said you have a message for me from Beric Gifford.' The eyes widened giving them the appearance of rain-drenched pansies. 'I – I haven't seen him, you know, not since the day he vanished, the . . . the day of . . . of the murder.'

I shook my head. 'Your man got it wrong, sir. He assumed too much. I have no message for you from Beric Gifford. But from what you've just said, I'm right, am I not, in thinking that you were at one time his friend? You are the person who told the Sheriff's officers that you saw Master Gifford near Sequers Bridge?'

Stephen Sherford nodded, now thoroughly bewildered. 'I am. But what of it?' The pale eyebrows arched themselves over those extraordinarily deep blue eyes.

Quite unexpectedly, I felt awkward and at something of a loss, for what possible reason could I give this young man for my interest in the murder of Oliver Capstick? I should have approached him sideways, like a crab, instead of tackling him face to face. I should have followed my usual course and gone to the kitchens, as the servant, Matthew, had instructed me to do, and while displaying the contents of my pack tried to discover what, if anything, was known by the cook and her helpers, or by the housekeeper, Dame Isabelle. I reflected wryly that I might also have made some money had I done so. The trouble was, I doubted if anyone but Stephen Sherford would be able to provide the answers to my questions.

'I – er – I'm a – a friend of Master Capstick's neighbours, John and Joanna Cobbold,' I floundered. Stretching the truth a little further, I added, 'They – er – they were fond of the old man. They – they're anxious to see his murderer brought to justice. I – I promised them I would make such enquiries as I could on my travels.'

'*I* don't know where Beric is,' my companion said sharply. 'And I don't want to, either. I want nothing to do with him. He was my friend, yes. But what he's done is inexcusable. If he's ever caught, he'll hang.' He shook his head. 'I can't think what got into him. Oh, he has a temper when he's roused, but I should never have thought him capable of murder! At least not that sort of murder. He might have killed someone in a fit of uncontrollable anger, but never in cold blood. It just shows that you never really know other people, not even when you've been friends with them for years.'

Master Sherford's sudden outburst began to put me at my ease. I realized that he probably needed to talk about his erstwhile friend in an effort to make sense to himself of what had happened; so I withdrew a few more steps into the shadows of the archway where it was more difficult to be seen, hoping that he would follow me, which he did. His initial irritation had vanished and he seemed as eager now to chat as he had been reluctant hitherto.

'That morning,' I said, 'the morning of May Day, when you saw him in the distance, near Sequers Bridge, do you remember if Beric was riding towards Plymouth or in the direction of Valletort Manor? Did you notice anything strange or odd about him?'

Stephen Sherford frowned and his eyes focused on me as though he had not really seen me before. He repeated the questions I was always being asked, had always been asked from my childhood onwards: 'Why are you so interested? What has it got to do with you?'

'I told you,' I answered smoothly. 'I promised John and Joanna Cobbold, who are Master Capstick's neighbours, that I'd try to find out anything I could that might lead to Beric Gifford's arrest.' (One thing seemed plain enough at any rate, and that was that Bartholomew Champernowne had not warned Stephen Sherford of my advent, nor tried to persuade him not to speak to me.)

Fortunately, my new acquaintance seemed happy to accept this explanation without further questioning on that particular score and merely nodded his head.

'What did you mean,' he queried, 'when you asked if I'd noticed anything strange or odd about Beric?'

I countered this with the question he had not yet answered. 'In which direction was he riding?'

'Towards Plymouth. It was very early. The dew was still thick on the grass, I remember, but I had been out maying with some of my father's tenants. We were coming up from the woods below Sequers Bridge when I saw Beric in the distance. I called out to him but he must have been too far away to hear.'

'You're certain it was your friend?'

'Of course! I recognized both Beric and his horse.'

'And there was nothing different about either of them that you can recollect?'

'No. I was a bit surprised that he didn't hear my shout, but perhaps it was because Flavius – that's his horse – was being especially mettlesome and it needed all Beric's skill and attention to quieten him.'

'Was there a particular reason for the horse's behaviour, do you think?'

The delicate eyebrows rose once again. 'Why should there have been? He's always been a difficult brute, and it's only Beric who can manage him. Moreover, he doesn't take kindly to crossing bridges. Never has done. I remember on more than one occasion, Beric cursing the fellow who sold him Flavius for not mentioning the fact before he parted with him. Said he wouldn't have bought him if he'd known.'

'But on that morning of the first of May, was the horse being more difficult than usual?' It had occurred to me that if Beric himself were jumpy and nervous because of his purpose when he reached his journey's end, then that edginess might have conveyed itself to his mount, making the animal more recalcitrant than was customary.

Stephen Sherford considered my question. 'Perhaps a little,' he conceded at length. 'Why do you ask? It can't possibly have any bearing on what happened subsequently, can it?' When I did not answer immediately, his irritation returned in full force. 'Why are you wasting my time with this stupid interrogation? What's the point of it?'

I nearly repeated to him what I had said to Jack Golightly about the dross and the diamond, but instead, I answered his query with one of my own.

'What do you think has happened to Beric Gifford in these months since the murder of his great-uncle? Where do you believe he's hiding?'

'He's escaped, of course. To France, if he's any sense.' The answer came all too pat.

'Without Katherine Glover?'

Stephen shrugged. 'Oh, I expect she'll join him, sooner or later. That's if he still fancies her after he's met all those attractive Frenchwomen.'

It was on the tip of my tongue to point out that Katherine Glover was a very pretty girl, but I didn't want to antagonize him further. Something in his tone, made me ask, 'Don't you like her?'

'She's his sister's maid, for heaven's sake!' he retorted impatiently. 'All right for a tumble in the hay, but not to marry!'

'Did you tell him so?'

'No, of course not! I wasn't such a fool. I've told you, he has the devil of a temper when roused, and he believes himself very much in love with Katherine Glover.'

'Is her lowly status the only charge you have against her, or is there some other reason?'

Stephen Sherford pursed his lips. 'I've only seen her twice, each time in Beric's company. But on both occasions it seemed to me that he was more in love with her than she with him. Oh, she was affectionate enough, kissing him and hanging round his neck, so I can't really tell you what gave me that idea. It just crossed my mind that she might be using him for some purpose of her own.'

'Such as?'

Again the irritation spurted. 'How in God's name should I know?'

I leant my back against the wall of the archway and waited while a carter with a full load of hay passed through. Once he was safely in the courtyard, with Sir Anthony's servants swarming about him, I said, 'Well, if you're right, whatever purpose she may have had in view must now lie in ruins. She can hardly have expected him to become a permanent fugitive from justice. And from all that I can gather, she seems, so far at least, to have remained true to her lover.' I did not add that I had received positive proof of Katherine Glover's affection for Beric Gifford only the night before last.

There was another interruption as a couple of kitchenmaids hurried past on their way indoors, vegetables from the garden held up before them, cradled in their aprons. The pair of them glanced sidelong at us, then broke into giggles once they thought themselves safely out of earshot.

My companion flushed and said angrily, 'I must be going. I've wasted enough of the morning as it is, talking to you.'

I remembered to be obsequious again, an objective I had almost lost sight of. 'You have been most kind. I can't thank you enough.'

He was mollified. '*Have* I been of any use to you?' he queried.

'I'm sure it will prove so,' I assured him, 'when I've had a chance to sort through all you've told me in my mind.' As he turned to go, however, I laid a hand on his arm. 'Forgive me, but there's just one thing I haven't asked on which I should be grateful to have your opinion. There are rumours, I've been told, that people claim to have seen Beric Gifford in this neighbourhood within the last few months. So could he, do you think, have eaten of Saint John's fern?'

Stephen Sherford blinked at me for a second or two, then gave a shout of laughter. But it had, I thought, rather a hollow ring.

'I don't believe in any of that nonsense, do you?'

I smiled. 'I have to admit that I've never met anyone who's actually known anyone who's eaten the hart's-tongue fern and become invisible. But is that proof positive that it hasn't happened to someone, somewhere, at sometime?'

'I should say so, yes.'

'Then where is Beric Gifford hiding? For he's still in the neighbourhood, you can take my word for it. I saw him the night before last.'

My companion gave me so incredulous a glance that I was forced for the sake of my own plausibility to explain the circumstances to him. When I had finished my story of Beric's encounter with Katherine Glover, he slowly shook his head.

'If what you say is true, then I have no idea where he can be. I thought him safe in France. Or in Brittany with Henry Tudor.'

It was the same answer that I had received from so many others. No one seemed able to suggest a hiding place close at hand where for months on end a man might defy all the forces of the law to find him. Stephen Sherford was plainly shaken by my revelation, and I exonerated him from any suspicion of pretence.

'I must tell my father what you have told me,' he said in trembling accents. 'I have sisters. My parents would prefer them not to walk abroad unattended with a murderer loose in the vicinity.' Friendship had obviously not survived the killing of an old man; nor, on reflection, did it deserve to. 'Where will you go now?' he added.

'To Modbury first, to glean what I can there, and then to Valletort Manor.' I picked up my pack and settled it on my shoulders. 'That, after all, is where the answers must finally lie. I shall have to see what Mistress Gifford and Katherine Glover are able to tell me.'

'You'll get nothing from either of them,' Stephen Sherford said as he began to move in the direction of the house. 'His sister dotes on Beric. He can do no wrong in her eyes. And Katherine Glover knows how to keep her mouth shut. Ah, well! God be with you, chapman!'

I called after him, 'You haven't received a visit from Bartholomew Champernowne today, I presume? At least, if you have, you haven't mentioned it.'

He paused, looking puzzled. 'He wouldn't dare to show his face here. My father and I dislike the fellow, and he knows it.'

'Then I'll wish you good day, Master Sherford.'

And I set out on the last leg of my journey.

Chapter Eleven

The little town of Modbury, running steeply downhill to the sequestered valley, has declined in importance since its Saxon heyday, when it was the moot burgh or chief meeting place of the district. It still boasts, however, a portreeve, steward of the market-place and the representative of the people in all their dealings with the lord of the manor; an ancient Saxon office.

Modbury Priory, high above the town, had, I learnt later, originally been a daughter house of the Benedictine Abbey of Saint Pierre-sur-Dives in Normandy, but thirty and more years ago, after many vicissitudes in its fortunes, the late King Henry had granted all its lands and revenues to his foundation of the College of the Blessed Mary at Eton. The priory had finally been dissolved ten years previously, and the last prior was happily living out the remainder of his days as a tenant of the college.

The Champernownes are still Lords of the Manor as far as I know, and have been since the reign of the second Edward, when they succeeded to the title after first the de Valletorts and then the Oxtons. The principal members of the family, at the time of which I speak, seemed to me to be generally well-liked, and had the great virtue, as far as I was concerned, of having supported the House of York during the recent civil wars. (I knew little at this juncture about Bartholomew Champernowne except that he belonged to a cadet branch of the family, and that I and at least two others felt some antipathy towards him.)

The population of the town was not large; less, I guessed, than that of either Totnes or Plympton. But it seemed to be a thriving place, its prosperity centred on the woollen industry with a fair proportion of Tuckers, Fullers and Weavers amongst its local surnames. It had a bustling marketplace and a cheerful, welcoming attitude towards strangers, if my experience was anything to go by.

This, then, was Modbury as I encountered it on that warm, sunny October afternoon, descending from the church and manor house atop the hill, to the huddle of shops and dwellings at its base.

I had no difficulty in finding the cottage of Anne Fettiplace. The first person I accosted, a bright, smiling youth with ruddy cheeks, was able to direct me straight to her door.

'Here, I'll show you,' he said. 'Follow me.' It was only a few steps further on and hardly worth his time and effort: he could have pointed it out from where we were standing. But, as I was soon to discover, he was typical of the townspeople, for most of whom nothing was too much trouble. 'She'll be pleased to see one of your calling,' the lad added. 'Indeed, we all shall. We've been starved for a good while now of fresh news from the outside world. Have you come far? From London, perhaps?' he suggested hopefully.

'From Bristol,' I said, and saw his face fall. 'But we do get London news,' I assured him. 'If you'll tell me where you live, I'll call on you and your goodwife later.'

'My mother and father,' he amended, but flushed with pleasure that I should think him old enough to be married. He pointed out his parents' cottage, wished me a courteous good day and sped off to spread the news that there was a stranger in the town.

My knock on Anne Fettiplace's door was answered by a woman as round and as plump as Mistress Trenowth and the Widow Cooper, and who, in looks, could only be their sister.

'Mistress Fettiplace?' I enquired, but without any doubt as to what her answer would be.

She gave me an apologetic smile and admitted the charge. 'But I'm afraid I'm not in need of your goods just at present, chapman,' she said. Then she paused, frowning. 'But how do you know my name?'

'I've come from Plymouth, where I met your sisters,' I explained. 'They bade me seek you out if I wanted a place to sleep in Modbury, so I'm taking the liberty of doing as I was instructed.'

Immediately her plump features were wreathed in smiles and she held the cottage door open for me to enter.

'Please walk in! If you're a friend of Ursula and Matty's of course I can find you somewhere to sleep. Put your pack and staff down there in that corner while I fetch you a cup of my best home-brewed ale. Are you looking to stay in Modbury long?'

While she spoke, she bustled about, filling a beaker from the ale-cask that stood in another corner of the room, and inviting me to sit down at the table. When I had slaked my thirst and complimented her, much to her gratification, upon an excellent brew, I said, 'Before I trespass on your time and good nature, Mistress Fettiplace, I must explain how I came to meet your sisters and what my business is hereabouts. You may not wish to have me as your guest when everything is made plain to you.'

'Have you eaten?' she interrupted. 'It's nearly suppertime. I was just about to get my meal and I should be most happy if you would share it with me. Whatever you have to tell me can wait until it's ready.'

I grinned. Anne Fettiplace was a woman after my own heart,

and one who had the right priorities.

'Nothing would please me more,' I answered, 'if you're certain you have enough for two.'

'More than enough,' was the reply; and in what seemed next to no time she had placed upon the table a large plate of meat pasties, a dish of damson tarts and another of oatcakes, some butter, still wrapped in its cooling dock leaves, and a big, round goat's-milk cheese. Then she replenished my beaker with more ale and bade me draw my stool closer to the board. 'You can tell me what you think I should know while we eat. But not just yet. Take the edge off your hunger first.'

I thanked her and pitched in, not realizing until I started eating just how ravenous I had been. Once my appetite was blunted, however, I wasted no more time and began my tale, commencing with my meeting, three days earlier, with Peter Threadgold and recounting faithfully most of what had happened since. There was something about Anne Fettiplace's open, gentle countenance that inspired my trust.

She listened carefully, asking only the occasional question when my narrative became unclear to her, and nodding her head repeatedly to show that she understood.

'So!' she exclaimed, when at last I had finished. 'The disappearance of Beric Gifford after his great-uncle's murder is a strange tale, sure enough, and I can see why you might be intrigued by it. But to think that you can solve a puzzle that's perplexed us all for so many months – well, I wouldn't be too certain about that.' She leant her plump elbows on the table, propped her several chins in her cupped hands and lowered her voice almost to a whisper. 'There's witchcraft at work here, or I'm very much mistaken. Beric Gifford has eaten of the Saint John's fern.'

'So I've already been told. But, Mistress Fettiplace,' I protested, 'do you *really* believe such a story? What I mean is, can the hart's-tongue fern *really* make anyone invisible, or is it just a . . . a . . . an old wives' tale? We all drink infusions of the leaves to ease our winter coughs and agues, and nothing happens to us. Nothing bad, that is. Why should *eating* the leaves make us disappear? Indeed, one of the people I met in the course of my journey here – I mentioned him just now, Jack Golightly – swore to me that he had once eaten a leaf without any ill effect whatsoever.'

'Oh, it wouldn't affect everyone who ate it,' my hostess replied with confidence. 'First, you have to make a pact with the Devil.'

'I've never heard that before,' I said, but found myself shivering, none the less, and hurriedly crossed myself to ward off evil. 'And you think that's what Beric Gifford has done? But why? Why didn't he simply run away, to France or Brittany? Or go north, to Scotland?'

'And become a penniless fugitive, having to shift for himself?' Anne Fettiplace was scornful. 'By staying here, by being able to make himself invisible at will, he can remain close to his home, to his doting sister and her newly inherited fortune and, most importantly, close to Katherine Glover.'

'And for such a reward, you think he'd sell his soul?'

'I think,' my companion answered solemnly, 'that Beric Gifford would do anything that that young woman told him to do. She has him in thrall.'

'You mean Mistress Glover?'

'I do indeed! He's a handsome lad and had girls in plenty before his sister was seized by the fancy to take that fisher-girl into her employ as lady's maid. Lady's maid! I ask you! But as soon as Beric set eyes on Katherine, or so I've been told, no one else existed for him. It's my belief she cast a spell on him, for the boy's besotted and that's a fact, as anyone around here who's seen them together can testify. One arm always draped about her neck and barely able to keep from fondling her, even in public.'

I pushed away my empty plate and swallowed the dregs of my ale. 'You said that he would do anything she asked of him. Are you suggesting, Mistress, that it was Katherine Glover who wanted Oliver Capstick dead, and that Beric Gifford was simply her instrument?'

Anne Fettiplace shrugged her ample shoulders. 'I think it possible. She may come of humble stock, but she's as proud as a peacock and thinks herself as good as the Queen, I dare say. She'd have been beside herself with rage when she learnt that Master Capstick thought her not good enough for his great-nephew. And according to my sister Trenowth, the old man spoke his mind in no uncertain terms, all of which I'm sure Beric would have reported to her.'

Here was a fresh view of the reason for the killing, one that I had not previously considered. And it might explain why Beric, having thought better of murdering his great-uncle one day, had returned the next in order to finish the job. So when my hostess had refilled my beaker and resumed her seat, I asked, 'What do *you* think happened after Beric returned to Valletort Manor on that last day of April?'

Mistress Fettiplace pursed her lips and gave the matter serious consideration. Then she nodded two or three times to herself and took a deep breath.

'I believe that when he returned home, he told Katherine and his sister all that had passed between him and Master Capstick; told them that his great-uncle wanted – or, rather, according to Mathilda, *demanded* – that he marry the granddaughter of some old friend of his, who had recently come back to Plymouth after years away; told them what he had said in reply, what the old man had answered and how, after that, there had very nearly been murder done.'

'And then?' I prompted.

'And then,' Mistress Fettiplace continued in a low and thrilling voice, her eyes widening in enjoyable alarm, 'Katherine Glover was so angry with old Master Capstick for insulting her in such a fashion that she insisted he deserved to die. She told Beric that he must avenge her, that he must kill his uncle the very next day. And also,' my hostess added in a far more practical tone, 'if Master Capstick had indeed carried out his threat to alter his will, Berenice would inherit his fortune without delay. They would all three of them be rich instead of having to pinch and scrape for every penny.'

'But,' I argued, 'could Katherine Glover have been so certain that Berenice Gifford would be prepared to share her great-uncle's money? Her future husband might, after all, have something to say to that.'

'Oh, yes!' Anne Fettiplace answered firmly. 'I told you, Berenice has always doted on her brother. Although she's only two years older than he, she has looked after him from the time that she could toddle. Without a mother, and with a father who was in his cups as often as he was sober, the two children were thrown into each other's company more than was customary for brother and sister. Neither was ever sent away from home; and since the death of Cornelius Gifford, the bond of affection between them seems to have tied them even closer. There were whispers at one time that the strength of their affection was abnormal.' She flushed slightly and went on, 'You know what I mean. But I never took any notice of such talk. And since Berenice announced her betrothal to young Champernowne, and since Beric became a slave to Katherine Glover's every wish and whim, the rumours have died a natural death,' she finished triumphantly.

'But surely,' I cavilled, 'if Berenice's affection for her brother is as great as you say it is, then she would never have allowed him to put his life in jeopardy by killing their uncle. Reflect a moment! This was not a murder carried out secretly, but in the full light of day with everyone looking on. There's little doubt in my mind that Beric's likely to end his life dangling at the end of a rope.'

'Not,' Anne Fettiplace urged excitedly, 'if he's never caught! And if he can make himself invisible at will, why should that happen? As for why his sister would let him do it, the money must have been an almost irresistible temptation. Here was a chance for Berenice to inherit all Master Capstick's wealth, and quickly.'

I was still unconvinced. 'But if one or the other of them had managed to murder Master Capstick by stealth, then both would have inherited his money and maybe no one would ever have been the wiser.'

My hostess considered this argument. 'Perhaps,' she suggested at last, 'Master Capstick had never said how he intended to leave his money until he told Beric that afternoon. The Giffords may have suspected they were his heirs, but did not know for certain.' She regarded me with bright, birdlike eyes. 'Don't you think that's possible?'

'Anything is possible,' I conceded with a sigh. 'Nothing about this murder seems to me to make sense.'

'That's because you're tired and in need of sleep,' Mistress Fettiplace smiled, rising to her feet. 'By your own telling, you've had precious little for the past three nights. First, trespassing,' she went on, not without a note of disapproval creeping into her voice. 'Then being a witness to Beric and Katherine Glover's midnight meeting. And, finally, someone trying to kill you while you slept.' She frowned. 'You know, I find it hard to believe that Master Champernowne would order his groom to do such a thing. And why?'

I shrugged. 'The why is easy enough. He doesn't want me making enquiries, jogging people's memories just at a time when the murder is beginning to fade from their minds. If Beric remains untaken, a year from now, perhaps less, it will be all but forgotten. That, I should guess, is Master Bartholomew's reasoning. And however fond he is of Berenice Gifford, he would prefer not to marry a woman so closely connected in the public consciousness with the murder of her uncle.' I got up from the table, stretching my cramped limbs. 'I must admit, I should be glad of an early rest. Tomorrow, I intend making my way to Valletort Manor, if you can give me directions how to get there.'

'Of course.' My hostess indicated the narrow stairway that twisted its way to the upper storey. 'My husband and son are both away from home at present, so you can use my son's chamber without the inconvenience of having to share it with him. It's the one facing you at the top of the stairs.'

I was surprised into silence. This was the first mention there had been of a family; but, looking back, I realized that I had merely assumed that Mistress Fettiplace was either a spinster or a childless widow, like her two sisters. In order to conceal my astonishment, I asked, 'Your husband and son, have they gone far?'

'Only to Exeter,' she answered cheerfully, 'on business.' She added, 'You'll find a chamber pot under the bed, and I'll bring you up a pitcher of water in case you want to wash away the dust and grime of the day.'

'I'll take it with me,' I said. 'There's no reason why you should wait on me. I'm grateful enough for your kindness as it is.'

She filled a large jug from the water barrel that stood just outside the cottage door and handed it to me. 'Have a good night's rest,' she smiled, 'and in the morning, I'd be glad to hear any news you might have gleaned on your travels.'

'I'm sorry,' I said. 'I seem to have talked of nothing but Master Capstick's murder. But, in truth, there's little news of any interest abroad at the moment. The Duke of Clarence is still under arrest in the Tower, but nothing, it appears, has been decided as to his fate. Other than that, there are no current rumours of any great doings. For the time being, at least, the country is quiet.'

'Well, we should thank God for that, I suppose,' Mistress Fettiplace said devoutly, but not without a trace of regret. 'There have been too many alarms and excursions during my lifetime, what with this noble at war with that one, and that one at war with the other. And kings coming and going and changing places like so many children playing at musical chairs. I'll say good night to you then, chapman, and hope that I don't disturb you when I come up to bed myself. I'll try to be quiet.'

Whether she was quiet or not, I had no idea, for I was asleep as soon as my head touched the pillow and knew nothing further until the sun, forcing thin, probing fingers through the cracks of the shutters, stroked me gently awake.

I felt completely refreshed and, getting out of bed, opened the window to reveal a beautiful October morning, hazy with autumnal sunshine, houses and trees outlined in gold against the rapidly dispersing mist. Modbury was already awake. I could hear the lowing of cattle as they were driven to pasture, voices upraised in greeting as people went about their daily business, and the ringing of the church bell as it summoned its citizens to the first worship of the day.

My conscience nudged me. It was some time now since I had last confessed myself or sought out God's House to ask His forgiveness for my sins. I decided, therefore, that I would visit the church after breakfast and rectify this omission. Over a plentiful meal of gruel and dried herrings, together with oatcakes warm from the oven, I asked Mistress Fettiplace if I might leave my pack and cudgel in her keeping until I returned, and was given her wholehearted blessing.

'It's nice to see young people mindful of their duty to God,' she approved. 'There's too much free thinking nowadays, and much of it not short of heresy, if you ask my opinion. Lollards,' she added darkly, nodding in a portentous way.

I have always been glad that God made our thoughts secret, kept them hidden from view, for I wouldn't like others to see too often inside my head. What's between God and me is a score only for Him to settle, but there are too many people in this world who think that they know His mind and have the right to speak for Him. Any poor soul who challenges their interpretation of His word risks his soul and maybe his life.

As I climbed the hill towards the church, I was greeted with the greatest friendliness by everyone I met; and by the time I had been stopped three or four times by locals anxious for news of the country in general and London in particular, the service was over and the worshippers beginning to disperse. Nevertheless, I pushed my way past them, determined to say a prayer for myself and my loved ones, and perhaps find a priest to hear my confession.

The interior of the church, which was dedicated to Saint George, was extremely dark, the more so because of the blinding sunshine out of doors. I stood at the back, just inside the porch, blinking at the distant chancel lights and waiting for my sight to clear. Above my head soared the arches of the nave. Slowly and carefully I inched my way forward into the gloom, pausing to bend my knee and cross myself as I approached the altar.

I looked for the priest, but he must have withdrawn to his house, eager for breakfast, as soon as the Mass was over, for there appeared to be no sign of him. So much, I thought, for my good intentions. I knelt down on the hard tiles and asked God to keep Adela and our children safe from harm during my absence, and could not help reminding Him that I was, after all, here on his business. 'For you know very well that it was You who sent me to

Plymouth in the first place,' I added sternly.

God, as usual, vouchsafed no answer, and I got up from my knees feeling slightly irritated. I was about to leave the church and return to Anne Fettiplace's cottage to collect my pack, when a sudden movement to my left made me start. Remembering the attempt on my life of the night before last, I spun around, hands clenched, ready to defend myself if necessary.

But it was not necessary. The figure that emerged from the North Transept was that of a woman, and my eyes were by now sufficiently accustomed to the darkness to recognize that she was richly dressed. I stood respectfully aside to let her pass before following her outside, into the sunshine. At the church door, she turned to thank me, and by the light of day, I saw that although she was not beautiful in the accepted sense of the word, she had finely chiselled features, with skin as brown as a hazel nut. Her eyes were also brown, dark and velvety, and the lashes that fringed them almost black. The effect was highly dramatic, and any man would have given her a second look.

'Berenice,' said a voice behind us, 'are you ready to go home yet?'

We both glanced round, and there, coming along the path towards us, was Katherine Glover.

Chapter Twelve

She did not see me at first. Her eyes were fixed upon her mistress.

'The horses are growing restless. You've been a long time,' she said.

'I stayed behind to pray after the rest of the congregation had left,' Berenice replied. 'I lit a candle for Great-Uncle Oliver.'

I saw Katherine Glover's unguarded look of astonishment and her open mouth, as if she would make some remark. But then she noticed me and her expression turned to one of shock, then of resentment.

'What are you doing in Modbury, chapman? Are you following me about?' Without waiting for my answer, she turned to Berenice. 'This is the pedlar I told you of. The one I met at the Bird of Passage Inn. The one who's so inquisitive concerning our affairs.'

Her mistress regarded me quizzically. 'So you're the man, are you?' The dark eyes were filled with sardonic amusement. 'But you omitted to tell us, Kate, how extraordinarily handsome he is.'

I felt the beginnings of a blush, and in order to change the subject I said quickly, 'When you refer to "us", Mistress, I take it that you mean yourself and your betrothed, Master Bartholomew Champernowne.'

The laughter vanished and the strongly marked eyebrows rose. 'Now how do you know that?' she asked.

'As far as your betrothal goes, I was told by someone in Plymouth that you and he were to marry. And because of what happened afterwards, I'm sure that he was with you when Mistress Glover returned home after our meeting at the inn.'

This time the eyebrows drew together in a frown.

'What happened afterwards?' Berenice demanded, and listened intently to my explanation. 'The fool!' she burst out angrily when I had finished. 'If any of this – the suborning of witnesses, attempted murder – comes to the Sheriff's ears, Bartholomew will be in very deep trouble indeed.' She glanced anxiously at me. 'Can I rely on your discretion, chapman, not to mention this story to anyone else?'

Wishing to conceal the fact that I had already confided in Anne Fettiplace, I prevaricated.

'I wasn't the only person involved, Mistress, as I've told you. But I assure you *I* have no intention of approaching any officer of the law.'

She mulled this over for a moment or two, before asking, 'What do you know of this man in whose cottage you were staying? This . . . This . . .'

'Jack Golightly,' I supplied.

Berenice nodded. 'This Jack Golightly. Is he likely, do you think, to make a report to the Sheriff's officers next time he visits Exeter or Plymouth?'

I shook my head. 'I should deem it highly improbable. The truth is that although, in general, he bears a grudge against all Champernownes, and wouldn't be averse to doing one of them a serious mischief if he could, he would be far happier committing that mischief himself. If you wish to keep your betrothed safe from harm, you'd do well to advise him to steer clear of Jack Golightly.'

'I shall certainly do so,' she answered. 'And I shall make it plain to him how exceptionally foolish his behaviour has been. Thank you for telling me.' Unexpectedly, she held out her hand. 'Will you come to visit us at Valletort Manor? Katherine and I are always ready to spend our money on ribbons and combs and all other such aids to vanity as I'm sure you carry in your pack.' The deep brown eyes were alight once more with mockery. 'And you can satisfy yourself that my brother is not in hiding there, which is what, I'm sure, you and half the rest of the world believes.'

I was taken aback by this frankness, and also by the fact that her proffered hand seemed to indicate that Berenice Gifford was prepared to treat me almost as a friend. But I did not trust her. She was laughing at me, secure in the knowledge of her ability to protect Beric from all prying eyes such as mine. Even Katherine Glover had shown no agitation at her mistress's invitation; and their confidence was a challenge that I could not refuse.

'Thank you,' I said. 'I shall be happy to visit you sometime within the next few days. I won't trouble you for directions, as I'm sure there must be someone who can tell me how to find Valletort Manor.'

Berenice Gifford threw back her head and laughed, this time seeming genuinely amused.

'Dozens,' she said. 'If our whereabouts were unknown to people in the past, you may be certain that there's not a person in Modbury and the surrounding countryside who doesn't know where to find us nowadays. Isn't that so, Kate?'

Katherine Glover grimaced sourly, pulling awry that little, flower-like face.

'Oh, they all come poking around,' she sneered, 'hoping to find Beric and claim the reward. None of our assurances that he's safely in Britanny manages to persuade them that he's not in hiding somewhere close at hand.'

'Nor,' added Berenice warmly, can they be persuaded that Katherine and I are not protecting him in this imagined concealment. And a few make it plain that they believe I egged my brother on to commit that heinous crime, so that I could inherit Great-Uncle Oliver's money.' She shuddered eloquently. 'It's true that we'd had our differences, the old man and I, but beneath that crusty manner, he was a kindly soul who'd been good both to me and to my brother. I had no reason to wish him dead: he was pleased with the news of my betrothal to Bartholomew and would have treated me well when the time comes for us to marry.' She sighed deeply and pushed back a lock of almost jet-black hair that had strayed from beneath her hood. 'Neither Kate nor I had any idea what Beric was plotting when he left home on May Day morning.' She turned to her companion for confirmation. 'Isn't that so, Kate?'

Katherine Glover nodded. 'Quite true. If we had had so much as an inkling, we should naturally have tried to prevent him, to reason with him, to discover the cause of his murderous rage. We should even have attempted to confine him to the house if persuasion had failed.'

'You don't think, then,' I suggested, 'that Master Gifford's anger had the same cause as his rage of the previous day, when he tried to strangle his uncle? You don't believe that he was still incensed by Master Capstick's refusal to contemplate you as his nephew's wife?'

She flushed uncomfortably and her look of resentment palpably increased.

'If you want the truth, yes, I think it did. But, given a chance, I might have been able to convince Beric that the old man's opinion was of no concern to me. That I was not offended by it.'

The tone of her voice was so sincere that I couldn't help wondering why I didn't believe her. I tried not to let my doubt show in my face, however; and, as her mistress was at last displaying some signs of wishing to be on her way, I bade both women good day and moved off in the direction of the churchyard gate, where their horses were tethered. The palfrey I recognized. The bay, with the two white front stockings, must therefore belong to Berenice.

Just at that moment, the lady herself called after me, 'Don't forget! We shall expect to see you soon, when you've finished selling your wares here in Modbury.'

I stopped and waved my acknowledgement, before walking on down the hill

I did not return at once to Anne Fettiplace's cottage, but waited until I was certain that I had not been followed. I had no clear idea why I felt this to be necessary, but for some reason I did not wish to draw the attention of either Berenice Gifford or Katherine Glover to my hostess, even though common sense suggested that I was being overcautious. On the other hand, although both women appeared to have been open and frank in their dealings with me, I knew for a fact that they were lying; that one of them, at least, had had recent contact with Beric Gifford, and that he was not in Brittany, but very much closer to home.

When I described the encounter to Anne Fettiplace and told her of my invitation to visit Valletort Manor, she looked worried.

'Will you go?' she enquired, serving me up a dinner of bacon collops and gravy, followed by apple fritters and goat's-milk cheese.

'Of course,' I answered, clearing my mouth with a swig of her home-brewed ale. 'I would have gone, in any case. To be asked can only be a bonus.'

'Then you must take great care,' she advised me. 'Will you go straight away?'

I shook my head. 'No. I've told Mistress Gifford to expect me within a day or two, but not immediately. She thinks the reason is because I wish to do some trading here, in Modbury, before setting out for Valletort Manor. But, in reality, I want to visit Burrow Island and the fishing villages along the coast.'

My hostess looked even more anxious, if possible, than she had done before.

'Then don't go asking too many questions,' she admonished me. 'Keep your eyes and ears open by all means, but stick to selling your wares. They're queer folk, the fishers, and don't take kindly to interference from the outside world. They protect their own, and Katherine Glover's one of them. Don't forget that!'

'I shan't forget,' I promised. 'I've had experience of what they're like. I had dealings with them once before, some years ago.'

'Well, remember that there are monks living on the island,' Mistress Fettiplace reminded me. 'They're Cistercians from Buckfast Abbey, and Abbot Kyng, so they say, is strict with his flock. If you do run your head into trouble, they'll protect you.'

I was dubious about this. Although I did not say so, it was my experience that monks separated from the Mother House tended to grow lax after a while, and disliked interfering in the entrenched ways and customs of the local community. But I had no intention of doing anything foolish. I was a married man now, with responsibilities, and I hoped that God would remember that as well as I did.

'Will you remain there long?' my hostess persisted, obviously still uneasy. 'My menfolk will be back from Exeter tomorrow. They'd always come to your assistance if you needed them. You'd only have to send me word.'

I thanked her, laughing, and took both her hands in mine.

'Mistress Fettiplace, I mean to be careful, but God bless you for your concern. As for how long I shall stay there, a day, perhaps two at the very most, is the limit of my expectations. The monks, if I recollect rightly, have a small hostelry on the island where I can sleep. At the end of that time, if I've not already discovered where Beric Gifford is hiding, I shall go on to Valletort Manor and see what I can find out there.'

When we parted, she reached up and shyly kissed my cheek.

'My lad's about your age,' she said. She patted my shoulder. 'Look after yourself and don't try anything foolish. Do you hear me, now?'

'I hear you,' I grinned, returning the kiss. 'I promise you I'll try to take care.'

With this she had to be content, and stood at the door of her cottage to wave me off.

It was still some while to noon, and I had the rest of the day before me; a beautiful October day, warm and sunny, but with a little breeze that fanned my cheeks and made walking easy and pleasant. The path that I had chosen was like its fellows on that peninsula of land between the rivers Erme and Avon; sometimes it led across open heath and at others plunged deep into dense patches of woodland; sometimes it led me uphill and at others, down. In several places, the track almost disappeared amongst great tangles of undergrowth, where long, snaking briars coiled around my legs as though loath to let me pass; and now and then, the trees drew back to leave a grassy space, their branches arching overhead, their trunks forming a circle like the pillars of some pagan temple. Little sunlight penetrated to these clearings, but on a fine day they were filled with a greenish, bronze-tinted, subaqueous gloom.

It was in one of these circles that I sat down to rest and eat the apple that Anne Fettiplace had insisted I take with me for the journey.

'You'll need something to sustain you,' she had said. 'You can't be sure when you'll get your next meal.'

So, blessing her thoughtfulness, I sat on a fallen log and bit into its bitter-sweet crispness. I was tired, for, by my reckoning, I had walked more than three miles by then and the going had been rough. The log was at the foot of a tree, and, when I had finished my apple and thrown away the core, I leant back against the bark, closing my eyes for a moment, letting my thoughts drift, dreaming of Adela and home . . .

I must have fallen asleep, for I was suddenly jerked awake by a violent bodily convulsion, and found myself possessed by an inexplicable sense of dread. I was sweating, but at the same time shivering with cold. I started to my feet, reaching for my cudgel, which I had propped against the tree-trunk, convinced that someone was in the clearing with me. But when I glanced around, there was no one to be seen. At first, I refused to accept the evidence of my eyes, and grasping my stick firmly in my hand, with two strides I was in the centre of the clearing, where I spun round and round on my heel, shouting, 'I know you're there! Come out from wherever you're hiding and show me your face!'

But nothing happened. There was neither sign nor sound of movement; no blurring on the edge of my vision to suggest that someone was trying to creep away unnoticed; no sudden snapping of a twig nor rustle of the last year's leaves that lay rotting beneath the roots of ancient, wind-blasted oak and beech. Finally, persuaded that I had been mistaken and that I had been awakened by possibly nothing more sinister than my head falling forward on to my chest, I lowered my cudgel and took a deep breath. The sense of dread had abated. I had ceased both to sweat and to shiver, although my skin was still cold and clammy to the touch, and a lingering sense of uneasiness continued to hold me in its grip.

Leaving my pack beneath a bush and screwing up my courage,

I decided to investigate the margins of the clearing. Taking as my starting point the coast-bound track that I was travelling, I prowled cautiously among the thick belt of trees and undergrowth that surrounded the circle of stunted grass. All was silent as the grave, and by the look of the ground no one had passed this way for several days. But halfway round, I suddenly came across yet another track, leading away from the clearing in a westerly direction; although this was more the ghost of a newly created trail, made simply by the trampling down of ferns and saplings.

On impulse, I followed it, my not inconsiderable weight cutting a deeper defile through the brushwood and leaving a more clearly defined pathway in my wake. I had not gone far, however, when I emerged into a small glade where the trees grew less densely, and where a little sunlight filtered through the foliage, shedding warmth and light into an otherwise desolate spot. But I had barely registered this fact before my eyes were caught and held by the sight of a crude tent, made by pegging down the lower branches of a tree and swathing them with a length of tarred cloth.

Cautiously, I advanced towards it, calling out, 'Is anyone there?' and, at the same time, raising my cudgel ready to defend myself, should the need arise. But there was no answer to my challenge and indeed, I already had the feeling that the tent was empty and that there was no one else about. Just to make sure, however, I bent down and peered inside, then, on hands and knees, crawled through the opening. It was dark within and smelled of rotting vegetation, and the grass was extremely wet. It must once have been used as a shelter of some sort, but all signs of habitation were gone. Not so much as a frond of bracken or a wisp of straw indicated that there might once have been a mattress to lie on.

I wriggled out again into the dappled sunshine, glancing around for anything else that I might have missed. But there was nothing, except for a more clearly defined continuation of the track on the opposite side of the little glade, wending its way down behind the makeshift tent and losing itself amongst the crowding trees.

Having come so far, I felt I had no choice but to discover its final destination. So, treading softly in order to make as little noise as possible, I pushed on through the undergrowth where last year's leaves still festered, where toadstools and puffballs sprouted between the roots of trees, and where saplings turned pale and sickly for want of light and air. I only hoped that I would eventually be able to find my way back again to the original clearing, and offered up a brief prayer for guidance when the time came.

By now, the ground was going rapidly downhill, and suddenly shelved away, bringing me up short on the edge of a steep ravine. Swags of ivy and other trailing plants poured down the rock face, while young trees clung on desperately by fragile roots, embedded precariously in the shallow soil. And some twenty feet below me on the valley floor, nestling in the lee of this miniature cliff, was a solid, granite-built house, surrounded by its outbuildings. Even as I watched, I saw a foreshortened Katherine Glover emerge from one of these to cross a cobbled courtyard and enter another.

Quite by chance, I had stumbled across Valletort Manor.

Quietly, almost stealthily, I made my way back up the slope and moved out of sight of the house as quickly as possible. Mistress Glover had not seen me; she had not glanced up and had obviously had no presentiment that she was being observed.

I found no difficulty in following the track back to the little glade where the tree-tent was, and reflected that the path to and from Valletort Manor must have been more frequently trodden than its counterpart on the other side, the track that led to the clearing. Whether this had any particular significance or not, I was uncertain, for I could not imagine that the crude makeshift shelter had ever been used by Beric Gifford. It was far too close to the house, and would easily have been found by the Sheriff's men during one of their many searches of the manor and its environs.

As far as Valletort Manor itself was concerned, it was plain that there had to be another approach to it on leveller ground. The rock face that backed the hollow in which it had been built afforded it protection, but not access. How to reach it from the front, I hoped to discover all in good time.

Before returning to the clearing, I explored the glade and the tree-tent yet again, just to convince myself that neither contained any clue to Beric Gifford's present whereabouts that I might previously have missed. But I could see nothing except the heavy, broken-off branch of one of the trees, lying half-concealed amongst the grasses. The shelter had been made for some purpose long since abandoned, and I guessed that no one had been near it for many months.

After one or two false starts, I found the trail I was looking for, and began pushing my way through the undergrowth, back towards the clearing. It took me some ten minutes or so to regain the perimeter of trees surrounding it, marked by the fallen log and my discarded apple core, now turning brown where it lay on the grass. I had been halfway round that circle when I had been lured away by the path leading to the glade, so I decided to complete the walk that would bring me once more to the shore-bound path and my pack, hidden under one of the bushes.

But there was only more scrub, more drifts of dead leaves, more beech and oak saplings growing up between the trees, and I was beginning to smell, faintly, the salt tang of the sea. I guessed that within five or six furlongs, this woodland, with its tangles of undergrowth, would give way to the flat open spaces of the downs that sloped down to the shingle and rocks of the shore.

This proved to be the case, but there was still a mile or so to go before I heard the distant hushing of the sea, and yet another half-mile and a steep descent to negotiate before I finally stood on the strip of sand that skirted the base of the cliffs. The track I had followed from Modbury had eventually brought me to a little bay opposite Burrow Island, the latter now in the process of being cut off by the tide. This swept around the rocky outcrop from both directions until the breakers merged and rolled shorewards together, the sand vanishing slowly beneath the waves. At present, however, a narrow strip of causeway still remained, although submerging fast. If I were quick, I could just make the shelter of the monks' rest-house and beg hospitality for the night. Once there, it was true, I should be unable to return to the mainland until the tide again began to ebb, but after my long walk I was tired and, above all, hungry. After only a few moments' indecision, I settled my pack more comfortably on my back and started across what remained of the sandy causeway towards the island.

Chapter Thirteen

I reached the island in the nick of time. The waves were already beginning to swirl around my feet while I was still some few yards distant from the shore, and I was ankle-deep in sea water before I stepped up on to one of the large, flat rocks that studded its narrow beach.

Fortunately, my stout leather boots had kept me dry, for I was fussy about keeping them soled and patched, learning from experience how needful it was in my calling to be comfortably shod. Wet feet were the devil, and watertight boots were therefore a necessity. When they were in want of repair, I always made a point of seeking out the very best cobbler in any town through which I happened to be passing, a policy that had so far repaid me well in my lack of corns, blisters and other ailments of the foot.

The October day was already starting to fade, and the sea shimmered in the dying light, gilded by the evening sun. On the grassy slopes above me, two white-habited brothers, crooks in hand, rounded up the community's sheep and herded them, slowly but surely, into the pen that stood in the lee of the monastery walls. On the island's crest, still clearly visible against the darkening sky, was the chapel of Saint Michael the Archangel patron saint of mariners, while to my right, at the top of some half-dozen worn stone steps, was the travellers' hostelry, where I hoped to be given food and a bed for the night.

I was about to mount these steps when a man came running down them, two large baskets grasped one in each hand. He pulled up short, a look of comical dismay on his face, when he saw the level of the tide.

'Oh, dear me!' he exclaimed in a rather high, fluting voice. 'I knew that would happen. I talk too much, that's my trouble. I was afraid that once I got chatting to Brother Anselm I should forget the time and find myself stranded here for the night. And I've left my cart on the mainland, too. Ah well! There's nothing in it but empty baskets. This was my last port of call.' He glanced at me and his eyes, a pale, clear blue, suddenly brightened. 'Still, I suppose you're going to be here, until the morning, aren't you? At least I shall have someone to share the hours until bedtime with me.'

'I shall be pleased to keep you company,' I said, holding out my hand. 'Roger Chapman, a pedlar, as you see. I've left it far too late to return to Modbury tonight, so, rather than trouble one of the fishermen and his wife, I decided to seek shelter with the brothers. And I've only just made it before the island is completely surrounded.'

My new acquaintance, returning my handshake, introduced himself as one, Bevis Godsey, a smallholder from a village some little way eastward, further along the coast.

'I visit the brothers about once a month,' he explained volubly, remounting the steps as the bell of the monastery chapel began to ring. He turned his head and winked over his shoulder. 'I bring them apples from my orchard and newly laid eggs. They're grateful for these little luxuries out here, perched on this rock. Supplies are not always as fresh as they might be by the time they've been transported all the way from the Mother House. When Brother Anselm and his flock are remembered at all, that is. Ah! Brother!'

He hailed a short, stout monk who had just emerged from a stone cottage next door to the hostelry. 'I was just talking about you. I've overstayed my time, as usual, and been stranded yet again, so I must once more beg accommodation for the night. And here's a chapman also wanting a bed.'

Brother Anselm waved flustered hands, flapping them in the direction of the cottage. 'I can't stop now. The bell for compline's ringing. Speak to Geoffrey, Bevis. He'll see you both safely bestowed and make certain that you have sufficient victuals for your needs. I may be able to join you later, but in case not, I'll wish you good night.' And he trotted off in the direction of the monastery as fast as his legs would carry him.

'Geoffrey Shapwick,' my companion informed me, 'is the lay brother on the island. He lights the lamp in Saint Michael's chapel every evening, to guide the ships out at sea away from the rocks, and during the day helps the other brothers to look after the sheep. He also hoes and weeds the vegetable patch, attends to the welfare of travellers and, in short, does all the odd jobs the monks themselves haven't the time – or say they haven't the time – to do. In return, he gets the cottage to live in rent free.'

'It sounds as if he earns his tenancy,' I laughed, and waited patiently while Bevis Godsey fetched Master Shapwick from his fireside and once more explained his continued presence on the island. The lay brother's total lack of surprise indicated that it was too frequent an occurrence to be worthy of comment, and within half an hour at the very most, we were ensconced beside a fire, a high-backed settle protecting our backs from the draughts that, together with the sand, seeped in under the hostelry door. A mazer each of ale stood at our elbows, while steaming bowls of fish soup and thick slices of black bread warmed our chilled limbs and filled our empty stomachs.

A tallow candle placed, in its holder, at one end of the table gave me my first real look at Bevis Godsey, and I decided that if there was one word that described him better than all others, it was 'dapper'. To begin with, he was neatly made; a small-boned man of some forty summers with, for one of his sex, delicate hands and feet. His clothes, cut from good woollen cloth, were neither patched nor mended and argued a certain financial status, elevating him above peasant or villein level. His teeth, too, showed white in the tanned face, with no blackening that I was aware of, and although he was short of stature, he held himself well, making the most of such inches as he had. But it was obvious, from the way he frequently displayed them, that his hands were his chief pride and joy. And as a smallholder, constantly working on his land, he had every reason to be proud of them, for the nails were rounded and unbitten, and the long, slender fingers almost completely free of ingrained dirt.

I noticed the ring which adorned his left thumb immediately, but it was some while before my hunger was sufficiently assuaged to allow my attention to wander for any length of time. When it finally did, however, I saw how the candlelight caught the ring and made it sparkle, and I began to suspect that tiny diamonds were set in the duller lustre of the gold. This fact intrigued me because it was surely too expensive a bauble for a man of my companion's worldly standing, even if he had accumulated some money over the years.

'A very fine thumb ring,' I commented, nodding towards it.

Bevis Godsey stopped eating and held his left hand close to the candle flame, spreading his fingers and regarding the ring admiringly.

'Beautiful, isn't it?' he said. He turned his hand so that its back was towards me, and I could see that the gold of the ring had been worked into an intricate pattern before being studded with the gems. 'Look closer,' he urged, 'and you'll note that the setting is in the form of my initials.' He advanced his hand closer to my face. 'There you are. B. G. Bevis Godsey. What do you think of that?'

What I thought, with a sudden, excited lurch of my stomach, was that I had seen the same arrangement of those two letters a day or so ago, in a hat brooch with a pendant, teardrop pearl; an ornament that was now nestling deep in the belt-pouch at my waist.

I reached out and took hold of my companion's hand, drawing it nearer to me, and my examination revealed that I had not been mistaken.

'A fine jewel, indeed,' I said, trying to keep my voice level. 'Was it made for you? A present, perhaps?'

He hesitated before replying, and his eyes could not quite bring themselves to meet mine.

'It . . . it belonged to my father,' he stammered. 'And his father before him. A family heirloom, in fact.' He must have seen my expression of incredulity, because he flushed painfully and jerked his wrist free of my grasp. 'It was given to my grandfather in thanks,' he said, 'by a gentleman to whom he had supplied some especially fine fruit for a special meal that he was giving. It so happened that their initials were the same.'

It must have sounded as lame an explanation to his own ears as it did to mine, and he looked even more uncomfortable than he had done hitherto. But, wisely, he decided that further embroidery of so improbable a story could only do more harm than good, and folded his lips together in defiant silence.

To his obvious relief, I made no attempt, for the time being at least, to press him further on the subject, and steered the conversation into less contentious waters. But although we chatted easily enough of this and that, and I was treated, inevitably, to his views on the present state of affairs between the King and his brother, the Duke of Clarence, my thoughts were busy elsewhere.

That the ring, like the hat brooch, had belonged to Beric Gifford, I had few doubts, but whereas I felt certain in my own mind that the latter had been accidentally lost, the thumb ring might well have been given to Bevis Godsey for a service rendered or to ensure his silence, or, in the absence of ready cash, in payment of a debt; and the coincidence of the two men's initials being the same would make the gift that much more acceptable. But first, for my personal satisfaction, I had to make sure that Bevis Godsey's story of his grandfather's acquisition of the ring was false.

This, in the event, proved to be much easier than I had anticipated, for he was a man seemingly unused to lying, and, having made up the story on the spur of the moment in order to combat my patent disbelief, he had failed to lay any foundations in his memory for it. An hour and some several cups of ale later, I managed, by devious means, to bring the talk round to the subject of given names, and the predilection of most parents for having their male offspring christened after husband or father or grandfather, thus sowing confusion in nearly every family.

'No doubt, you were so called for that reason,' I added with apparent innocence. 'Bevis is an uncommon name.'

'It's from an old Norman word, meaning "bull",' my companion said proudly. He went on, 'My mother heard it somewhere or the other, and liked it. It was entirely her choice, and had nothing to do with either my father or grandfather. They were not so baptized.'

'You surprise me,' I lied.

Bevis shook his head reminiscently. 'My father always complained that it was far too fancy a name. He and his father were both called John, which, he maintained, being the name of

Our Lord's most beloved disciple, was good enough for any man.'

He seemed completely unaware of the fact that he had just destroyed his explanation about how his family had acquired the thumb ring, and continued to smile at me, more than a little drunk by now, from the opposite side of the table.

To make assurance doubly sure, I said, 'Your grandfather was a fruit grower, you say, as you are. Who was the gentleman he served?'

Again, no warning bells sounded in my companion's sleepy head; no recollection, however hazy, of the story of the matching initials.

'He was one of the very last of the Oxton family,' he answered. 'A distant kinsman, I believe, of the Oxtons who were Lords of the Manor of Modbury after the de Valletorts and before Champernownes.'

'Ah, yes! I've heard of them.' I rose and stretched my arms above my head. 'I'm bone-weary. I think I'll go to bed, if you've no objections?'

Bevis also got to his feet, having swallowed the dregs of his ale.

'I'm ready to join you. I don't think we shall see Brother Anselm tonight, after all, and it's been a long day. I was abroad before first light this morning. Come with me, and I'll show you where to sleep.'

I followed him into a neighbouring room, where two straw-filled mattresses had been laid side by side on the floor and covered with rough woollen blankets. Bevis and I appeared to be the only guests staying in the hostelry that night, for which mercy I was thankful.

I began pulling off my boots. 'Which route did you travel today,' I asked, 'to get here?'

And now, unexpectedly, he grew wary. In the flickering radiance of the candle that we had brought with us from the ale-room, I could see the sudden tension in his face. Those alarm bells which had failed to alert him twenty minutes since, were now ringing loudly.

'Oh,' he answered vaguely, 'I kept to the usual paths. They're safest.'

I remembered something he had mentioned earlier. 'You said that you've left your cart on the mainland. What about your horse? Where is it stabled?'

'It's – er – it's a handcart,' he replied as casually as he could, but I heard the note of chagrin in his voice.

I mentally reassessed his position in the social scale, as he must have known I should. Bevis was not as well off as I had supposed. He did not own a horse, and it was therefore highly probable that neither his father nor his grandfather had done so either. This information made it even less likely that the latter, presented with a valuable gift such as the thumb ring, would not have sold it and turned it into money. I needed no further proof. I was totally convinced by now that the ring had been, until recently, the property of Beric Gifford. But where had Bevis met him, and under what circumstances?

Having stripped down to my shirt and hose, I lay down on one of the mattresses and pulled the blankets up around my chin. My companion did likewise and blew out the candle.

'Did you sell your fruit in Modbury market before coming on to the island?' I asked, hoping that my interest in his movement sounded offhanded enough to prevent suspicion. Bevis made a sort of grunting noise that I took for assent, so I continued, 'I understand that there's a house of some size between Modbury and the coast. I thought I might try to find it on my return journey tomorrow. The women of the household might be glad to buy from me. Do you know the place I mean?'

'Valletort Manor,' he answered reluctantly. 'Yes, I know it. I've visited it once or twice in the past, but not today. I went nowhere near it today.' And with this strangely overemphatic statement, my companion turned on his side, humping his back towards me, and would respond to no more of my questions on the subject. Within minutes, he was either fast asleep, or feigning to be so.

Although extremely weary, I lay awake a while longer thinking about the thumb ring and wondering how it came to be in Bevis Godsey's possession. Even on such a short acquaintance, I did not believe him to be a thief, and anyway, how on earth would he have managed to pilfer it from off Beric Gifford's hand? No, I felt certain that it had been given to him in payment for some service rendered, but what sort of service, I could not imagine.

But where and when had he met Beric? Bevis's urgent denial that he had been anywhere near Valletort Manor today suggested the opposite to my already distrustful mind. Yet, if it had been within the manor pale that the two men had encountered one another, why had it been necessary for Beric to pay for any kind of favour with a valuable ornament, when he had easy access to his doting sister's purse?

There might be an answer to that question, I eventually decided. If Bevis Godsey had not known who Beric was, had met him at a sufficient distance from Valletort Manor not to guess at his identity, then Beric had probably wished to keep him in the dark. A visit to the house and his return with money, could well have alerted Bevis to the truth, or, at the very least, made him curious. On the other hand, the initials in the ring would provide a clue as to Beric's identity.

It was an unsatisfactory explanation, but then, the whole

situation was as muddied as a village pond. For instance, what sort of favour was Bevis Godsey capable of rendering Beric Gifford that could not be performed by either Katherine Glover or Berenice? I had seen little of the former and even less of the latter, but for all that, both had struck me as being strong-minded women, perfectly able to carry through any task, however formidable, in the name of love.

But that was as far as I got in my deliberations that night, because sleep overtook me; and apart from a resolve to confront Bevis Godsey with my suspicions on the following day, I knew nothing else until morning.

I was awoken by the faint, sad crying of the gulls.

Suddenly alert and vigorous, I heaved myself off my mattress and threw wide the shutters, letting in the grey light of an early dawn. The stars were paling fast, some of them already snuffed out, and there was the damp, delicious smell of dew-drenched grass. The air was fresh and easy to breathe, and I could hear the eternal murmuring of the sea.

I turned to my companion, ready to rouse him to the delights of this brand-new day, only to find his mattress empty, the blankets neatly folded at the foot, himself nowhere to be seen. I scrambled into my clothes, snatched up my pack and cudgel and went in search of Geoffrey Shapwick at his cottage.

'Bevis Godsey?' he said, when I eventually ran him to earth on the hillside, driving the sheep from pen to pasture, in company with two of the brothers. 'He left early, before it was light; as soon as the tide had receded enough to allow him to cross dryshod to the mainland. He asked me to give you his good wishes and to say that he had enjoyed your company. He was sorry he couldn't stay until you woke, but he had urgent business at home and wanted to be there by midday.'

I cursed silently. If I had not slept so soundly, worn out by my long walk and the sea air, I might have been disturbed by Bevis's stealthy rising, and been able to question him further about the ring. But at least, now, I felt sure that he had something to hide. Probably, waking with a clearer head, he had recalled our conversation of the previous night and realized that he had given the lie twice over to his original story. And he would guess that I had realized it, too. The only course, therefore, was flight before I tried to satisfy my curiosity with yet more questions.

I stripped off and waded into the sea to wash away yesterday's dirt, then dressed again, cleaned my teeth with my willow bark and begged some of the monks' fresh water, brought to the island in barrels, in which to shave. By this time, Geoffrey Shapwick had returned to his cottage and prepared me a breakfast of a couple of fried bacon collops between two hunks of coarse, oaten bread, washed down with yet more ale.

'You'll be on your way as well, I dare say,' he remarked as I stuffed the last mouthful of bread and meat into my mouth and wiped my lips free of grease on the back of my hand. 'Now that the tide's out.'

I nodded, then, when able to speak, enquired thickly, 'Bevis Godsey, does he come here often?'

'About once a month,' was the answer, thus confirming what Bevis himself had told me. 'He brings us fresh fruit and such vegetables as we can't grow ourselves on the island. He sells also to the fisherfolk along the shore.'

'What about Valletort Manor?' I asked. 'Does he call there, do you know?'

Geoffrey Shapwick hunched his shoulders. 'Probably. Now and then.'

'Did he visit it yesterday, do you know?' I persisted.

I was given an odd look for my pains. 'If he did, he didn't

mention it to me, but he was talking to Brother Anselm for most of the time before you arrived. You're an inquisitive fellow, I must say.'

'I always have been,' I answered cheerfully, humping my pack on to my back and preparing to take my leave. 'God be with you, Master Shapwick. Where can I find Brother Anselm at this hour of the morning?'

'He went up to Saint Michael's chapel to douse the lamp for me, as I had your breakfast to see to. He might still be there. He doesn't move very quickly nowadays.'

The chapel was very small – no more, I should guess, than some five paces long and four paces broad. Brother Anselm was indeed still there, staring out to sea through one of the windows set in the eastern wall.

'I've come to take my leave of you, Brother,' I said, 'and thank you for your hospitality.'

'I trust you were comfortable, my child.' He patted my arm with an avuncular smile. 'You passed a good night?'

'I slept like a log,' I assured him. 'I had pleasant company, too, for the evening. Bevis Godsey,' I added.

'Ah yes! Bevis! A bit of a chatterer, but a good man, for all that. It was because he stayed talking to me that he was caught by the tide.'

'He comes once a month, I understand, to bring you fresh fruit and vegetables.'

'Yes. We have a few things from him, but not enough I'm afraid to make it worth his while to travel this distance, unless he had another reason to do so.'

'And does he?' I prompted.

'Fortunately! He has kin amongst the fisherfolk. His mother was a member of one of the families hereabouts. And they are very clannish, very tightly knit communities, you know. They never lose touch with one another, not even when they go some miles away to live, as did Bevis's mother, Susan Glover. Indeed you might say that the Glovers are the most clannish family of the lot.'

Chapter Fourteen

I walked back across the slowly widening causeway of sand that linked Burrow Island to the mainland at ebb tide. Above me, the gulls wheeled and called, or floated aimlessly like scraps of torn parchment, while oystercatchers and redshanks waded in the shallows, pecking hungrily at whatever flotsam had been thrown up by the sea. Ahead of me, thin grasses crested dunes that gave shelter to a cluster of slate-roofed cottages, built just above the high-water line. Boats lay upturned on rocks veined with yellow seaweed, fishing nets stretched across them to dry. And I knew that on the far side of the headland was another fishing community, larger, because more protected, than the one directly in my line of vision, where I could already see and hear signs of life. Smoke rose into the still air through the holes in the cottage roofs and early morning sounds threaded the silence.

I had been in no hurry to reach the mainland, my feet dragging as my thoughts raced, trying to assess the significance of what Brother Anselm had told me. Bevis Godsey was related to Katherine Glover, which solved the problem of how he was acquainted, or had come into contact, with Beric Gifford. It also explained why he would be willing to do some service or favour for a man whom he must know to be wanted for cold-blooded murder. What was less clear was why he had been paid with Beric's thumb ring rather than with money from Berenice Gifford's purse.

Enlightenment dawned with the realization that Bevis himself might well have chosen this method of recompense. Such a possession would give him status, confer on him an aura of that prosperity which had, in fact, eluded him. At the same time, he could not admit how he came by the ring without revealing Beric's presence close at hand, so a story had to be concocted for friends and neighbours that would satisfy their curiosity. But the story with which I, a nosy stranger, had been regaled had been a spur-of-the-moment tale, neither well thought out nor well rehearsed, fading from his memory almost as soon as it was told. This strongly suggested to me that Bevis had not owned the ring for very long, and that he had done the favour for Beric Gifford only that previous day, probably sometime within the last twenty-four hours. Beric, therefore, was not very far away, possibly skulking within the pale of Valletort Manor, which, in itself, would have sparked Bevis Godsey's emphatic denial of having been there yesterday.

I recalled the strange feeling of lurking evil that I had experienced on waking up in the clearing. Had Beric been close to me then, observing me from some concealed vantage point amongst the trees? And later, when, from the bluff above the manor house, I had seen Katherine Glover crossing the courtyard, had he been hiding in one of the outbuildings? Was it possible that she had actually been on her way to visit him then? At the thought, the hairs rose on the nape of my neck and I shivered.

It was now fully daylight, and a fisherman had emerged from one of the cottages to mend his net, which clearly showed two gaping holes. I hailed him as I approached.

'Good morning! Do either you or your goodwife need anything from my pack, I wonder?'

He jumped when he heard my voice and demanded belligerently, 'Where have you sprung from?'

'The island. I spent the night as a guest of the monks.'

'It was you, then.' His tone was surly. 'I was told that a stranger had crossed the causeway late yesterday afternoon. One who was nearly caught by the tide.'

There was very little, probably nothing, that passed unnoticed, or that was not immediately made common knowledge, in this tiny, tightly knit community of fishermen.

'I got wet feet, certainly,' I admitted. 'But the brothers were hospitable, as always. I was soon fed and made comfortable again.'

The man peered at me suspiciously. 'Been here before, have you?'

'Once. A long time ago. Now, would your goody be interested in my wares, do you think, or shall I try elsewhere?'

He gave a nod of his head towards the nearest cottage. 'You can ask her,' he conceded grudgingly, and returned to mending his nets.

The goodwife, a plain, almost ugly woman, proved far friendlier and more loquacious than her husband, a fact that was explained within the first few minutes of our acquaintance, when she volunteered the information that she was a 'foreigner' from Plymouth.

'You must find this existence extremely lonely, then,' I said, drawing up a stool and opening my pack. I spread out its contents on the rough wooden table.

'I do,' she sighed, before adding frankly, 'but when God has given you my looks, and you've no money either, you can't pick and choose a husband. You take what's on offer and are thankful for it.'

Not for the first time, I reflected how unfairly the dice were loaded against women in the game of life; how brutally their fate was governed by chance. (This is true of men also, I suppose, but to a far lesser degree. Far less.)

I watched while she lovingly fingered some lengths of damask ribbon before sadly abandoning them in favour of more practical considerations, like needles and thread. While she examined the rest of the items, I glanced around the single, sparsely furnished room in search of some means of pushing our conversation in the direction in which I wished it to go, and found inspiration in a row of apples set out to finish ripening on a shelf.

'Fine fruit! You've had Master Godsey here, I can see. He certainly gives value for money.

The goodwife glanced up. 'Do you know Bevis?' she asked in some surprise.

'We spent the night together in the guesthouse on the island. He was caught by the tide because he stayed talking too long with Brother Anselm.'

She laughed. 'That makes good sense. He's a great talker, is Bevis.'

'And a member, or so I'm told, of the Glover family. Are they among your neighbours hereabouts?'

The woman shook her head. 'They live in the cove on the western side of the headland.' She looked sideways at me, a furtive gleam in her dark eyes. 'You know the history of Katherine Glover, I suppose? Nowadays, there aren't many folk from these parts who don't.'

I didn't enlighten her as to my origins. 'You mean since the murder of Master Capstick,' I suggested, 'and the subsequent disappearance of Beric Gifford?'

My companion crossed herself hurriedly and whispered, 'The Sheriff's men won't find him, you know. He's eaten Saint John's fern.'

'So I've heard it said.' I rested my elbows on the table and cupped my chin in my hands. 'A fisherman's daughter seems a strange choice of a wife for a young man such as Master Gifford.'

'Everyone predicted that no good would come of it. But it was really *her* fault. Berenice Gifford's, I mean. *She* was the one who took a fancy to Katherine in the first place, and insisted that she go to live at the manor as her maid.'

'How did she come to notice the girl?' I enquired.

'The Glovers have always supplied Valletort Manor with fresh fish every Friday, and on fast days in general. Whenever it's been safe for the boats to put to sea, that is. Jonas Glover or his wife used to carry part of the night's catch up to the house themselves until about a year ago, when Katherine started doing it for them. And not long afterwards, Berenice Gifford asked her to be her personal maid. It was a recipe for trouble, everybody said so. Katherine's a very beautiful girl. It was inevitable that Beric would be attracted to her, although no one expected that he would want to make her his wife.'

'Why was Berenice Gifford in need of a maid?' I wondered. 'What happened to her previous attendant? She must have had one, surely?'

'Oh, yes! A woman who had been at the manor in her father's lifetime. Constance Trim. But Constance's own father died and his widow was left with very little money to live on. Constance felt it her duty to go back to Modbury and look after her mother. She's an excellent seamstress, I believe, and can earn enough to support them both.'

'Have you ever seen Beric Gifford and Katherine Glover together?'

'Three or four times,' the goodwife admitted. 'Maybe oftener. The last occasion was a couple days before the murder. I'd been picking mushrooms in the meadows and woods near Valletort Manor.' She broke off, eyeing me askance, guessing that I knew as well as she did that it was against the law then, as it is now, to gather field mushrooms, because the death cap can so easily be slipped in among the rest; a simple way to poison

165

someone and make it seem an accident.

I returned her gaze blandly. 'Beric and Katherine must be very much in love,' I prompted, ignoring the latter part of what she had just told me.

'He certainly is with her,' the goodwife agreed, smiling gratefully. 'On each occasion that I saw them together, it seemed to me that he couldn't make enough fuss of her. I reckon he dotes on her, and that's a fact.'

'And would you say that she is as affectionate as he is?'

My companion hesitated. After a moment's reflection, she said, 'Perhaps not. But then, there's always one of every twosome who's more loving than the other.' The touch of bitterness in her voice suggested that she spoke from personal experience. 'Don't misunderstand me, though,' she went on quickly. 'She appears fond enough of him. But I suspect that she was even fonder of the prospect of being mistress of Valletort Manor. It was something she would never have believed possible, not in her wildest dreams. But, of course, that's all over now.'

I suddenly recalled Stephen Sherford's words. 'It seemed to me that he was more in love with her than she with him.' And now here was corroboration of his suspicions. But he had also implied, in contradiction, that Beric would tire of his betrothed before she did of him, although that, I was sure, had been mere wishful thinking. Stephen Sherford had made it plain that he did not like Katherine Glover, and I had a feeling that the goodwife, if pressed, would agree with him. If it came to that, I was uncertain whether or not my own impression of her had been favourable, but was unable to make up my mind.

'What do you think they will do?' I asked. 'As you've just pointed out, there's no prospect of their ever being master and mistress of Valletort Manor now.'

My companion shrugged. 'Who can say? There's only one thing

certain: Beric Gifford's thrown away his uncle's fortune, his home and his safety all for the sake of a moment's revenge, a momentary satisfaction. But he'll live to rue it. He's bound to. No man could let all that slip through his fingers and not go mad with regret. In time, he'll probably grow to hate Katherine Glover, and then I wouldn't give a fig for her life. A man who's committed one murder won't balk at a second.'

'Don't you think he might have gone abroad?' I said. 'Don't you think he might be in France or Brittany?'

'No,' was the positive reply. 'He's eaten Saint John's fern and made himself invisible.'

'You seem very sure of that.'

The goodwife hesitated, obviously debating with herself whether or not to say more. Then she took a deep breath and, lowering her voice, confided, 'My husband doesn't like me to talk about the murder because it involves one of our community. One of *their* community,' she amended wryly. 'I'm not one of them, and never have been. One day, I'll run away, back to Plymouth, and they'll never see me again.'

'Go on,' I urged, when she seemed inclined to fall into a reverie of escape and freedom. 'What is it that you were going to say?'

'Say? Oh, yes! Well, I go for walks. Long walks, inland, picking berries and . . . and mushrooms,' she added defiantly. 'They help eke out our diet of fish, and more fish, in between Bevis Godsey's visits. A week or so gone, near Valletort Manor, I saw Beric Gifford's cloak hanging on the broken branch of a tree. It scared me almost witless. He could have been standing right next to me, invisible, and I shouldn't have known so I took to my heels as fast as I could. But then, when I'd gone a little distance, curiosity got the better of me, although I can hardly believe now that I was such a fool. But I was. I crept back, scarcely able to breathe because I was so frightened, to see if he'd materialized once I was out of the way.'

'And had he?' I asked, carried along on the tide of her credulity.

'No,' she was forced to admit. 'But his cloak had gone!' Her eyes glistened with excitement. 'He'd been there all right, visible or not, and taken it away with him when he left.'

'And you're sure that the cloak belonged to Beric Gifford?'

'I've seen him wearing it. Brown velvet, lined with pale blue sarcenet. A bit shabby and rubbed around the neck, but otherwise smart enough.'

At that moment, the cottage door opened and her husband came in, his leathery features puckered in suspicion.

'You've been a fair while, chapman. What's going on? There can't be that much that my goody's needing.' He eyed the woman sharply. 'You've not been gossiping, I hope! I've told you! We keep ourselves to ourselves here. We don't want every passing traveller knowing all our business.'

The goodwife picked up a reel of coarse thread. 'I'll take this,' she said, looking at me imploringly, begging me to reveal nothing of our conversation.

I thanked her and began putting the rest of the things back into my pack.

'We've been talking about London,' I lied cheerfully. 'I was there a few months ago and your wife wanted to know all about the latest fashions.'

The fisherman snorted in derision, but made no further comment. He was determined, however, not to leave us alone together any longer, and waited doggedly for me to quit the cottage, following me outside and closing the door behind us. I wished him good day and, as the tide had not yet receded far enough for me to walk round the headland, I scrambled up the rocky, boulder-strewn path to the top of the cliff and made my way across the promontory until I could look down into the cove on its other side.

A similar, but larger, huddle of slate-roofed cottages nestled against the rising ground at its back, and now that the sun was beginning to mount in the sky, there was greater activity amongst the fishermen and their families. This was a slightly more prosperous community than its neighbour because a little less exposed to the elements. And in one of those cottages Katherine Glover had been raised.

I hitched up my pack and started on the rocky descent to the shore.

Of the dozen or so dwellings that straggled around the cove and a little way up the hill behind it, I discovered, in the course of the next hour, that no less than seven were occupied by Glovers and their kinsfolk, all related to one another by either blood or marriage. And it was rapidly made plain to me that any mention of the murder, or the Giffords, and especially of Katherine herself, would be met with instant expulsion from whichever cottage I happened to be in. Indeed, by the time I reached the seventh one, I was met on the threshold by an angry deputation, led by a middle aged couple, whom I guessed to be Katherine's parents.

'Get out! Go on! Leave us alone! We don't want you here!' the man said, in a voice that was all the more threatening for being quiet and restrained.

There was a muttered assent from the score of people gathered at his back, and I noticed uneasily that several of the men were brandishing some evil-looking clubs, three or four of them exactly like the one described to me by Mathilda Trenowth as being the murder weapon.

'Be off with you!' exclaimed the woman, whom I felt sure was Katherine's mother; a fact that she confirmed a moment later. 'My daughter warned us about you. She said that some nose-twitching pedlar might be around, asking questions about things that are none of his business. So we suggest that you go now, before we do something that you might live to regret.'

'Or not live to regret,' her husband added softly.

Once more, I felt the hairs rise on the nape of my neck. Years ago, I had had experience of the ruthlessness of these people, and I had no wish to be the victim of their prejudice and hatred.

'Very well!' I said, with as much bravado as I could muster. 'If that's how you feel, I shall leave at once. I've no desire to stay where I'm unwelcome.'

'Good,' replied Katherine Glover's father. 'And don't let any of us catch you round here again.'

I moved off, walking, I hoped, with dignity, but conscious all the while of those menacing figures behind me, and of those itchy fingers lovingly caressing their sticks. The rocky path led me upwards through a narrow ravine to the cliff top, and from there a track ran across the headland to disappear eventually into a belt of wind-blasted trees. Once within their shelter, I allowed my pace to slacken and then, feeling tired or, to be honest, somewhat weak-kneed from fright, I sat down on the damp, sandy ground, bracing my back against the trunk of an oak.

I was just recovering my composure and a little of my self-esteem, and wondering if the track I was on would eventually lead me to Valletort Manor, when I became aware of someone standing beside me. I glanced up to see a young girl, perhaps twelve or thirteen years of age, whom I had noticed a quarter of an hour earlier, on the edge of the crowd on the beach, and whose hazel eyes were now regarding me thoughtfully through a tangled mass of dark brown hair.

'Do you want to know about Beric Gifford?' she demanded baldly. 'Well, I'll let you into a secret. He's invisible. He's eaten Saint John's fern.'

I sighed deeply. 'So everyone keeps telling me.'

'Oh.' She sounded disappointed. She had obviously hoped that she was apprising me of something that I did not already know. She frowned, obviously cudgelling her brains for other information with which to capture my attention, and succeeded when she said, 'I saw him. Beric Gifford, that is. On the day of the murder, it must have been, because the front of his tunic was stained with blood.'

'You're sure?' I demanded excitedly, scrambling to my feet. 'Are you positive that this was on the day of the murder?'

'It was May Day.' She smiled, delighted at having achieved her object. 'He didn't see me. He was with that Katherine Glover. All over one another, they were, pawing each other and kissing until it made me feel sick. I hate the Glovers,' she added confidentially, thereby revealing the reason for her willingness to talk.

'Where was this?' I asked. 'Where did you see Katherine and Beric Gifford?'

'In the woods above Valletort Manor.' Her frown returned and she thrust out her lower lip. 'They were covered in dirt. They must have been rolling about on the ground. I can just imagine what they'd been up to!'

She spoke with the self-righteous disapproval of love-making that I have frequently noted in girls shortly before they blossom into womanhood. I reflected that given another year, or maybe even less than that, my young lady would have discovered for herself the pleasures of rolling about on the ground with a boy.

'Why are you smiling?' she demanded crossly.

I stooped and, parting the tangle of hair, kissed her gently on the forehead.

'No reason,' I lied. 'Are you certain that the front of Beric Gifford's tunic was stained with blood? Could you see it properly? How far away from him were you?'

'I hid behind a tree when I saw them coming. They didn't notice me, though they passed as close as I am to you now. They were too busy whispering and laughing together. I could see dark stains on the front of Beric's tunic. At the time, I thought they were just more dirt, but later, when everyone was talking about the murder, I guessed what they must be.'

Here was confirmation of what Mathilda Trenowth claimed to have seen.

I asked, 'Was Master Gifford wearing a hat?'

The girl nodded. 'That black velvet one he always wore. Why do you want to know?'

I ignored her question and put another of my own. 'And was this cap ornamented in any way?'

She thought for a moment or two before shaking her head. 'No. I'm sure I should have noticed, because he'd pulled the cap right down over his head, almost covering the tips of his ears.'

'What time of day was this?'

The girl laughed. 'Jonas Glover was right about you. You're a nosy one, aren't you?'

'What time of day?' I persisted.

'Nearly noon, I reckon. Most people had gone to the May Day feasting in Modbury, but my mother was angry with me about something or the other. I forget what. So I had been left behind.'

I sensed that she was beginning to lose interest, and felt that I had tested her patience long enough with my catechism. So, having ascertained from her that I was on the right track for Valletort Manor, I wished her good day and set off along the path.

Chapter Fifteen

Once, Valletort had undoubtedly been one of the most important manors of the district; but the great disaster of the previous century, the terrible outbreak of bubonic plague that had ravaged the whole of Europe and decimated its population, in some instances wiping out entire villages, had led, as in so many other cases, to its decline. Many of the fields surrounding it stood fallow, or, having ceased to be tilled altogether for lack of manpower, were reverting rapidly to wasteland, being reclaimed by the encroaching woods. For, like many another family, the Giffords had of necessity stopped farming their demesnes because of soaring labour costs and the plunging market prices of crops and livestock.

Much of this I could see and guess for myself as the track from the cove brought me directly into the heart of the manor lands. A number of dwellings and smallholdings at which I halted in order to sell my dwindling supply of goods were occupied by tenants who, with practically no encouragement, delighted in admitting that their forefathers had been villeins, owing feudal allegiance and manorial service to the Giffords, and contrasting their own lot favourably with that of their ancestors. They were also eager to boast about the many shifts and ploys used by them to thwart the rent collectors; and it took very little imagination on my part to see how a lazy, self-indulgent landlord, such as Cornelius Gifford seemed to have been, would have preferred to live on his

173

wife's money rather than incur the expense and inconvenience of imposing a distraint upon his tenants' goods.

I was urged to rest, eat and gossip so often that it was late afternoon, and the light already fading, before the manor house itself came into view, sheltered by its wooded bluff, its approach overgrown with scrub and thickly crowding trees. The entrance was through an archway, beneath a gatehouse showing dangerous signs of crumbling masonry. Beyond that lay the courtyard that I had observed the previous day. This was bounded on three sides by outbuildings and on the fourth by the house itself, the latter, in places, in almost as parlous a condition as the lodge.

I walked into the centre of this cobbled square and waited to be challenged, but for a while, nothing stirred. The silence was so intense that I could almost hear it, and even the birds seemed to have stopped singing. The wind, which had been blowing strongly across the open ground of the headland, barely ruffled my hair.

I remembered Jack Golightly telling me that there was a paucity of servants at Valletort Manor. His estimate had been only three, apart from Katherine Glover: an old nurse, an ancient, semi-blind steward and a groom who had been in the Giffords' employ for many years. It was with considerable surprise, therefore, that, after what seemed like several minutes but was probably no more than one, I saw a woman approaching me across the courtyard, elderly, certainly, judging by the many lines on her face, but with an upright and vigorous carriage. At the waist of her dark grey homespun gown hung an imposing bunch of keys, indicating that she must hold the post of housekeeper.

'Who are you? And what do you want?' she demanded.

I explained my errand. 'Mistress Gifford invited me here. She hoped, I think, to buy some of my goods if there was anything that took her fancy.' I favoured the woman with my most ingratiating smile, but there was no lightening of her rather sour expression.

'Indeed?' she queried. 'She has said nothing to me about it.'

'Ask Mistress Glover,' I suggested. 'She knows. She was present when the invitation was given.'

The housekeeper's features set in lines of rigid disapproval. 'I ask Mistress Glover no more than I have to,' was the uncompromising answer.

'Thank you, Mistress Tuckett,' said a quiet voice behind her, making the housekeeper jump and spin round. Neither of us had heard or noticed Katherine Glover's approach.

The two women glared at one another with such naked hatred in their eyes that I wondered how Berenice Gifford could tolerate the presence of both under one roof. But it was the elder of the two who eventually backed down and moved away, proceeding at a stately pace towards one of the outbuildings and vanishing inside it.

'Berenice has been expecting you,' Katherine Glover said. 'Follow me.'

I supposed the familiarity was natural since they were future sisters; but at the same time, I couldn't help wondering what the relationship between them might be if the marriage of Beric and his betrothed never took place. Would Katherine Glover one day find herself returned to the poverty and squalor of her parents' cottage, all her erstwhile hopes and dreams lying in ruins?

The main entrance to the house led straight into the great hall with its high-raftered roof and old-fashioned, central hearth. Large, tapestry-covered screens stood at either end of the room. The one inside the door by which Mistress Glover and I had just entered was, presumably, to keep out the courtyard draughts, whilst I supposed that the second helped lessen the smells of cooking that emanated from the kitchens. A minstrels' gallery ran the length of one wall, above the high table on its carpeted dais. The remainder of the floor was rush-strewn, with a couple of chairs and stools providing the only alternative seating to a stone bench set beneath the windows. These latter displayed the hall's only attempt at modernization, the upper halves having been glazed to let in more light. The lower, however, were still covered with the original oiled parchment.

I had seen a greater parade of wealth and material comfort in ordinary gentlemen's homes in any town that I had ever visited; and there was little evidence to suggest that Berenice Gifford had so far spent much of her recently inherited wealth on Valletort Manor. But then, I reflected, she had not expected to be the recipient of her great-uncle's fortune and would have made no plans what to do with the money when it was hers. She was probably still getting used to the idea of being a rich woman.

Berenice herself was sitting in the single armchair that the hall boasted, close to the spluttering fire. Some logs had just been added, temporarily smothering the flames, and the smoke, rising towards the louvre in the roof, was causing someone to cough. As I approached, I saw that this someone was none other than Bartholomew Champernowne, leaning nonchalantly over the back of Berenice's chair. I was somewhat discomfited. I had not expected to meet him there.

'Here's the chapman,' Katherine Glover announced. 'Nurse was doing her best to prevent him entering.'

So, I reflected, the housekeeper and the nurse mentioned by Jack Golightly were one and the same person, although the lady was neither as old nor as decrepit as he had described her. She looked, in fact, rather formidable. I wondered if the groom and the steward had suffered similar slander from the tongues of the gossips.

'Ah! Chapman!' Berenice did not rise, but, again to my surprise, extended her hand, this time in greeting. 'I expected you before this.' Without giving me a chance to reply, or to point out that I had arrived earlier than promised, she continued, 'And, as you can see, I have persuaded Master Champernowne to await your coming. He feels he owes you an apology.' She slewed around to smile up into the scowling face of her future husband. 'Don't you, my heart's dearest?'

There was something so mocking in her tone that it very nearly turned the endearment into an insult, and for the first time, it occurred to me that her acceptance of Bartholomew's proposal might have been solely in order to win her great-uncle's approval, and not because she was in love with the young man. But if that were the case, why should she have persisted with the betrothal after Oliver Capstick's death and after she had inherited all his money? Moreover, I could not help but remember Mathilda Trenowth's description of Berenice at the time when the girl announced her forthcoming marriage: 'I don't recall ever having seen her look so happy. She was obviously very much in love.'

So I must be misreading the signs, a fact that seemed to be confirmed a moment or two later when Berenice lifted her hand and stroked Bartholomew's cheek. 'Say you're sorry, like a good little boy. You promised me you would.'

I heard Katherine Glover give an impatient snort, but her mistress ignored her.

Bartholomew Champernowne said sulkily, 'I'm sorry I sent my man to try to kill you, chapman.'

Feeling that there was no adequate answer to this, I maintained my silence. I saw Katherine curl her lip, and even Berenice suddenly seemed to realize that attempted murder could hardly be brushed aside with an apology, even supposing it to be sincere. She rose abruptly to her feet and, once more patting her betrothed's cheek, said, 'Go home, now, dearest. We'll meet again tomorrow.'

'It's nearly dark,' he protested indignantly. 'I thought I was to stay the night!'

'You haven't seen your parents now for two whole days,' she reminded him. 'You were to stay until the chapman arrived, that was our bargain. Go home, Bart! Please.' She kissed his lips. 'We'll be married very soon, then we can be together all the time. Goodbye, my sweet.'

'Sweet' was hardly the right epithet for young Champernowne, who took his departure in a very acid frame of mind. At the door, he paused and flung over his shoulder, 'You may not see me tomorrow! It will depend on how I feel!' The hall door slammed shut behind him.

The two women looked at one another, then Katherine said, 'You'll see him. While he can sponge off you, he'll never stay away long.'

Berenice frowned. 'Hush, Kate! That will do! Go after him for me and make sure that he leaves the manor. He's quite capable of sneaking back again in an effort to persuade me to change my mind.' She waited until the other woman had left the hall before turning to me. 'Now, chapman, draw up that stool and show me what you have to sell.'

An hour later, I was sitting in the kitchen in the company of the groom and housekeeper, eating a belated supper.

Greatly to my astonishment, after buying all my ribbons and a length of Italian silk that I had carried in my pack all the way from Bristol, Berenice Gifford had insisted that I spend the night at Valletort Manor.

'It's far too dark now to make your way back to Modbury,' she had said. 'You would never find the track. You can sleep in one of the outbuildings. There's plenty of clean straw in the stables that will make an excellent bed and keep you warm, as well. But first,' she had added, 'you must have food. Kate, ask Nurse to come here, would you, please?'

Katherine Glover had returned from seeing Bartholomew Champernowne off the premises some time earlier. I had noted, without seeming to do so, Berenice's raised eyebrows as her maid had re-entered the hall, and the curt nod with which Katherine had answered the unspoken query. She had been absent for well above half an hour, if not longer, and I wondered what she could have been doing to detain her all that while. I immediately suspected that Beric Gifford was somewhere on the manor, and that his betrothed had been with him. So the last thing I had expected was an invitation to stay for the night.

Now, as I ate my way steadily through two large pastry coffins filled with meat and gravy, followed first by savoury, and then by apple dumplings, I did my best to winkle some information out of Mistress Tuckett and the groom, but without success, as both were adept at parrying unwanted questions. The latter, who was indeed elderly and also extremely taciturn, was particularly good at it, and on more than one occasion cut the nurse-housekeeper short when her tongue showed an inclination to run away with her. Finally, I was forced to accept that there was nothing to be got from either of them.

My only consolation was the prospect of a night free to roam about the stables and other outbuildings in the hope of a glimpse of Beric Gifford. But, with an inward sigh, I had to admit to myself that even this was unlikely. I should hardly have been offered the freedom of the courtyard unless Berenice and Katherine were absolutely certain that Beric was safely within doors and away from my prying eyes.

I wiped my mouth on the back of my hand and stood up.

'Thank you, Mistress Tuckett,' I said, presuming, in the absence of anyone else, that she must also be the cook. 'The pasties and dumplings were delicious.'

'It's good of you to say so. A word of appreciation never comes amiss. But it's too much for one woman,' she continued. 'In the days when I was the nurse here, we had a cook *and* a housekeeper *and* maids besides. And it's high time we had them again, if you want my opinion, now that my young lady can afford them. But we all know where *her* money goes!' she added angrily.

'That'll do!' the groom warned; and Mistress Tuckett, with a white-eyed look, pressed her lips together.

'The apples,' I went on, 'were especially fine. You must have had a visit yesterday from Master Godsey.'

'Oh, Bevis! Yes, he was here. Went away very pleased with himself, after talking with his cousin. I don't know why.'

'Do you mean Mistress Glover?' I enquired. 'I was told that she and Master Godsey were kinsfolk.'

But the housekeeper only tightened her lips still further and started to clear away the dirty dishes. So I stretched my arms above my head and gathered up my almost empty pack and my cudgel.

'I'll be off to the stables, then,' I said. 'Good night to you both.'

'There's no need to go through the hall.' The groom detained me, indicating a door in one of the further corners of the kitchen. 'There's a passageway on the other side that leads out into the courtyard. You'll find the stables easily enough, I reckon. They're next to the laundry.'

The passageway, when located, I discovered to be dimly lit by a single cresset set high on the wall, close to the outside door. This was still unbolted, and I was about to lift the latch, when I was seized by the powerful conviction that someone was watching me. I stood for a moment, frozen into immobility, my heart pounding, my breathing all but suspended. Then, slowly, very slowly, my right hand curling convulsively about my stick, I turned my head first to the right, where there was nothing to be seen except the blank wall, then to the left, where I suddenly noticed a narrow arch and a flight of stairs, rising into the darkness beyond it . . .

My heart stopped its pounding; in fact it almost stopped beating altogether as I found myself staring straight into the eyes of someone lurking in the shadows.

Robert Steward, as he duly introduced himself, was, unlike the groom and Mistress Tuckett, as old and as frail as Jack Golightly had portrayed him. He claimed that he was almost ninety years of age, having been born, so his mother had told him, in that year when the Scots beat the English at the battle of Chevy Chase, somewhere in the north. But although his sight and hearing were both impaired, I found it possible to hold a perfectly rational conversation with him provided I faced him when talking and spoke with clarity and care.

To begin with, I have to admit, all was confusion and muddle until I established who he was and the fact that he wanted me to accompany him to his bedchamber.

'Don't know who *you* are,' he mumbled, laying a withered hand on my shoulder, 'but it's good to see a new face. An honest one, too.' He shivered, gathering the skirts of his patched and darned woollen robe about his emaciated ankles, and turned to lead the way upstairs. He shook his head so that the thinning grey locks became even more untidy. 'I don't know what's going on in this house. There's something evil abroad. I'm frightened.'

I was instantly intrigued by these words and followed him with alacrity to the top of the flight, where an iron-studded door opened

181

into a tiny room under the eaves. A bed took up most of the floor space, and the only other object was a cedar wood chest, standing in one corner. The whole was illumined by a solitary rushlight, placed next to a tinderbox on a shelf.

My host invited me to sit on one side of the bed while he sat on the chest, facing me. 'Now, tell me your name,' he demanded, 'and what you're doing here.'

Once I had disposed of my pack and cudgel by the simple expedient of pushing them under the bed, I obliged on both counts, not disguising my interest in the murder of Oliver Capstick and the present whereabouts of Beric Gifford. When I had finished speaking, Robert crossed himself.

'Something evil,' he repeated. 'Here, in this house.'

I leant forward, resting my forearms on my knees. 'Beric's still here, is that what you're saying? He hasn't gone abroad? He hasn't run away? But are you sure about that? The Sheriff's men couldn't find him when they came looking, now could they?'

'No, nor never will,' he answered, staring at me with his rheumy, faded blue eyes.

'Why not? Do you also believe that Beric's eaten of Saint John's fern?'

Robert's gaze, which had been sharply focused on mine, now slid away from me, looking at some point beyond my right shoulder.

'He was a sweet little lad,' he said sadly. 'Grew up into such a happy child. Everyone doted on him, especially his sister.'

'So why do you think he bludgeoned his great-uncle to death?' I asked. 'What turned him into a murderer?'

The steward thought about this, sucking his toothless gums. 'She did,' he said at last. 'Things were never the same after she came here to live.'

'Do you mean Katherine Glover?'

'Yes. Her! The fisherman's daughter.' His gaze returned to my face.

'Why do you say that? Why were things never the same?' I persisted.

He shrugged, the bony shoulders beneath his robe looking as brittle and as fragile as a bird's. 'They just weren't. She became mistress of this place. We all had to do as she told us. All of us.'

If this were true, it explained Mistress Tuckett's animosity.

'But what about Mistress Berenice?' I said. 'She appears to me to be a strong-minded woman, one who would never tolerate such an untoward situation. And now, surely, there can be no question of Katherine Glover ever becoming mistress of Valletort Manor. Mistress Gifford's position in the house has to be unassailable.'

Robert Steward shook his head dolefully. 'The master's disgrace doesn't seem to have made any difference to that trollop's position. It's as though the mistress still regards her as the true chatelaine of the manor. Oh, don't mistake me!' He flapped his bony, brown-mottled hands in one of those displays of irritation that old people indulge in every now and then. 'Katherine Glover would never presume to take liberties with the mistress. But the rest of us have to do as she says. She was the one who evicted me from my room next to the hall and pushed me away in this piddling little cupboard, and all because I'm too old now to carry out my duties properly.' He added with a venom that sent the spittle flying from the corners of his mouth, 'She'd have turned me out altogether if Mistress Berenice would have agreed to it.'

It crossed my mind that Robert might be exaggerating Katherine Glover's part in his humiliation, but his story raised a more interesting question.

'Why do you suppose a new steward has not been appointed in

your place?' I asked. 'The omission seems strange to me, especially as you were made to vacate your old quarters. And why does Mistress Berenice not employ more servants in general? Money can no longer be an object with her. Mistress Tuckett was complaining about the lack of help while we were eating our supper.'

Robert considered the problem for a moment or two. 'Maybe she can't get people to come and work here,' he said at last. 'Maybe she never will until Beric's caught and sent to the gallows. It's lonely here.' He shuddered suddenly and gave a whimpering cry. 'And there's a murderer loose.'

It was an explanation that I should have thought of for myself and I was ashamed that it hadn't occurred to me. I prayed that my powers of deduction were not deserting me.

'Of course. You must be right,' I said, and rose to my feet. 'Well, I'd best be off. Your mistress has offered me accommodation in the stables for the night. I'd hoped for a warmer berth, like the kitchen, but, alas, beggars can't be choosers.'

'You could stay here, with me,' my new acquaintance suggested with a pathetic eagerness. 'I'd be grateful for your company. You're a big, stout lad. I'd feel safe. For this night, at least.'

'What is it you're afraid of?' I asked gently.

But he didn't seem able to say, simply repeating that there was something evil in the house. 'You can share the bed with me,' he added hopefully. 'There's room for two.'

I looked at the softness of the mattress, but regretfully shook my head. He followed me, shuffling and wheedling, as I descended the stairs to the outer door.

But this had now been securely bolted top and bottom. Furthermore, the key had been turned in the lock and then removed. While I had been upstairs, Valletort Manor had been secured for the night.

I smiled ruefully at my companion. 'Well,' I said, 'it seems that I have no choice. Master Steward, you've got yourself a bedfellow.'

Chapter Sixteen

I could easily have returned to the kitchen to inform Mistress Tuckett that I was still in the house, and ask her to unlock the outer door. But the suspicion that I had been deliberately relegated to the stables because Beric was sleeping inside that night had taken a firm hold upon me. I suddenly felt sure that this was a God-given opportunity to bring me one step closer to Oliver Capstick's murderer.

'They've locked up early tonight,' Robert volunteered as I followed him back up the stairs to the room beneath the eaves, once more stowing my pack and cudgel under the bed, where neither of us could hurt himself by tripping over them. My companion resumed his former seat on the chest, beaming his toothless smile.

'You didn't answer my question just now,' I said, also sitting down again on the edge of the mattress. 'I asked you if you thought Beric Gifford had eaten of Saint John's fern.'

'He may have done,' was the dismissive answer. 'I suppose it's possible. But it doesn't make you invisible for ever, you know. Leastways, not that I've ever heard of. You have to keep on eating the leaves if you want to stay unseen for any length of time.'

'Well, the plant grows plentifully around the manor,' I pointed out. 'And no one would want to remain invisible for very long, surely. In Beric's case, just long enough to help him evade the

187

law and justice.' I added, 'You're an old man and have lived a great many years upon this earth. Honestly, now! Have you ever known anyone who's become invisible through eating the hart's-tongue fern?'

Robert Steward thought this over. 'A distillation of the leaves is a well-known cure for the hiccoughs,' he offered at last.

'I'm aware of that fact,' I retorted irritably. 'But what I'm asking you is: does eating the raw leaves cause you to vanish?'

'Everyone says so.'

'I know everyone says so! But have you, in all your long life, ever come across someone who's done it? Eaten the leaves of the Saint John's fern, that is, and been made invisible?'

Of course, I could guess his response even before he shook his head, sad at having to acknowledge defeat. 'But,' he added, brightening, 'that doesn't mean to say it hasn't happened, does it?'

It was an argument I had heard before and which was virtually unanswerable, so I let the matter drop. Instead, I enquired, 'Where are the other bedchambers in this house? How do I get to them from here?'

Robert looked alarmed and a scrawny hand shot out to grasp my wrist. 'You're not leaving me alone!' he exclaimed. 'You promised to stay the night with me!' When I indignantly protested that I'd made no such commitment, his grip on my arm tightened; and although I could have shaken him off easily enough, there was a wild expression in his eyes that made me uneasy. 'You're not going anywhere,' he continued. 'I'll have one night's good sleep, even if I have to lock you in to get it.'

He was as good as his word. Before I had time to realize what he was up to, he had slid off the chest, rounded the corner of the bed and turned the key in the lock of the chamber door. He then put the key inside the breast of his food-stained gown, pushing it up under his left armpit and clamping that arm to his side.

Again, it would have taken little effort on my part to overpower him and seize the key, but it would have involved me in an unseemly brawl with a man old enough to be my grandfather, and one, moreover, who was in some sort my host. Besides which, there was the distinct possibility that if I went searching for Beric against Robert's will, he would raise the household and reveal my purpose. I had learnt that crossing a very old person is like crossing a very young child, and often produces the same results: tantrums and tearful recriminations. (I shall be like that myself, one day. Indeed, the hour is already fast approaching, if my behaviour towards my children and their children is anything to judge by. But then, when you're over seventy, why shouldn't you have your own way occasionally? Time's running out, after all.)

I considered arguing with him, pleading, cajoling, but eventually concluded that it would be a wasted effort. I could see that he wasn't open to reason. Force was my only option, and I had already rejected that. So I took off my boots, swung my legs up on to the bed, stretched myself out, arms linked behind my head, and stared up at the ceiling.

'You're angry,' he said with an attempt at pathos. But he made no effort to remove the key from its unsavoury resting place.

'No, I'm not,' I lied; but found, after a moment or two, that this was the truth. I was suddenly dog tired, caught in a lethargy of mind and body induced by the long day's walk, the salt sea air and the fact that I had overeaten at supper. 'Lie down and let's get some sleep.'

Robert nodded happily, turning to open the chest with his right hand and pulling out an assortment of old garments. These, once he had produced the key and carefully placed it under his half of the pillow, he proceeded to pile on over his ancient house-gown.

'It starts getting chilly at nights this season of the year,' he explained. 'And I can't stand the cold like I used to. You'd do well to get under the blankets before you fall asleep.' I did as he suggested, but he kept a sharp eye on me, just to make sure that I wasn't feigning weariness, and wasn't about to make a sudden grab for the key.

The last item he fished out of the chest was a flat-crowned, black velvet hat with which he covered his head, pulling it down by its narrow brim until it covered his ears.

'This is better than an ordinary nightcap,' he said happily. 'Much warmer.'

I had been almost asleep, politely holding my eyes open with a tremendous effort, but suddenly I was wide awake again, raising myself up on one elbow.

'Who does that hat belong to?' I demanded. 'Where did you get it?'

'I didn't steal it,' was the indignant reply, 'if that's what you're thinking. It's Beric's. Not that it's any of your business, but it was given to me by the mistress after he disappeared. She told me he didn't want it any more, and as we both have small heads, I might as well have it. It's my guess he was wearing it when he killed his great-uncle, and now can't bear the sight of it.'

I digested this, coming to the conclusion that Robert was more astute than he looked. I must be on my guard.

'Was there an ornament in the hat when Mistress Gifford gave it to you?' I asked, again already knowing the answer.

'No,' he said. 'Should there have been?'

'Don't young men usually wear a jewel of some sort in that kind of hat? They're so plain, otherwise.'

Robert sniffed. 'Well, there was nothing pinned to this. I don't remember that there ever was, although I might be wrong. Beric was a fashionable dresser, I grant you. Liked to follow the London trends, when he could find someone to tell him what they were.'

He closed the shutters tightly, then clambered into bed. A sourish, musty odour emanated from the motley collection of garments he was wearing, and I hurriedly turned my back on him. I am not naturally squeamish – I cannot afford to be in my calling – but this was a particularly unpleasant smell. Some of it came from the clothes, but I suspected that it was many a long month since Robert himself had washed any part of his person. My stomach heaved. The stuffy darkness was all-embracing, and I knew a moment of unaccustomed breathlessness and panic.

'You have the door key safe?' I demanded.

I heard him pat the pillow. 'No one can get in – or out,' he assured me.

'In that case, why don't you lock yourself in every night? Surely, you'd feel safer?'

'If a person's invisible, locked doors are no bar,' Robert claimed, thus revealing Beric to be the source of his fear. 'But tonight,' he added confidently, 'I have you to protect me.'

I was either too tired or too cynical about the magical properties of Saint John's fern to be alarmed by his words. I merely grunted and let the first wave of sleep wash over me, sinking thankfully into its billowing folds.

I was awakened by a cock crowing somewhere on the manor, its piercing cry penetrating even the tightly closed shutters of the steward's by now fetid little room.

I lay quietly for a moment or two, gathering my wits about me, but my overfull bladder was making me extremely uncomfortable and I slid out from beneath the blanket, groping for the chamber pot under the bed. When I had relieved myself, I opened the window and stared down into the still silent courtyard.

In a prosperous household, at this time of the morning, it would have been bustling with life as the servants prepared for the coming day. But Valletort Manor was deserted, and I decided that now was my chance to poke about on my own. Unfortunately, the thought had barely entered my head, when Mistress Tuckett appeared, hurrying across to one of the outbuildings. The groom followed hard on her heels, making his way to the pump that stood in a corner of the yard.

My plans being thus thwarted, I glanced behind me at the figure in the bed, but Robert Steward was still snoring, and I decided to wait until he awoke naturally, rather than ferret about beneath his share of the pillow in order to find the bedchamber key.

It was many years since I had been what my mother scornfully termed 'a lie-abed' (with the inevitable rider about laziness and the Devil), but this morning I had an ulterior motive for once more closing the shutters and climbing back beside my night's companion. I wished to prolong my stay at Valletort Manor, but had no real excuse for delaying my departure. Berenice and Katherine had bought as many of my wares as had taken their fancy the previous evening, and they would therefore expect me to be on my way this morning as soon as it was light. I felt, however, that if I were able to postpone my leaving for as long as possible, something – some unforeseen opportunity, perhaps, or some piece of luck – might eventually lead me to Beric. So I stretched out beside Robert Steward without any expectation of going back to sleep, and with every intention of rousing him within the next half-hour or so if he failed to awaken of his own accord. I closed my eyes and began to mull over the events of yesterday . . .

It was the babel of upraised voices and the clattering of horses' hoofs that eventually roused me from this second slumber, and I opened bleary eyes to see my bedfellow, still wearing his motley collection of garments, the shutters flung wide, leaning halfway out of the window, his mouth agape, staring down into the courtyard. The position of the sun told me that the morning must be well advanced; probably almost ten o'clock, and dinnertime.

I sat up and swung my legs out of bed. 'What's going on?' I demanded.

Robert turned. 'Oh, you're up at last, are you? You were sleeping like a baby and I didn't like to wake you.' He nodded in the direction of the window. 'I don't know what's happening down there, but something's wrong. I recognize the Sheriff's man from Modbury. And I heard him say that perhaps he ought to send to Plymouth for more men.' He sucked his toothless gums in alarm.

My interest was by now thoroughly aroused, and I rather rudely elbowed him aside, taking his place at the open window. Below me I could see an agitated knot of people: Berenice Gifford and Katherine Glover, still, surprisingly, not dressed and with cloaks flung on over their night-shifts; Mistress Tuckett, fully clothed but with her hood slightly pulled awry; the groom, dismounted but holding the reins of Berenice's bay horse, which showed signs of having recently been ridden hard, judging by its heaving flanks and the flecks of foam around its mouth; and, finally, a man, a stranger to me, whom I presumed to be the Sheriff's officer, still up in the saddle. He it was who was speaking, his words clearly audible in the windless air.

'He can't have got far, although I have to confess neither John Groom nor I had any sighting of him on our way back from Modbury.' He dismounted abruptly, revealing himself to be a stocky, powerful, barrel-chested man. 'I'd best take a look at the body.'

His last words failed to register with me as they should have done, and it was without any great sense of urgency that I leant out of the casement and called down, 'What's happened, Mistress Gifford? Is anything amiss?' Five faces were lifted to mine, frozen in amazed disbelief. 'Is something wrong?' I repeated.

'What . . . what are you doing up there?' Berenice asked huskily, stammering as though her voice was reluctant to obey her.

'I slept here,' I answered. 'Your steward invited me to share his bed last night. When I refused, he locked me in and hid the key. It didn't seem worth the effort or discourtesy of forcing him to give it up, so here I am. Isn't that right, Robert my friend?'

He squeezed under my arm and poked his head out of the window.

'I don't like this room, Mistress,' he complained querulously. 'You know I don't. I don't like being up here all on my own. I've told you so a dozen times, but you refuse to listen to me. There's something evil in this house and it frightens me, so I made the chapman keep me company last night.' He let out an ear-splitting cackle of laughter. 'I hid the key. He couldn't get it from me. I was too cunning for him. I put it under my pillow, where he couldn't get at it.'

The Sheriff's officer asked, 'Master Steward, are you sure the chapman couldn't have stolen the key and returned it again without your being aware of it?'

Before Robert could reply, Mistress Tuckett cut in, shaking her head and addressing the lawman. Her back was towards me and I couldn't catch all that she said; but I heard enough to know that she was explaining how the key of the outer door, leading from the kitchen passage to the courtyard, was removed for extra safety once it had been turned in the lock.

I saw Berenice and Katherine glance at one another. Then the former addressed her quondam steward.

'Robert, do you know if Roger Chapman had left the house at all before you first spoke to him?'

I butted in furiously. 'No, I hadn't. What's all this about? What are you suggesting?'

'Allow the steward his say,' the Sheriff's officer demanded.

'Come on, old man! Let's hear you! Did you understand your mistress's question?'

'Of course I did!' Robert snapped. 'I'm not senile.'

'Well then? What's your answer?'

Robert waved a gnarled hand at me. 'He's already told you. I saw the chapman come out of the kitchen and spoke to him before he had time to go outside. He followed me upstairs and I wouldn't let him out again. I was too quick for him. Too clever!' He sniggered and began rocking to and fro in a paroxysm of self-congratulatory mirth.

I was half afraid he might reveal why he had locked me in in the first place, and I felt that my desire to go poking and prying around Valletort Manor would not be well received by its mistress, But the old man was by now too far gone in his own conceit to remember what, to him, were merely trivial details.

I called down peremptorily, 'Would you mind, Mistress Gifford, telling me what this is about? It seems more and more as if I am suspected of some crime or misdemeanour.'

She stared up at me and, for a fleeting second, I thought I saw a look of baffled rage and frustration cross her face. Then, suddenly, it was gone and she gave me a tremulous, apologetic smile.

'I'm sorry, Roger. I must confess that I've wronged you. I hope that you can find it in your heart to forgive me, considering the circumstances.' She covered her eyes with both hands, and I could see that her whole body was shaking. Katherine Glover slipped a comforting arm about her mistress's shoulders.

'What is it? What's happened?' I cried, on fire with curiosity and impatience.

'It's Master Champernowne,' Mistress Tuckett said, as Berenice seemed in no fit state to reply. 'He's been murdered.'

* * *

We were all gathered in the great hall, standing or seated about the high table on its dais. The Sheriff's officer had accompanied us, for now that I was no longer his quarry, he seemed uncertain what course to pursue.

'But what made you suspect me?' I asked angrily, my first flush of bewildered indignation beginning to turn to a slow-burning fury.

'Because Bartholomew had tried to kill you,' Berenice said. 'And because his body was found in the stables.'

I was momentarily diverted. 'How could it be? Last night, Mistress Glover saw him off the manor at your request.'

'He must have come back after I'd returned indoors,' Katherine put in. 'It's the only explanation. He restabled his horse in one of the stalls and then . . . and then, before he could cross the courtyard to knock at the door, he was set upon by his attacker and murdered.'

'But why would he come back?' I asked. 'What would be his purpose?'

Berenice sighed. 'Because he prefers – preferred,' she corrected herself, with a catch in her throat, 'being here with me to returning to his parents' house. Until I inherited Great-Uncle Oliver's fortune, neither Sir Walter nor Lady Champernowne approved of Bartholomew's choice of bride, and he had quarrelled bitterly with them on the subject. Things are different now, of course, and recently, I've been trying to get him to go home more often. But he still hasn't – hadn't – forgiven his mother and father.'

'And you really thought,' I said, recalling my grievance, my anger flaring up again, white-hot, 'that I would stab a man in the back?'

I had been allowed to see the body where it lay, face downwards, in one of the empty stalls, a ring of dried blood encircling a neat wound made by a weapon that had been driven cleanly through the heart. I had carefully examined the ground all around, and was of the opinion – an opinion which I had so far kept to myself – that Bartholomew Champernowne had been killed outside the stall and dragged in there after he was dead; although why the murderer should have felt it necessary to do so, I had not yet worked out to my satisfaction. A faint glimmer of light was, however, beginning to dawn.

The murder weapon, I surmised, could have been a dagger or an ordinary long-bladed knife of the sort that most men, myself included, always carry with them for cutting up meat. Equally, such a knife could be found in every kitchen the length and breadth of the land. The killer had taken the knife away with him, and it was unlikely now that it would ever be positively identified.

'If the chapman here didn't murder Master Champernowne,' the Sheriff's officer said, 'who did? Did he have any other enemies, Mistress Gifford, that you know of?'

Berenice slowly shook her head and pressed a hand to her temples. 'Bartholomew was generally very well liked. I can't think of anyone who bore him a grudge.' But at the last word, she suddenly lifted her face to mine. 'Wait! Chapman, what is the name of that man who told you that he hated Bartholomew? Indeed, you said he hated all the Champernownes? Jack . . . Jack something-or-other . . . Yes, I have it. Jack Golightly!'

I was so shocked that I was unable to find my voice for a moment or two; long enough, at any rate, for the Sheriff's officer to express his interest.

'Where is he to be found, this Jack Golightly?'

Katherine Glover answered promptly, 'Roger Chapman can tell you.'

'Now, hold hard!' I exclaimed hotly. 'You have no cause, Mistress Gifford, to accuse Jack in this manner. Besides, it's impossible. How could he have gained access to Valletort Manor last night? You're careful enough about locking up the house.

Surely you must be equally careful about locking the courtyard gates.'

'There's a wicket door beside the gate,' Berenice said quickly. 'It's always left open. That's obviously how Bartholomew got in when he returned after Katherine had waved him off home. He must have dismounted and led his horse through.'

'That's as maybe,' I retorted angrily. 'But how does that implicate Jack Golightly? He was undoubtedly tucked up in his bed, several miles away.'

'Not necessarily,' the Sheriff's officer said heavily. 'There's plenty of thieving and poaching going on in these parts at night, you can take my word for it. Suppose this man was out and about yesterday evening and came across Master Champernowne. Perhaps Master Champernowne saw him and words were exchanged. It might be that they even came to blows. This Golightly fellow then decided to follow Master Champernowne. The tracks hereabouts don't allow for fast riding and a fleet-footed man could easily keep pace with a horse. So, he followed him back here, entered by the wicket, there was another quarrel and your friend drew his knife.' The office nodded to himself as though well satisfied. 'Yes,' he said thoughtfully, looking at me, 'that could be it. Now, chapman, tell me where I can find this Jack Golightly.'

Chapter Seventeen

It was Mistress Tuckett who gave the Sheriff's officer directions, as she seemed to know Jack and where he lived. I could only watch in confusion as the man strode purposefully from the hall. Then I sat down on the edge of the dais while my companions dispersed, the two younger women presumably to get dressed, the housekeeper and groom about their daily business.

I felt as though I were trapped in the middle of some absurd nightmare. How had Jack Golightly suddenly become a suspect for the murder of Bartholomew Champernowne? It made no sense. It was as if a name had been plucked out of the air because a killer must, and would, be found.

I could understand why the Sheriff's officer was so eager to make an arrest. Sir Walter and Lady Champernowne were most probably of some importance in the district, and for the wilful murder of their son they would undoubtedly demand that the perpetrator be brought to justice without delay. Woe betide the lawman who failed to catch the villain! But why were Berenice Gifford and Katherine Glover so anxious to identify the criminal that they must seize upon any possibility, however unlikely? Why must they try to make palpably implausible facts fit their theory? I was momentarily baffled . . .

Then the light that had been slowly dawning at the back of my mind burst into full and glorious radiance. Of course! *I* had been intended for the part of the murderer. Bartholomew had been detained here on the pretext that he owed me an apology and then I had been invited to pass the night in the stable. *I* was the one who would have been found there with the body this morning, but for the unwitting intervention of Robert Steward. Who, then, was the real villain? For me, there could only be one answer: Beric Gifford.

But if this were so, it meant that both Berenice and her maid must be party to Bartholomew's murder; that they had had prior notice of Beric's intention. Why he needed to dispose of his future brother-in-law I as yet had no idea, but that puzzle could wait. First, I had to work out the details of the deed itself, and my guess was that Bartholomew had never left the manor, but been stabbed to death within minutes of his arrival at the stables. Katherine had been dispatched by Berenice, under the pretence of making sure that he had quit the premises to establish that the killing had been successfully accomplished and the body concealed in one of the stalls, so that I should not accidentally stumble across it when I put in my expected appearance. I recalled Berenice's raised eyebrows and Katherine's answering nod, both of which now took on a new significance.

There had been an element of risk involved, it was true, for I might have chosen to sleep in the very stall where the corpse was hidden and, having discovered it, raised the alarm. But would that really have made any difference? Yesterday evening or this morning, I could still have been accused of the crime.

My appearance at Robert's window, and the subsequent revelation that I had been locked in with him all night, must have been a great blow to the two women. It explained the expression of anger and frustration that I had glimpsed on Berenice's face, and why another scapegoat for the murder had to be found, and quickly, before the suspicions of the Sheriff's officer could begin to centre on Beric Gifford. Like manna from heaven must have come the memory of all that I had said in Modbury churchyard concerning Jack Golightly and his hatred of the Champernownes. Berenice gave me the impression of being an intelligent, perceptive woman, and no doubt she, too, had sensed that the Sheriff's officer wanted a swift arrest; something with which he could confront Sir Walter and Lady Champernowne when he informed them of their son's untimely death. Moreover, and of great importance to Berenice, who had been the object of their disapproval, the culprit would have no connection with Valletort Manor.

Which brought me back to the reason for Bartholomew's murder. Assuming that I was right, that Beric Gifford was indeed the killer, why had his death been necessary? And why would Berenice concur? I recalled again Mistress Trenowth's words when she told me how happy Berenice had seemed the day she announced her betrothal. So what could possibly have happened in the meantime to make it necessary for her to agree to his being killed? What threat had he posed to her beloved brother, or to Katherine Glover, that she accepted he must forfeit his life?

'Are you still here, chapman?' asked a voice behind me. 'I thought you would be on your way by now.'

I glanced round, startled, to find Berenice standing just behind me, dressed from crown to toe in funereal black. I could see nothing of her face except as a pale oval behind her gauze veil, and there was something so sinister about her sudden appearance that a shiver of apprehension coursed down my spine. Nevertheless, nervous as I was, I felt compelled to say something in defence of Jack Golightly. I rose clumsily to my feet and turned to confront her.

'Why have you sent the Sheriff's officer on a fool's errand?' I asked accusingly. I drew a bow at a venture. 'You know Master Golightly didn't kill Master Champernowne. You know it was your brother.'

There was a moment's silence, during which the air was charged with menace. Then Berenice laughed, a low, musical sound, and put back the veil from her face. I was struck anew by her unusual looks; the dark complexion, the deep brown eyes and the strong, almost mannish cast of countenance. No, she was not beautiful in any accepted sense of the word, but beside her, the small, flower-like features of Katherine Glover paled into insignificance.

'I've told you before, Roger –' the use of my name was almost sensuous – 'Beric's long gone. Why should he stay? It would be madness. I assure you, he isn't here. And even if he were, why would he want to kill Bartholomew? He has no reason to wish him dead.' She moved closer to me as she spoke and laid a hand against my chest.

I recoiled from her touch as if stung. I could not explain my reaction, except that, just for a second, I had the impression that I was looking into the face of someone, or something, not quite human.

She laughed again, but this time it was a harsher, less pleasant sound.

'Don't worry, I have no wish to seduce you. Well? You haven't answered my question yet. Why should my brother want to kill my betrothed, even if Beric was here, instead of far away, in Brittany or France?'

'That's not true,' I blurted out. 'He's in neither of those places, and I think you know it. I don't understand why he murdered Master Champernowne, but I do know that he hasn't fled abroad.'

'And what makes you so certain of that fact?' Berenice demanded, descending the two steps of the dais, so that we now stood on a level.

'Because,' I answered recklessly, 'I witnessed Mistress Glover's meeting with your brother five nights ago, outside the Bird of Passage Inn at Oreston.'

The strong, well-marked eyebrows flew up in surprise and I heard her sharp intake of breath. 'Did you, indeed?' the lady asked softly. Her eyes shifted to a point beyond my right shoulder. 'Ah! Kate! Your arrival is most opportune. The chapman here has just informed me that you met my brother at midnight, five nights ago, outside the inn at Oreston. What have you to say to that?'

I had turned as soon as she addressed her maid, in time to see Katherine emerge from a small door in the tapestry-covered wall behind the dais. This was the same entrance that Berenice must have used a few minutes earlier, and explained her abrupt, almost magical appearance behind me. But there was nothing supernatural about it, after all, and immediately I began to feel better. I had allowed myself to become the prey of foolish fancies.

Katherine Glover was also arrayed in unrelieved black, although she had released her hair from beneath its hood, letting it flow in a golden-brown mane across her shoulders. She was indeed a very pretty woman, and the luminous grey eyes that she turned on me were brimming with innocence.

'I'm sorry, chapman, but you're mistaken. I was tucked up in my bed and fast asleep from the moment that my head touched the pillow.' The soft red lips curled into a smile. 'My aunt and uncle will tell you that they heard and saw nothing. You dreamt it. There's no other explanation.'

I opened my mouth to argue with her, then realized that to do so was pointless. It was Katherine's word against mine, and in any case, Berenice would pretend to believe her, even though she knew the truth. There was nothing further I could do here for the present, and I needed to find out what had happened to Jack Golightly. Perhaps he could prove beyond the shadow of a doubt that he was miles from Valletort Manor the previous evening. But then again, perhaps he couldn't. Suddenly it was imperative that I should leave as soon as possible in order to pursue my own enquiries.

'I must go,' I said. 'With your permission, Mistress Gifford, I'll retrieve my pack and stick from Robert Steward's room and then be on my way. Thank you for your hospitality. I'm deeply sorry that my visit here should have ended in such a tragedy. You have my sympathy.' I tried to sound sincere, but failed miserably.

Neither woman answered, but watched in silence as I disappeared from their sight around the kitchen screen. Once again, I shivered. I should be glad to shake the dust of Valletort Manor from my feet. But I should be back. I was sure of it. I felt it in my bones.

I paused, listening intently, then, slowly, turned my head and looked over my shoulder.

All was quiet except for the chirping of an occasional bird, but I could have sworn that, a moment earlier, I had heard a twig snap. Was someone following me? Had Berenice gone straight to her brother, wherever he was hiding, to inform him that I knew too much? That I was dangerous?

My departure from the manor had been delayed by Robert Steward, who not only wished to discuss the murder, but also to detain me for as long as possible.

'I told you this place was evil,' he kept muttering. 'I don't want to be left alone here. I don't like it any more. It's not the same since *she* came.'

In the end, I had to break free of the hands grasping my sleeve and escape down the stairs before he hit on the idea of locking me in again. But as I followed the track that led up to the high wooded ground behind the house, I was made uneasy by my late start, and wished fervently that I was at the end of my journey and safely back in Modbury.

I told myself not to be so foolish: no one would harm me. Another murder, especially one coming so soon on the heels of Bartholomew Champernowne's, would divert suspicion back to Valletort Manor, and that was surely something that neither Beric nor his sister could tolerate. But then I reflected that only the two women need concern themselves with an alibi. Beric had eluded justice for so long, it seemed impossible that he should be caught now. And whether he could make himself invisible or not, he had certainly perfected the art of lying low. It was a talent that many a woodland creature would envy him.

I resumed my walk, my now almost empty pack allowing me to quicken my pace considerably. A piece of dry wood snapped under my feet; but then, like an echo, came the crack of another twig somewhere along the track behind me. My heart began to thump and I could feel the prickle of sweat all over my body. It was a coincidence I told myself; I was hearing things. There was no one following me. Nevertheless, I started walking faster still, my strides lengthening.

Without warning, I found myself in the little glade where stood the shelter made of pegged-down branches covered with tarred cloth. On a sudden impulse, I dropped to my knees and crawled inside, dragging my pack and cudgel after me. It appeared even danker and darker than it had seemed the day before yesterday, as I waited for I knew not what, hardly daring to breathe. Had I been mistaken? Was there really someone dogging my footsteps? Or was I letting an overripe imagination run away with me? I laid hold of my stick, gripping it tightly, and tucked my long legs more carefully underneath my body, making certain they couldn't be seen . . .

Someone was in the glade. I knew it by the slight vibration of the ground and the rustle of feet in a drift of dried leaves. Then all noise and movement ceased, and I guessed that whoever was there had paused to glance around. Would he look inside the tent? But why should he? He had no cause to think I knew that I was being followed.

Suddenly, however, he was standing right outside. Through the narrow, triangular opening I could see his boots; soft brown leather that must have reached to his knees, for the tops were hidden from my view. The framework of branches, clearly visible from within, trembled slightly as he placed a hand on the outer covering. Any moment now, he would stoop and peer in . . . I withdrew as silently and as sinuously as I could until I came up against the trunk of the tree and found it impossible to retreat any further.

Then, abruptly, the owner of the boots moved away, but I wondered what he would do when it dawned on him that I was no longer travelling the path ahead. Would he come back? Would he realize where I was hiding? Probably. It behoved me, therefore, to abandon the shelter as soon as possible. I gave my pursuer a minute or so to get clear of the glade before wriggling out, shouldering my pack again and setting out after him.

Beric Gifford – for who else could this man be? – and I had now changed places. I was the one with all the advantage of pursuit and surprise. But still, I must be cautious. He had twice shown himself to be a ruthless killer, and I had no doubt that, if he could, he would rid himself of me. Once I had recklessly owned to seeing him and Katherine Glover together, five nights ago at Oreston, I had sealed my death warrant as far as Beric was concerned. I should have thought of that before making my admission; and perhaps I had in one corner of my mind. Perhaps, without fully realizing it, I had decided to flush my quarry into the open, for how else was Beric ever to be brought to justice?

Suddenly the trees drew back and I found myself in the clearing where, the day before yesterday, I had eaten my apple whilst sitting on the log, and where, afterwards, I had fallen asleep. On the opposite side of the grass circle was the path leading to the main track that stretched from Modbury to the sea. But where was Beric? I had walked quickly and should surely have caught up with him by now. Yet there seemed to be no sign of him.

Suppose he really was able to make himself invisible! Suppose the story about the Saint John's fern were true! I had managed to convince myself that it was just an old wives' tale, but I could be wrong. Beric could have discarded his clothes and be standing alongside me now, and, at any minute, I should feel his hands about my neck, squeezing the life from my body. Or, more likely, a knife would be plunged between my shoulder blades as had happened to Bartholomew Champernowne. I had been all kinds of a fool not to consider this possibility before setting out in pursuit of such a dangerous opponent. I had allowed what I thought was common sense to gain too firm a hold over my mind. All at once, I was afraid to move. My feet felt as if they were rooted to the ground.

Something moved on the edge of my vision. I whirled about, my stick clasped in both hands, ready for action, only to be brought up short by the sight of a swineherd, followed by three fat pigs, as they emerged from the trees where the animals had been rootling for mast.

'Hey up!' the man said, looking alarmed, as well he might. 'No need to be so quick with that cudgel of yours, chapman. There's no one about here as would wish to harm you. Especially not a great hulking lad like you.'

I heaved a sigh of relief and lowered the stick to my side.

'I beg your pardon,' I said. 'But all the way here, between Plymouth and Modbury, I've been fed with stories about someone by the name of Beric Gifford, who's committed a murder seemingly and has made himself invisible in order to escape justice, by eating the hart's-tongue fern.'

The man's face darkened. 'Ay, that's true enough,' he agreed. 'Battered his poor old uncle to death, so they say. And has been cheating the hangman ever since.' He lunged at one of the swine who showed signs of wandering away in search of some more succulent morsel than he had yet managed to discover. 'If you like, I'll walk with you part of your way. It'll be company for us both, and between us we should be able to tackle even an invisible man.'

'I'd be grateful,' I answered. 'I've just come from Valletort Manor, and Bartholomew Champernowne was stabbed to death there, last night. The groom found his body, cold and stiff, this morning in one of the stalls in the stable.'

My companion looked aghast and let out an oath. Under his questioning, I told the story as far as I knew it; although I didn't repeat my suspicion that I had been intended for the role of the murderer. Not only did I have no proof to support my theory, but it would have made the tale too long and too complicated, and needed too many explanations regarding my prior involvement. But I did add that the Sheriff's officer had gone in pursuit of Jack Golightly, and also stated my own opinion concerning the identity of the killer; an opinion with which the swineherd wholeheartedly concurred.

'Though why he should have wanted to do away with Master Champernowne, who was to be his brother-in-law, I'm sure I can't fathom. But Beric Gifford's proved himself to be an evil man. I'm sure he never showed any signs of it when he was young. A happy-go-lucky youth, I always thought him. A touch arrogant, maybe, considering he was so feckless and forever on his beam ends. But then, that's normal for those who don't have to earn their daily bread, and live on expectations from others. They've never heard the old rhyme, I suppose, "When Adam delved and

Eve span, who was then the gentleman?".'

The woodland had now closed about us again as my new friend and I, followed by the pigs, still rootling and snuffling at the base of every promising tree-trunk, slowly progressed along the narrow path leading to the main track. I said, 'I can't imagine why the Sheriff's officer didn't immediately name Beric Gifford as the culprit as soon as the murder was discovered. It seems obvious to me. Instead, he allowed himself to be cozened by Mistress Gifford into believing that Jack Golightly was to blame, simply because the man is known to have a grudge against all Champernownes.'

'Oh, I'm acquainted with that officer,' the swineherd sneered. 'He's called Guy Warren. He's a bit of a simpleton, easily persuadable, especially by a good-looking woman. And Berenice Gifford has always been that. Strong-willed, too. Used to protect the boy when they were young. Sometimes you'd have thought she was his mother, not his sister, although she was only two years the elder.'

'Do you know the family well?'

He shook his greying head. 'No. I'm swineherd to the Champernownes, like my father and grandfather before me.' He yelled at the largest and fattest of the pigs, who had turned aside, deep into the trees, and was determinedly digging at the base of an oak, using both snout and feet. 'Drat the animal. Come on, Jupiter! You can come back later and find whatever it is you think you're looking for.' He added, 'My goody's none too clever, so today I'm going home to see how she is.'

'Nothing serious, God willing?'

'No.' He lowered his voice confidentially. 'Women's troubles. But your news'll have her on her feet again, mark my words! A murder! And the victim a kinsman of the master's! I'll be very surprised if she doesn't find that she can walk into Modbury as soon as we've eaten. She'll want to visit her sister and find out what's happening . . . Jupiter!' He turned to yell once more at the recalcitrant pig, who, unnoticed by my companion, had now been joined by the other two. Cursing roundly, the swineherd went after his charges and, with much flailing of his arms and liberal use of his stick, drove the three animals out of the undergrowth and back on to the path. 'Dratted, obstinate creatures,' he complained, when he had again caught up with me. 'Vicious, too. Never get on the wrong side of a pig. If they don't like you, they'll attack you. They're partial to human flesh.'

I nodded and the conversation began to flag. 'Your wife has kinfolk in Modbury, then,' I said idly, in order to fill the breach.

'Only the one sister and her daughter. Eulalia and Constance Trim.'

The latter name stirred a chord of memory. Where had I heard it mentioned, and recently? Constance Trim. Constance . . . Ah! Now I had it! The fisherman's wife had told me that Berenice Gifford's former maid had been called Constance Trim. I turned to glance at my companion.

'I've heard tell of your niece,' I said. 'She was employed at Valletort Manor, but quit to return to Modbury, to look after and support her widowed mother.'

The swineherd snorted as loudly as any of his pigs. 'Whoever told you that isn't in possession of the true facts, that's all I can say. Eulalia's more than capable of taking care of herself. No, Constance didn't leave Mistress Gifford's service of her own free will. She was told to go. And for no good reason that she knew of, other than to bring that Katherine Glover into the house.'

Chapter Eighteen

Shortly after imparting this interesting piece of information, the swineherd bade me farewell and proceeded, together with his animals, along a tributary path that, he said, led to his cottage and his ailing wife.

'I hope you find your goody well on the road to recovery,' I shouted at his retreating back, and he raised a hand to show that he had heard me. But he was too much occupied with his pigs to spare more of his attention. They were all soon lost to view amongst the trees, and I continued onwards for the remaining two hundred yards or so before emerging on to the main track to Modbury.

I suddenly realized that for the last quarter of an hour I had forgotten about Beric Gifford and his pursuit of me, and I paused, glancing around warily, my heart beginning to thump against my ribs.

He was no figment of my imagination. Those legs and feet, encased in their long leather boots, that I had glimpsed through the opening of the tree-tent, had been real enough. Beric had followed me from Valletort Manor, with what fell purpose in mind I could only hazard a guess; but I was convinced that I had been saved from a violent confrontation solely because of my encounter with the swineherd. Beric must have been ahead of us at that point, but our voices, raised in conversation, would have given him ample warning of our approach, and he could easily have stepped aside into the shelter of the trees. The question remained, had he decided to tail the pair of us and bide his time until the swineherd and I parted company? Or had he given up and returned, balked of his prey, to Valletort Manor?

Somehow, knowing Beric's ruthlessness, the ease with which he killed for seemingly very little reason, and the enjoyment that he appeared to derive from it, I thought the former option the more likely of the two; and fear slithered across my skin like water as I took stock of my present situation. I was not far from safety. If memory served me aright, this belt of woodland would soon give way to open ground; the heath and meadows used by the people of Modbury to graze their sheep and cattle. But I was not yet clear of the trees, and although they were beginning to thin, there was still sufficient cover from which Beric could launch a surprise assault. But then again, he would have no need of cover if he were invisible.

I moved slowly forward, my cudgel at the ready, but it was impossible to guard both front and rear, however many times I swung around in circles. Finally, I backed up against an ancient, broad-trunked oak, dropped my pack to the ground and waited. And once more, from somewhere not too far away, came a sound like the snapping of a twig, but whether from the opposite side of the track or from my own, it was difficult to judge. All I could say for certain was that I was once more gripped by that sense of an all-pervasive evil, and the conviction that Beric must be very close at hand. I braced myself for an assault.

The thudding of horses' hoofs and the jingle of harness made me glance to the right as a small, sombrely dressed cavalcade appeared around a bend in the path, a bullish, thick-necked man, arrayed all in black, riding at its head. It needed no one to tell me that this must be Sir Walter Champernowne, apprised of his son's death and now on his way to Valletort Manor. This surely meant that the Sheriff's officer – Guy Warren, the swineherd had called him – must have informed Bartholomew's parents of his murder and of the identity of his suspected killer. And they, in their turn, had probably raised the hue and cry after Jack Golightly. I had to find out as soon as I could what was happening.

Without further ado, I shouldered my pack and left the shelter of my oak, pushing forward, past Sir Walter and his retinue of household officers who, as I expected, did not deign to acknowledge anyone so lowly as myself. A pedlar and one, moreover, on foot, would have been beneath their notice even if they had not had weightier matters on their minds. And by the time that all sight and sound of the horsemen had dwindled and died away, I had, by dint of rapid walking, managed to leave the woods behind. Almost at once, the feeling of impending danger, of evil, of menace, lifted as I stepped from shadow into sunlight; and as I neared Modbury, my spirits insensibly rose as well.

The little town, as I had anticipated, was in a state of ferment, news of the murder having preceded me by some considerable time. All trading and work appeared temporarily to have been suspended, with knots of people gathered on every street corner, at every cottage door and outside every ale house, discussing such unlooked-for tidings. There was about the place the air of excitement, overlaid with the half-genuine horror that such events usually provoke.

My appearance at Anne Fettiplace's cottage was greeted with a shriek of welcome and relief by the lady herself, and a demand that I immediately tell everything I knew, so that she could pass it on to her neighbours.

'And don't pretend you weren't at Valletort Manor when the murder happened!' she exclaimed. 'Sergeant Warren has already told us that there was a chapman present. It couldn't have been anyone but you.'

I grabbed her arm and shook it urgently. 'Is there talk of an arrest yet? Have you heard if the Sheriff's officer named anyone specific in connection with Bartholomew Champernowne's murder?'

She nodded vigorously. 'He did. That man you mentioned – I forget what he's called – but the one you said had a grudge against the whole family.'

'Jack Golightly?'

'Ay, that's right. Sergeant Warren's gone after him with a posse.'

'And what will be done with Master Golightly?' I asked. 'If he's unable to prove his innocence, what will happen to him? Will he be hauled off to Plymouth, or is there somewhere here, in Modbury, where he can be confined?'

But she was not attending. Her countenance had lifted into a smile as she glanced at someone behind me.

'Here are my husband, and son, Simon. They'll know,' she said proudly.

It seemed that her menfolk had arrived home from Exeter as expected the previous day, and, having done a morning's work without stopping at the appointed time for dinner, had now returned to the cottage hungry for a belated meal. They were both easy-going, good-natured men, and the older Fettiplace immediately extended an invitation to me to eat with them.

'Mother's told us all about you,' the son added, shaking me warmly by the hand.

Mistress Fettiplace ushered us all indoors, saying excitedly, 'You don't know the half of it, my lad! Roger *did* sleep at Valletort Manor last night, and was still there this morning when Master Champernowne's body was discovered. Didn't I say, when there was mention of a pedlar being present, that it must be him?'

'You did, Mother,' the young man agreed, treating me to a broad wink as he seated himself at the table. 'You'll have to give us all the details, chapman, if you please, so that we can lord it over the rest of Modbury with our superior knowledge.'

My first impulse had been to refuse Master Fettiplace's kind invitation to join him at table, but my gnawing hunger – for I had had no dinner, none having been offered me at Valletort Manor – combined with the savoury smell of his wife's cooking, was too strong an inducement to accept. I should be of little use to anyone, I reasoned, with an empty stomach. So, while we ate our meat pasties and drank our ale, I recounted all that had passed during my brief sojourn with Berenice Gifford, and also made the Fettiplaces free of my own version of what I thought had really happened.

When I had finished, Master Fettiplace rubbed his chin thoughtfully. 'You may well be right, chapman, in your assumptions, but you've precious little proof to go on as far as I can see. Why would Beric Gifford, even allowing for the fact that he's already a murderer, want to kill Bartholomew Champernowne? He was pleased with his sister's betrothal. Everyone in Modbury'll tell you that. While this Jack Golightly, on the other hand, is an avowed enemy of the family, and, if I've got the story correctly from my goody here, bore Master Bartholomew an additional grudge for what took place at his cottage a few nights back. I dare say you'll find yourself called on as a witness.'

'That's true enough,' his son agreed, tearing a hunk from the loaf and cramming it into his mouth. He added thickly, his speech only just intelligible through the mass of bread, 'We must pray that your friend can prove his innocence beyond all doubt, otherwise I'm afraid matters could go very ill with him.'

'Suppose he can't,' I said. 'Where will he be taken?'

'To Exeter eventually, most likely for trial at the Winter Assize.'

'But in the meantime?' I urged.

Master Fettiplace, whose name I had by this time learnt was Ivo, cleared his mouth with a swig of ale before giving me an answer.

'Plymouth would be my guess, to the lock-up underneath the Guildhall. There's only a very small cell here, and if it should happen to be already occupied . . .' He shrugged and let the sentence hang.

I chewed my lip. 'How soon shall I be able to find out if an arrest's been made?'

Simon Fettiplace snorted with laughter. 'Don't worry! You won't have to wait very long, believe me. News fairly flies around in these parts. I always say we know what's happening on the other side of the Tamar before the good people of Cornwall know it themselves.'

'True enough,' his father concurred. 'If this friend of yours has been charged with Bartholomew Champernowne's murder, I reckon you'll be bound to hear of it before nightfall. But,' he went on, 'I don't know what you can do about it. You won't be able to alter things, for the reasons I gave you just now. And once that fool Guy Warren has got an idea in his head you won't shift it easily, not unless you can offer him proof positive to the contrary.'

I glanced at Anne Fettiplace, who nodded in agreement with her husband's words. 'Guy's a stubborn man,' she added on a note of warning.

I took another pasty and bit into it, letting the juices run down my chin. 'Then I'll just have to prove to Sergeant Warren that he's made a mistake,' I said.

'Do you *really* think that Beric Gifford is the killer?' Simon Fettiplace asked me. 'I'd have bet my life that he'd fled abroad by now. But I'm forgetting! My mother told us that you claim to have seen him at Oreston, and only a few nights since.'

I nodded. 'Outside the Bird of Passage Inn.'

Ivo Fettiplace probed his back teeth with his tongue while considering this statement.

'Are you absolutely certain that it was Beric Gifford you saw?' he enquired at last.

'If it wasn't Beric,' I answered with some asperity, 'then Katherine Glover has found herself another lover in a very short space of time.'

'How was he dressed?' Mistress Fettiplace wanted to know.

'It was too dark to see much, and, besides, I was looking through a narrow gap in my bedchamber shutters. He was muffled in a cloak and had one of those flat-crowned caps pulled forward over his eyes.'

'He did have such a hat, it's true,' my hostess confirmed. 'Made of black velvet. Wore it a lot, he did. In fact, come to think of it, he was rarely without it.' She paused, staring at me. 'Now, what have I said to make you look all whichways, like that?'

'I don't know,' I answered slowly. 'Indeed, I'm not sure if it was something you said or that I said. Or maybe something we both said.' There was a silence while I racked my brains, trying to discover what was bothering me. Then, 'No, it's no good,' I sighed. 'I can't quite put my finger on it.'

We all spent the next few minutes recalling as accurately as we could the more recent utterances of Mistress Fettiplace and myself, but to no avail. My memory refused to be jogged a second time, and, in the end, we were forced to abandon the attempt.

'You'll remember whatever it was later,' Anne Fettiplace said comfortably, beginning to clear away the dirty dishes. 'That's the way it always happens. If I can't recollect where I've put a thing, I let it go, and the answer always comes to me when I'm not even thinking about it.'

'True, true,' nodded her husband. He refilled all our cups with ale. 'So,' he continued, 'you're satisfied, Master Chapman, that the man you saw outside the Bird of Passage Inn at Oreston must be Beric Gifford.'

'I can't understand why he didn't escape abroad as soon as he'd murdered his uncle,' Simon objected, loosening his belt and sighing with repletion. 'What sane man would wait around to get his neck stretched? Or to spend the rest of his life in hiding?'

'If he's willing to risk eventual madness by eating Saint John's fern and constantly making himself invisible,' Ivo Fettiplace said after a moment's silence, 'then I suppose there's no reason why he shouldn't defy the law and stay at Valletort Manor until he dies.'

'Do either of you know him well?' I asked.

Father and son exchanged glances, each waiting for the other to speak, then the older man shrugged.

'I suppose everyone in Modbury knows him and Berenice. They are – or rather were, before this terrible business – in and out of the town ever since they could ride a pony. And I suppose we, as a family, took a greater interest in them than most folk, on account of Anne's sister being housekeeper to old Master Capstick.'

'Do you like them?'

'They're a civil enough young couple,' Simon Fettiplace conceded. 'She can be bad-tempered if anyone thwarts her or she isn't treated with the deference she thinks she's due, but I've never had a cross word from Beric. I've always thought him a pleasant young fellow, and I was shocked beyond measure when I heard what he'd done.'

'We all were,' his mother added, overhearing this last remark as she came back into the cottage with a full pail of water. She poured some of the liquid into a pan which she then hung over the fire to heat, and set down the bucket and the rest of its contents on one end of the table, announcing her intention of making water-cider with the pippins she had bought the day before yesterday from Bevis Godsey. 'It's high time you two were getting back to the sawmill,' she reprimanded her menfolk.

But neither man seemed inclined to heed her words, turning deaf ears to her suggestion.

'Beric's always been a good horseman,' Ivo Fettiplace remarked cutting himself a wedge of the goat's-milk cheese that had not yet been cleared from the table.

'He is that,' agreed Simon, following his father's example. 'When he bought that horse of his – that great black brute with as evil an eye as I've ever seen in an animal – everyone said as how he'd break is neck. But not Beric!' Simon crammed the cheese into his mouth. 'He had that creature eating out of his hand before he'd had it a fortnight. Together, they were like one of those mythical beings I've heard tell of, half man, half horse. But I forget their name.'

'You mean centaurs,' I said.

'Do I?' He swallowed convulsively, regarding me with some curiosity. 'You're probably right. You've pretty good book learning for a chapman.'

'I was given an education by the monks at Glastonbury,' I explained. 'My mother intended me for the religious life, but I had other ideas.' I turned to Ivo. 'Would you agree, Master Fettiplace, that Beric Gifford is as good a horseman as your son claims he is?'

The elder man helped himself to another slab of cheese. 'I would that. There's not been the horse foaled that he couldn't ride. Never a second's trouble with any of them that I've ever seen.'

'And what about Mistress Berenice? Is she as fine a horsewoman as her brother is a horseman?'

'Very nearly,' Mistress Fettiplace cut in. 'Though you won't find men giving her the credit that's her due.' She whisked the cheese off the table and put it away in a cupboard, with a muttered animadversion about insatiable appetites.

Husband and son ignored the stricture and continued to dwell on the riding skills of the Giffords.

'Mistress Berenice is a good enough horsewoman, I grant you,' Simon admitted. 'But she hasn't the same confidence as her brother.'

'Almost!' Anne Fettiplace protested indignantly as she ladled some of the hot water into a bowl in order to begin washing the dirty dishes.

'But not quite.' Her husband rose from his stool and stretched his arms above his head until the bones cracked. 'Come on, Simon, my lad. This won't get the wood cut. At this rate it'll be nightfall before we've sawn up that load of timber.' He held out a calloused, leathery hand. 'In case we don't meet again, Master Chapman, I'll wish you God's blessing. Will you be staying much longer in Modbury?'

'I'm not sure,' I answered. 'I must certainly remain until I get definite news of my friend.' I did not add that if Jack Golightly had indeed been arrested, then my self-appointed mission to track down Beric Gifford would become of the greatest urgency.

'Of course! Of course!' agreed my host genially. 'And you must remain here with Anne for as long as you wish. She'll be glad of your company, won't you, my dear?'

'I'm depending upon his staying for a while at least,' his wife responded. 'I want you to meet all my neighbours, Roger, and tell them the story of your visit to Valletort Manor. Only,' she cautioned, 'I wouldn't repeat your theory concerning Beric Gifford until you have amassed more proof. Besides, they won't be interested in that.' She gave me her most winning smile. 'I hope you'll agree to do this for me.'

I promised, although a little grudgingly, for I wanted everyone to know that I considered Jack Golightly innocent. Ivo and Simon Fettiplace both laughed and wished me well as they left the cottage, while Mistress Fettiplace bade me sit down again while she finished the dishes. She indicated a rough, wooden armchair that I guessed to be her husband's seat, for it was not only swathed with a piece of red cloth, but also boasted a cushion, covered in the same material. I was conscious of the honour done to me and sat down carefully, at first bolt upright, but gradually slipping down until my legs were stretched at full length in front of me.

I was full of pasties and good ale, having overeaten as usual, not knowing when I might get my next meal. The food and, in addition, the warmth of the fire were making me drowsy, and I was aware that my eyelids were heavy. I made a valiant effort to stay awake, but could not. Within five minutes of sitting down, I was fast asleep.

Even as I closed my eyes, I knew I was going to dream. Since our meal, I had been suffering from one of the oppressive headaches that sometimes afflict me and are harbingers of those strange visions that crowd my unconscious mind. I was in a wood, shrouded by a clinging, rain-drummed mist, and I knew I must be near the sea, for in the distance, I could plainly hear the gentle sobbing of the waves. Suddenly the wind rose sharply, tearing aside the curtain of rain, tossing the spidery twigs of the trees and making them rattle so loudly that I was not at all surprised, on closer inspection, to discover that they were in fact dry, bleached bones.

Without warning, the swineherd was standing beside me, while his pigs rootled and snuffled at the base of one of the trees, showering us both with the earth from their digging. The muffled sound of hoofs made us look round, and there, riding towards us on his big black horse was Beric Gifford, his flat-crowned, black velvet cap pulled forward over his eyes, wrapped in a cloak and struggling to control his mount, which showed a strong tendency to unseat him. Beside him, holding the animal's rein, walked Robert Steward, also wearing a flat, black velvet cap exactly like his master's.

They had almost drawn level with us, where we stood at the side of the track, when I stepped full into their path to halt them. Then I reached into my pouch and pulled out the hat ornament with its entwined letters, B and G, and its pendant, teardrop pearl, handing it up to Beric to take from me. But he shook his head, pushing my hand aside with an impatient gesture. As he did so, I noticed on the middle finger of his right hand the ring that I had last seen adorning that of Bevis Godsey.

Just at that moment, Berenice Gifford and Katherine Glover came out of the trees, side by side, their heads close together and laughing. When they saw the rest of us, they laughed harder than ever until, somehow or other, we were all joining in. And yet, horribly, our gaping mouths made no sound, but from one corner of Beric's there oozed a thin, dark trickle of blood . . .

Someone was shaking my arm violently and calling, 'Wake up, chapman! Wake up!' Blearily, I opened my eyes, uncertain of my surroundings, to find Mistress Fettiplace bending over me, her face puckered with concern.

'What is it?' I managed to ask at last.

'It's your friend, that Jack Golightly,' she said. 'He's been arrested for Bartholomew Champernowne's murder!'

Chapter Nineteen

For a moment I was too bewildered to know where I was or what I was doing. I must have stared at Mistress Fettiplace like a veritable fool, for she shook my arm again, but harder this time.

'Your friend, Jack Golightly,' she repeated, 'has been arrested and charged with the murder of Bartholomew Champernowne. One of my neighbours has this minute brought me word.' And she pointed to a woman standing just behind her, in the open doorway of the cottage.

My mind was beginning to clear, although I was still somewhat bemused. I had been sleeping deeply and the dream had seemed very real. I had had no time to interpret it, and was conscious that its message was already fading, lost in this more pressing anxiety.

I heaved myself out of the chair. 'Are you certain of this?' I demanded.

Anne Fettiplace clicked her tongue in exasperation. 'This is Mistress Cordwainer. Ask her yourself.' And once again she waved her hand towards the other woman, who had now ventured a few paces into the room.

'It's true enough,' the neighbour confirmed. 'I saw Sergeant Warren come back not a quarter of an hour since, and he had a prisoner in tow. Tethered to the horse, the poor soul was, and forced to walk alongside it. His wrists were bound and he had a gash above one eye. Someone who knew him said that it was Jack Golightly.'

'He's been brought back here, then?' I asked unnecessarily. 'He's not been taken to Plymouth?'

'Seemingly not. He's locked in the roundhouse.'

'I must speak to him at once.' I pulled on my leather jerkin. 'Where can I find Sergeant Warren?'

'He's gone off to seek out Sir Walter and Lady Champernowne to inform them of the arrest. He's left Nick Brown on guard.'

'Well, Master Warren won't find Sir Walter at home,' I said. 'I passed him an hour or more ago, presumably on his way to Valletort Manor. Indeed, I feel sure that he could have been going nowhere else. What sort of a man is this Nick Brown? Could he be persuaded to let me have a word with the prisoner, do you think?'

'Don't you worry your head about that,' Mistress Cordwainer told me. 'Nick's my husband's cousin's son. He'll oblige me, if I ask him.' She gave me a gap-toothed grin. 'And I'd do more than that for a big handsome lad such as you.'

I thanked her and stooped to kiss her cheek. She coloured up fierily and giggled, as self-conscious as a young girl. 'That'll be enough of that,' she protested. 'Come along with me.'

Ten minutes later, after a mere token resistance to his kinswoman's demands – for it was plain that in this closely knit community family bonds were paramount – Nick Brown, a smiling, tousle-headed youth, unlocked the roundhouse door and let me inside.

'But don't be too long,' he urged.

I gave him my promise and then stood still as the door closed, letting my eyes grow accustomed to the darkness.

'Who is it?' asked Jack Golightly's voice as, at the same moment, I stumbled over his knees. He swore fluently. 'I hope you're not a prisoner, too. This hole isn't big enough for more than one.'

I made myself known to him, and he eagerly seized my hand, the chains that shackled his wrist to the wall making a dismal rattle as he did so.

'Is it really you, chapman? What are you doing here? How did you get in? Sergeant Warren hasn't arrested you as well, has he?'

'No, no!' I assured him, before embarking on my explanation. When I had finished, I added, 'Was there no way in which you could convince that fool of a sergeant that you had nothing to do with Bartholomew Champernowne's death?'

I had by now grown used to the gloom and I saw Jack shake his head.

'I was alone all that night, as I am most nights. Who was there to vouch for me?' He went on bitterly, 'As you say, Warren is a fool. A blind, bigoted fool! I had the feeling that it wouldn't have mattered what I'd said in my own defence, he'd still have taken me in charge.'

'It should have been me,' I admitted, 'sitting here in your place. I was the intended victim, not you.'

'What do you mean?' he asked. 'You're talking in riddles.'

So, as briefly as possible, I told him all that I knew and all that I guessed. When I had finished, he drew in a sharp, hissing breath.

'Of course!' he exclaimed. 'You must be right. The murderer has to be Beric Gifford. But why? Why would he want to kill his future brother-in-law?'

'That's what I don't know,' I said. 'That's what I have to find out.'

'Then you've no time to lose, for I'm to be taken to Plymouth tomorrow.' He added with a sudden spurt of anger, 'And since, on your own admission, it was you who brought me and my hatred of the Champernownes to Berenice Gifford's attention, I think you owe me something.'

I placed a hand on his shoulder and pressed it. 'I pledge you my solemn word that whatever I can do shall be done. Rest easy. God won't permit an innocent man to be punished for the crime of another.'

I only wished that I could have felt as confident as I sounded but I took heart from the fact that God had surely sent me on this mission to find Beric Gifford, just as he had used me to bring villains to justice in the past.

'But You'll have to show me the way, and quickly,' I told Him as I left the roundhouse, thankfully breathing in fresh air once more.

In my heart of hearts, however, I knew that God must already have shown me the way, and that I was just being slow at interpreting His signs and signals. I was about to make my way to the nearest inn to drink a cup of ale and ruminate quietly, when I recollected having given my word to Mistress Fettiplace that I would allow her to parade me before her neighbours as someone who had been present at Valletort Manor that morning. I was reluctant to fulfil my promise, but she had been very kind to me and I owed her some sort of return for all her hospitality. The brief delay was a small price to pay for the satisfaction she would derive from showing me off, and something that would cost me very little effort.

Consequently, I retraced my steps to her cottage where her surprise at seeing me again was mingled with delight once I had explained my purpose.

'That's good of you, Roger,' she said, pausing in her task of chopping apples for the water-cider she was making. 'Wait while I wash my hands, and then I'll take you to meet three of my closest friends. I'll make certain they don't detain you long, for I can see you're champing at the bit and want to be about more important business. Leave your pack here, with me. I'll take good care of it until you come back to collect it again.'

She was as good as her word, calling on only those three of her neighbours with whom she appeared to be on terms of the greatest intimacy. I was persuaded to repeat my story to each one in turn, and did my best to answer all their questions in so far as I was able. But I said nothing concerning my thoughts on Beric Gifford; and Anne Fettiplace, sensible woman that she was, gave no hint of them, either.

We had just left the last of the three cottages, and I was about to take my leave of my hostess yet again, when a woman came out of a dwelling on the opposite side of the alleyway and called across, 'You're Roger Chapman, aren't you?'

My heart sank at the prospect of further delay, but I could hardly deny the charge with Mistress Fettiplace's friend standing not two feet distant, in her doorway.

'I am,' I acknowledged.

The woman nodded. 'I'm Eulalia Trim. And this –' she half turned to indicate the young woman behind her – 'is my daughter, Constance. She was maid to Mistress Gifford before she was dismissed to make room for that Katherine Glover. Rumour has it that you were at Valletort Manor this morning when Master Champernowne's body was discovered. She'd be interested to hear the tale.'

My reluctance vanished, and I'm ashamed to say that I muttered a rather hurried farewell to Anne Fettiplace before following the two women into their cottage. In spite of the swineherd's conviction that the Widow Trim was more than capable of looking after herself without any help from her daughter, there was, nevertheless, an air of poverty, a hint of straitened circumstances about the interior that I had not encountered in the other dwellings

I had visited that morning. And both women made it plain that they harboured an understandable grudge at Constance's loss of a place that had provided her with food and lodging at no cost either to herself or to her widowed parent.

I decided to stir up their animosity even further to see what result it produced. 'I heard that you begged leave from Mistress Gifford to come here to look after your mother,' I said, addressing Constance.

'Nonsense!' she replied angrily. 'Whoever told you that was either lying or has been misinformed. I was sent packing to make way for Katherine Glover! That's the truth of it!'

'At Beric Gifford's insistence?'

The younger woman shook her head emphatically. 'Oh no! He may have grown besotted with Katherine in time, but that was after she became Mistress Berenice's maid. In any case, he would never have thrown me off the manor. He wasn't like that. But no doubt he believed what his sister told him, as he always did.'

I frowned. 'Why is it that everyone who knows Beric speaks well of him? This is the man who murdered his great-uncle in cold blood.'

'Oh, he has a temper when he's roused,' the widow cut in. 'But he's very loyal and could never bear to hear any of his family or friends spoken of unjustly. He would never have let the old man belittle the woman he was in love with.'

I shrugged. 'I can understand that and applaud him for it. I can even understand why he attacked his great-uncle in the heat of the moment when, by all accounts, Master Capstick insulted Mistress Glover and tried to force Beric into marriage with another woman. But to return the following morning, when a night's sleep must have cooled his temper, to set out for Plymouth with the sole purpose of bludgeoning an old, defenceless man to death while he slept, that I can neither understand nor excuse.'

'Perhaps he didn't,' Constance Trim said with a defiant obstinacy. 'Perhaps, after all, somebody else committed the murder.'

I said impatiently, 'You know that's foolishness. The housekeeper saw and recognized Beric. Besides –' I fished in my pouch and brought out the hat-brooch – 'he dropped this on the floor of Master Capstick's bedchamber. I found it there, amongst the rushes.'

The Widow Trim was more interested in how I had gained access to Oliver Capstick's house than in the ornament, and was already asking eager questions to that effect when her daughter abruptly waved her into silence.

'This doesn't belong to Beric,' she said. 'He never wears a jewel in his hat. But Berenice does. This brooch is hers. She has a black velvet cap exactly like her brother's. She used to borrow his clothes sometimes to go riding in, when she wanted to be very daring. They're much of a size, except for their heads. His is smaller than hers. She could never wear his hats.'

I stared at her in stupefaction. At last, 'Are you absolutely certain,' I asked, 'that Beric has never worn this ornament?'

'I'm positive,' was the answer. 'I recognize it. It's Berenice's.'

Against all reason, I found myself believing her. Why, however, when confronted with the jewel, had Mistress Trenowth identified it as belonging to Beric? Yet even as I silently asked myself the question, I recalled the way in which the housekeeper had hesitated as she looked at the brooch, and the constraint in her voice as she made her reply. But why should she lie? Why should she wish to protect her late master's murderer? Then I remembered the Widow Cooper's words. 'Over fifteen years Mathilda looked after that man . . . and then to be left nothing in his will! It's disgraceful and so I told her, although she pretends she doesn't care. But, of course, she does. She's bound to!' And she had. Mistress Trenowth must deliberately have misled me out of resentment.

Had she guessed that the murderer might be Berenice dressed in her brother's clothes right from the beginning? Or was I letting my imagination run away with me again? Maybe there was another explanation. Maybe Beric had been unable to find his hat that fateful morning and had borrowed his sister's instead . . .

But another memory was surfacing in my mind. Robert Steward had told me that the black velvet cap he wore in bed had been given to him by Berenice soon after her brother's disappearance. Yet the person I had seen outside the Bird of Passage Inn had been wearing just such a piece of headgear! A flat, dark cap that fitted its owner perfectly. But Beric's cap had been for some months in the possession of the former steward. It followed, therefore – it had to – that it was not Beric whom I'd seen.

To this day, I cannot remember bidding farewell to Mistress Trim and her daughter. I suppose I must have done so, and also taken my cudgel from where I'd propped it against the wall, before I quit the cottage. But my next recollection is of sitting beside a stream, staring into the depths of the clear running water as it purled over its rocky bed. I can still remember the delicate, opalescent colours of the pebbles.

Gradually, my rioting thoughts began to steady, to form a pattern that was at last beginning to make some sense of the story of Beric Gifford. I recalled, as I had done once before, Mistress Trenowth telling me how happy Berenice had been when she told her great-uncle of her betrothal. 'She was obviously very much in love,' the housekeeper had said. But this had not been my impression when I had seen Berenice and Bartholomew Champernowne together. Indeed, my feeling had been that she rather despised him. So who was really the object of her affections?

I dipped one hand in the stream, letting the water run like satin between my fingers. An idea was forming uneasily at the back of my mind and for a while I tried to repulse it. But it would not be kept at bay, the unwelcome facts relentlessly pushing their way forward. It was Berenice, not her brother, who had taken such a fancy to Katherine Glover that she had dismissed her own maid in order to create a place for the girl, not merely in the household, but as her close companion. Beric, that young man of whom most people had something good to say, had only fallen in love with Katherine after she had gone to live at Valletort Manor. Moreover, he was spoken of as the one who was the most in love of the two. But was Katherine Glover the beloved not only of Beric, but also of Berenice?

My mind jibbed at the idea, for such a liaison was against all the teachings of the Church and punishable by death. Yet I knew that these relationships did exist between both men and women, (and had, indeed, sensed something of them whilst I was a novice at Glastonbury Abbey). The young girl with whom I had spoken yesterday, on my way to Valletort Manor, claimed to have seen Katherine Glover and Beric on the day of the murder 'All over one another, they were, pawing each other and kissing until it made me feel sick.' But supposing the person she had seen dressed in male clothing, with blood stains on the front of the tunic, had not been Beric, but Berenice!

A horse and rider clopped by on the path behind me, the man nodding a perfunctory greeting. I barely acknowledged it, however, for the sight of them had set up yet another train of thought in my mind. All those people who had seen Beric on the morning of the murder had mentioned that he was not entirely in control of his mount; but Simon and Ivo Fettiplace had spoken of him as the perfect horseman. 'There's never been the horse foaled that he couldn't ride. Never a second's trouble with any of them that I've ever seen.' Until now, I had, like everyone else, concluded that

Beric's excited and agitated state had somehow conveyed itself to the animal, or made him less able than usual to master the creature. But might there not be a simpler explanation? If it had been Berenice riding Flavius that morning, she might well have found a little difficulty in handling him. Mistress Fettiplace gave her the credit of being a fine horsewoman, but had admitted that she was not quite as good a rider as her brother. 'Very nearly,' had been her reply when I had put that question to her.

And then there was the thumb ring worn by Bevis Godsey. He had lied about how it came into his possession, and when he realized that he must have given himself away by his own stupidity, he had sheered off in a hurry, before I was awake, leaving me to wonder why Beric would have given him such a valuable jewel, or what the latter might have done to earn it. But I now knew Bevis to be a kinsman of Katherine Glover, one with the same initials as Beric. Perhaps, when he had called at Valletort Manor, she had given it to him. But why? More importantly, why would Beric allow her to make such a gift? And where had he really been ever since the murder?

I withdrew my almost numbed hand from the stream and dried it on the grass before settling down to consider what might have happened on the morning that Oliver Capstick was murdered; but I soon realized that, in order to get a true picture, I must go back in time to the previous day. On that occasion, Beric, incensed beyond measure by his great-uncle's criticism of his intended bride, and also by his attempt to coerce him into marrying Jenny Haygarth, had attacked Master Capstick in a fury of red-hot rage by trying to throttle him. But his own better nature, as much, I suspected, as Mistress Trenowth's intervention, had prevented him from committing murder. He had told the old man to alter his will and be damned to him, and had ridden home to Valletort Manor, safe, as he thought, in the knowledge of Katherine's affection.

So far I was reasonably sure of my ground. But what had followed? Had he discovered that Berenice and Katherine were really lovers? Had he gone searching for them, anxious to tell them what had taken place, only to find them locked in one another's embrace? I remembered the tree-tent in the woods. Was that where they had lain together, out of the sight of prying eyes? And if my surmise proved to be correct, what would have been Beric's reaction? Disbelief, horror, the sense of betrayal – surely he would have felt all these things? And when he had recovered from the first awful shock, when the truth had finally sunk in, would he not, in his anger and humiliation, have revealed all that he had been prepared to sacrifice for Katherine Glover, even consenting to his sister becoming their great-uncle's sole heir? And would he not then have threatened to return at once to Plymouth, to tell Oliver Capstick the truth and to reinstate himself in his kinsman's regard by consenting to marry Jenny Haygarth?

Or might he, in his bitter rage, have attacked the women, so that they were forced to defend themselves? Two to one, they could well have overpowered him. But then, of course, they must have begun to realize what a danger this furiously angry man was to them and their forbidden love. There was only one way to make sure of his silence, and that was to kill him! It was possible that Beric's death had been accidental, but in the light of what must have happened next, I doubted it.

For what happened had surely been Berenice's decision to murder her great-uncle and enter into her inheritance without delay. The next morning, therefore, early, dressed, except for the hat, in her brother's clothes and mounted on Flavius, she had ridden to Plymouth, bludgeoned the old man to death while he slept and ridden home again. She had no hope of escaping notice but to be seen from a distance was an essential part of her plan. Beric would be blamed for Oliver's murder while she and

Katherine played the parts of horrified, but still devoted, sister and betrothed.

But why had Bartholomew Champernowne had to be killed? Was it possible that he had found out about Berenice's love for Katherine, or was on the verge of suspecting the truth? In that case, where would this murderous course end? For the two women must stand in constant danger of discovery, the more so because Berenice took foolish and unnecessary risks, like dressing in her brother's clothes and riding to a midnight rendezvous with Katherine at the Bird of Passage Inn.

And yet they had a sort of protection so long as it was widely believed that Beric had not fled abroad, but was eating Saint John's fern in order to gain invisibility and stay close to his betrothed. And that, I saw with sudden clarity, was perhaps the real reason why it had been necessary to remove Bartholomew Champernowne. I had told Berenice that he had been going about the countryside trying to force witnesses to change their testimony; to say that it was not Beric whom they had seen on the day of Oliver Capstick's murder. And if Beric was exonerated, the finger of suspicion would inevitably begin to point at the person who had benefited most from Oliver Capstick's death: Berenice, herself.

Chapter Twenty

Even if I was right, and Beric was dead, what chance had I of proving it? His body could be buried anywhere in the acres of woodland that surrounded Valletort Manor. What hope did I have of locating the exact spot? But I had to try for Jack Golightly's sake. I couldn't let an innocent man go to the gallows for want of effort on my part.

I got to my feet and wandered a short way along the bank of the stream, lost in thought and unaware of the direction in which I was walking. I was only vaguely conscious that I was leaving Modbury behind me and plunging once more into the belt of trees that swathed the countryside between town and sea; and I failed to notice the all-embracing silence until it was broken by a voice, addressing me by name and returning me abruptly to my surroundings.

'We meet again, Roger Chapman, but you're a fair way off the main coastal track.'

It was the swineherd. 'God's Fingernails, but you startled me,' I accused him breathlessly. The three pigs brushed past me, preoccupied with their never ceasing quest for food. 'How did you find your goodwife?' I added more calmly.

'Fair! Fair!' was the cheerful response. 'She's well enough, at all events, to get up from her sickbed and leave the house in order to catch up with the latest gossip. As a matter of fact,' he went on, lunging with his stick after one of the pigs that showed a tendency to stray too far into the trees, 'she'd already heard rumours of the murder. One of the local woodsmen had called at the cottage to tell her what he knew.' He regarded me curiously. 'Are you feeling all right? I don't believe you've heard a word I've said.'

'I was remembering a dream I had about you and your pigs,' I said slowly, 'while I was dozing today, after my dinner. The animals were digging under a tree and . . . and . . . Yes, I can see it clearly now!' My excitement began to mount. 'That's what they were doing this morning, just before we parted company, all three of them rootling around under an oak as though their lives depended upon it. And you said . . . Let me see . . . You said what vicious creatures pigs are. You said never get on the wrong side of them or they'll attack you. They're partial to human flesh.'

'Well, so I might have done,' the swineherd admitted, puzzled. 'I don't recollect saying anything of the sort, mind you, but if I did, it's nothing but the truth. Nothing to get worked up about.'

'Do you recall the whereabouts of that oak tree?' I demanded, laying an urgent hand on his arm. 'Think, man! Think! I know it's a lot to ask, but—'

'I dare say I could find it again if I had to,' he replied, freeing himself somewhat peevishly from my grip. 'You're right. It is close to where we said goodbye, and that was within fifty yards or so west of the main track to the sea. But why? What's the purpose of all this?'

'I'm not certain yet,' I answered. 'It's just that . . . Well, it's just that I believe something may be buried there. Are we any distance from your cottage? Do you have a spade that I could borrow?'

'I might.' He paused, frowning, reluctant to retrace his steps, but consumed by the curiosity that my words had aroused in him. 'You'll have to keep your eye on the pigs, though, while I fetch it.

And don't let 'em stray too deep into the woods, or we'll never see hide nor hair of them again, dratted creatures! Here,' he added, 'you'll need my stick. I'll be as quick as I can.'

He was as good as his word, returning with a stout spade after less than ten minutes, plainly relieved to see all three of his charges still within view. He handed me the implement to carry, retrieved his stick and, with words of encouragement to the animals, continued along the track that we were on, myself close at his heels.

He was obviously familiar with all the woodland paths for, within a very short space of time, and after taking a number of extremely narrow, tortuous and occasionally almost nonexistent trails, we emerged on to the main road leading from Modbury to the sea. Some thirty or so yards further on, we turned at a right angle along another track, and I recognised the spot where I had taken leave of my companion earlier in the day. We proceeded a little further in a westerly direction and then, like a small miracle, the largest of the pigs, the one my companion referred to as Jupiter, left the path and trotted off into the trees towards an ancient oak. Here, after only a few seconds, he began snuffling and digging at its base, the other two pigs lending him their assistance in a great state of excitement.

'What is it?' the swineherd asked uneasily. 'What is it they've found?'

'I think,' I replied cautiously, 'that it could be a body – or what remains of one after nearly half a year.'

My companion swallowed noisily. 'Who . . . Whose body?' he stammered.

I did not answer at once, except to request him to move the pigs away from the tree if he could. This was no easy task, but he finally managed to drive them off, and while he kept them under his eye, some few yards distant, I peered closer to inspect what had already been uncovered. I could see little at that stage, but there was something there for I could smell the stench of putrefaction, and although it made my flesh creep, I resolutely began to dig with the spade.

The grave was quite shallow as, had I stopped to think about it, I might have expected. It was doubtful if even two women, digging alternately, would have had the strength to make it deeper. A hand, with tatters of flesh still clinging to the bones, was the first thing to emerge, and then an arm, partly concealed by the rags of a disintegrating shirt. I fell to my knees and manually scraped away the final thin blanket of earth and leaves to reveal a now almost fleshless corpse. The shirt had been its shroud, for there was no sign of any other clothing. The women must have stripped Beric nearly naked before putting him in the ground, Berenice probably having reasoned that she would be more likely to be mistaken for her brother if she were wearing the same garments that Beric had had on the previous day.

But it was the corpse's head, once I had overcome my revulsion that interested me most. The skull on the left-hand side was shattered into fragments, and had obviously received a very heavy blow. I wondered which of the two women had administered it, and with what. Then I noticed some fragments of bark embedded in the wound, and I remembered the broken branch that I had found in the little glade, lying on the ground. Had they intended to kill Beric? Or had it been merely a fortuitous accident? Either way, it had not taken them long to perceive the advantage of his death to themselves.

I realized that the swineherd had approached and was looking over my shoulder. Just at that moment, some maggots crawled out of the undamaged eye-socket and he had to turn aside in a hurry to be sick.

'God in heaven!' he exclaimed as soon as he could speak,

wiping his mouth on his sleeve. 'You might have warned me. Who is it, do you know?'

I sat back on my heels. 'Not for certain, but I believe it to be Beric Gifford.'

'What? You mean him that murdered his uncle?'

'Was thought to have done so, yes. But I'm pretty sure now that he was innocent of the crime.'

'Then who did kill the old man?'

'His sister and Katherine Glover,' I answered. 'Beric was also their victim.' I added, 'I think Berenice and Katherine are lovers.'

It took a moment or two for my words to sink in, then a look of horror spread across his weather-beaten features. 'They could be put to death for that,' he whispered.

'A fact of which I suspect they are fully aware,' I said. 'I believe Beric discovered their secret and threatened them with exposure. Exposure, if not to the law, at least to Oliver Capstick.'

The swineherd was still looking ill, a fact for which I was grateful as it prevented him from asking too many questions. But the pigs were beginning to show an interest in the corpse, and I had to beg his help in covering it up again. When it was once more decently shrouded in earth, I had another favour to ask him.

'Will you stay here with your animals and keep guard over the grave? I'm going to Valletort Manor to confront Mistress Berenice with her crimes.'

He agreed, albeit reluctantly, once I had convinced him that I now knew where I was, and that I could find my way to the house without the necessity of a guide.

'Keep close to the edge of the track,' I instructed him, 'and if Sergeant Warren should pass this way in pursuit of Sir Walter Champernowne, whom I believe to be at the manor, you may tell him what you know and invite him to take a look at the body himself.'

'And if he doesn't pass this way?'

'I shall meet up with him eventually and bring him here. Now I have to be off. We must put our trust in God to make all right.' And I waved my hand in farewell before setting out along the track that led to Valletort Manor.

As I passed through the little glade, I looked at the tree-tent with new eyes, now that I knew its true purpose. It also occurred to me to wonder why I wished to confront Berenice Gifford and Katherine Glover before first going in search of Sergeant Warren. Was it because I was not absolutely certain that my version of what had happened last spring was the correct one? Or was it because they were women and, heinous as I believed their crimes to be, I wanted to give them a chance of escaping the full rigour of the law? The more I thought about it, the less I was able to decide.

When I reached Valletort Manor, the courtyard was full of those riders, together with their horses, whom I had met on the road from Modbury earlier in the day. The men looked bored and the animals fretful, as they might well be after several hours of enforced inactivity. There was no sign however of the man I believed to be Sir Walter, and I presumed him to be indoors, comforting the bereaved Berenice.

The Champernowne servants looked at me with indifference as I threaded my way amongst them and entered the great hall by the main door. The remains of a meal stood on the table on the dais, but the participants were now gathered together in the middle of the room, seated beside the fire. At least, Sir Walter and Berenice were seated, with Katherine Glover standing behind her mistress's chair. Sir Walter's stern countenance had mellowed a little since I had last seen it, and his head was inclined towards Berenice, whose cheeks were becomingly tear-stained, although her eyes, I noticed, were not in the least swollen or red.

The knight was in the middle of uttering some consolatory remark, in a low, grief-stricken voice, when he happened to glance up and see me.

'Who's this?' he demanded in quite another tone.

Berenice and Katherine Glover both stared in astonishment, but then I saw something very like a gleam of fear in both pairs of eyes.

'Roger Chapman, what are you doing back here again?' Berenice asked, rising slowly to her feet. 'We thought we'd seen the last of you.'

'I'm sorry to disappoint you. I've come to tell you that I've found your brother,' I announced baldly. 'That is, I've discovered Beric's grave.'

I think Berenice would have faced me down and poured ridicule on my story, but at my words, Katherine Glover gave a scream and clapped both hands over her mouth. She began to sob hysterically.

'Stop that at once, Kate, d'you hear me?' her mistress shouted slapping her hard across the face.

But the admonition was useless and the other woman sank to the floor, clutching her reddened cheek.

'I told you we'd be found out in the end,' she moaned. 'You always took such risks.'

By this time, Sir Walter Champernowne was also on his feet, looking dazed and bewildered. 'What's going on? What's this all about?' he entreated.

As briefly and succinctly as I could, I told him of my suspicions and of my gruesome discovery in the woods. 'And I think you'll find that one of these two women also killed your son,' I added. 'I suspect Mistress Glover of being responsible for that particular murder. As pretty a pair of cold-hearted killers as you're likely to find anywhere in England.'

Berenice, who had been bending over her friend, suddenly straightened up and flew at me, her mourning draperies billowing out around her, giving her the appearance of a great black crow. I prepared to defend myself, but it was only when Sir Walter shouted a warning, that I realized she had a knife in her hand. Where it had come from I had no idea, but it must have been concealed somewhere about her person.

Fortunately, there was a stool close by and I grabbed it, holding its seat in front of me as a shield. The blade stuck fast in the wood, and with a curse Berenice let go the handle. Sir Walter Champernowne, recovering his wits and convinced by her actions of the truth of my accusations, lunged at her in an effort to seize her by the skirt, but she whirled out of his reach. Gripping Katherine Glover's arm, she hauled her to her feet and literally dragged her friend across the floor and through the door at the back of the dais. Sir Walter and I, both still shocked by the speed and turn of events, were slow to move in pursuit. The door was slammed in our faces, and we heard the rasp of bolts being shot home on the other side.

'Where does it lead?' the knight demanded, breathing heavily. 'To what part of the house?'

'I don't know,' I admitted, turning in the direction of the kitchen. 'We must ask Mistress Tuckett.'

But the housekeeper, disturbed by the sudden noise, had already emerged from the kitchen to discover the cause. At the same moment, Sergeant Warren burst in through the main door of the hall, followed by several of Sir Walter's servants who had also been alarmed by the uproar within. I left the knight to put the Sheriff's officer in possession of all the facts, while I dealt with Mistress Tuckett, pointing to the door at the back of the dais.

'Where does that go?' I demanded, explaining that it had been bolted on the other side. And when I was told that, behind it, a flight of steps led up to the mistress's bedchamber, I insisted on being taken there at once.

The astonished housekeeper was inclined to jib at this, until Sergeant Warren added the weight of his commands to my request. So, leading us through the kitchen to the passageway beyond, and from thence ascending a flight of stairs to an upper corridor, Mistress Tuckett pointed out the door to Berenice's bedchamber, situated halfway along.

'There's her room, and there, at the other end, is the staircase that leads down again to the great hall. But before anyone of you goes another step, I'd like to know what all this is about.'

Sergeant Warren and Sir Walter Champernowne ignored her and strode forward to hammer at the bedchamber door. When there was no response, the former tried the latch, but although it lifted, the door refused to yield.

'Bolted from within,' Sergeant Warren announced unnecessarily. 'We must break it down. Somebody fetch an axe.'

'No need for that,' said Sir Walter brusquely. 'Here we are, you, myself and the chapman, not to mention three or four of my men. We're all big enough and strong enough. Surely we ought to be able to break it down between us, if we all rush at it together.'

It was not quite as easy as he made it sound, but in the end two panels of the wood splintered under our combined assault and we were able, one at a time, to squeeze through the gap that we had made . . .

We were too late, as I had feared we might be. Both women were already dead, sprawled across the bed yet still, in death, enfolded in one another's arms. After the first, shocked stillness, Sergeant Warren stooped and picked up a small glass bottle from the floor.

'Poison,' he said, pouring the few remaining drops into the

palm of his left hand. He sniffed it warily. 'Probably an infusion of deadly nightshade berries.' He sighed heavily, then added with a venomous snarl, 'I hate to see a murderer cheat the gallows.'

But his words were almost lost as Mistress Tuckett, finally penetrating the room through the gap in the splintered door, let out an ear-piercing scream.

Jack Golightly embraced me with the tears coursing down his cheeks.

He had been released from the roundhouse an hour or so earlier and had immediately sought me out at the Fettiplaces' cottage, where I had been made more than welcome for yet another night. Indeed, I had the feeling that neither Anne Fettiplace nor her husband would ever have forgiven me had I not accepted their offer of hospitality, for they and Simon were basking in the reflected glory of my exploits. Everyone in Modbury wanted to hear the story and have the mystery explained, as well as to congratulate Jack on his freedom. Besides which, the sensation of the day's events at Valletort Manor would probably never again be repeated: a murder in the morning and a double suicide in the evening was more than anybody felt that he or she had a right to expect in a lifetime. I was the hero of the hour.

The swineherd, too, his pigs now safely penned in their sty for the night, merited his share of interest. He had been able to waylay Sergeant Warren, riding to seek out Sir Walter at Valletort Manor, there to boast vaingloriously of his swift arrest of Jack Golightly.

'He didn't believe me, you know,' the swineherd confided later when all the Fettiplaces' neighbours had at last gone home to sleep off the excitement and a generous quantity of good, home-brewed ale. He himself was just setting off for his own cottage within the manor pale. 'At least, put it this way: Sergeant Warren didn't want that body to be Beric Gifford's, for he knew that if it were, Jack's arrest was going to make him look an almighty fool.'

I smiled and clapped the swineherd on the back. 'Well, in the end he had no choice but to believe it. And thank you, my friend, for all your help, for without you and your pigs I doubt if I'd have guessed the truth.'

He looked pleased, but reluctantly disclaimed the honour. 'God would surely have illuminated your mind by some other means,' he said.

He left the cottage, nevertheless, with a jaunty gait and whistling a tune under his breath.

'You've given him something to tell his children and grandchildren,' Anne Fettiplace remarked, closing and bolting the cottage door for the night.

'And his goody and her kinswomen, the Trims, will treat him with a new respect,' Ivo Fettiplace observed as he began damping down the fire.

'Are you set on beginning your homeward journey tomorrow?' his wife asked wistfully.

'I am,' I answered. 'I'm sorry, but there's nothing to keep me here any longer. I'm more than happy for Sergeant Warren to take the credit with the Sheriff for what has been discovered concerning these dreadful crimes. Moreover, it will be a long journey back to Bristol, for I must visit both Plymouth and Tavistock on my way home to let some friends know the outcome of my labours. And I've a family, a wife and son and daughter, whom I've not seen for very many weeks. They'll be looking for me. And I miss them.'

'Of course you do.' Mistress Fettiplace planted an affectionate kiss on my cheek. 'And don't forget, while you're in Plymouth, to seek out my sisters and let them know what has happened, as well.'

I nodded. I had said nothing to anyone of my suspicions that Mathilda Trenowth might have guessed that the murderer was

245

really Berenice, and not Beric. After all, I couldn't prove it. She would deny it if challenged, and in the event it hadn't prevented the truth from being discovered.

I had to share Simon's bed that night, and as I picked up my candle to join him upstairs, my hostess tapped me on the shoulder.

'By the way,' she said, 'there's talk that Bevis Godsey's come forward to volunteer evidence to Sergeant Warren. He's been frightened, I dare say, by the news of another murder and the two women's suicide. It seems he's confessed to catching Berenice and Katherine together in an unguarded moment and guessing the truth. He was given a valuable thumb ring belonging to Beric Gifford in order to buy his silence.' Anne Fettiplace gave a mirthless snort of laughter. 'A good job for him, I reckon, that things have turned out as they have. Otherwise, I wouldn't have bet a fig on him living to a ripe old age.'

I lay awake for a long time that night, listening to my bedfellow snoring, unable to fall asleep myself. My longing to see Adela again, and to hold her in my arms, was overwhelming. I wished that God had not picked on me as the fittest person to solve these mysteries for Him and bring those responsible to book, but at least He had provided me with a loving wife and children as the calm, constant centre of my occasionally dangerous life.

But then, not for the first time, I found myself admitting that I shouldn't really like to lead a simple chapman's life. I should miss the excitement and the thrill of foiling evil and righting wrongs. In three or four weeks, with luck and lifts from friendly carters, I should be home, surrounded by every domestic happiness and comfort that Adela could provide. But I knew very well that after a few days I should begin to grow restless, all my senses alert, waiting to hear God's next call. And, secretly, I should be only too eager to obey.

The Brothers of Glastonbury

Kate Sedley

August, 1476: Roger the travelling chapman – whose sharp wit and tender heart have been involved in affairs touching the mightiest and humblest in the land – ought to be on his way home to Bristol after a peaceful summer's peddling. But a request from the Duke of Clarence to escort a young bride travelling to meet her betrothed takes him instead to Wells – and an extraordinary adventure. For the bridegroom has vanished, and his brother soon follows.

Roger links the disappearances to the discovery of an ancient manuscript written in a strange language. But as he gradually deciphers the manuscript's meaning, he concludes that a greater mystery still may lie at the heart of the brothers' disappearance . . .

'Weaves a compelling puzzle into the vividly coloured tapestry of medieval life' *Publishers Weekly*

'An attractive hero and effective scene-setting' *Liverpool Daily Post*

0 7472 5877 5

HEADLINE

The Holy Innocents

A Roger The Chapman Medieval Mystery

KATE SEDLEY

As Roger the Chapman, novice monk turned pedlar, makes his way towards Totnes, he learns that a gang of cutthroats is terrorizing the surrounding district. After he himself is playfully ambushed by some country women, he is inexorably drawn into the spider's web of a local tragedy.

Rescued by the handsome Grizelda, he is told of the terrible fate of the Skelton children. Recently deprived of their wealthy mother, they were left to the care of their unpopular stepfather – who by chance becomes Roger's temporary landlord. For Roger is given charge of the very town house from which the two youngsters mysteriously vanished.

But how had they left this house? Why had they left it? And were the outlaws really responsible for their dismal deaths? These are the questions that will increasingly haunt the chapman.

'Compares well to Ellis Peters's Brother Cadfael tales'
– *Publishers Weekly*

'Sedley skilfully interweaves romance, intrigue, and authentic period detail' – *Booklist*

'An attractive hero and effective scene setting'
– *Liverpool Daily Post*

FICTION / CRIME 0 7472 4665 3